He turned to study me.

"Have you ever attended any sort of formal event?"

I thought of how I must look, and I could see the doubt in his eyes. "Not since I was a kid, sir," I answered, then added, "but I swear, I'll do whatever you say. I learn fast and I promise I'll make you look lucky, and I'll be obedient and perfect, I promise!"

Bobby laughed. "Come on, Cash, I bet he cleans up all right! Take him home and try him out!"

"He is rather personable," he admitted, scrutinizing me. "A slave might even rectify my image, and he might not look too bad once he's cleaned up."

I wasn't sure whether to stand tall and display my bruises and welts, or shrivel to the floor to hide from his gaze. I stood there, frozen, instead.

Also recommended...

You may also enjoy these other ForbiddenFiction works:

Nicholi's Vengeance by J. A. Jaken
Nicholi's world goes up in flames when soldiers invade his country, leaving chaos in their wake. Captured and enslaved in a foreign land, Nicholi struggles to cope with the nightmare of slavery and adapt to the terrifying and inexplicable world he is thrust into. He draws courage from a steadfast determination to get justice for his murdered family and—he hopes—peace to himself by finding and killing the man responsible for the destruction of his village. Yet, through it all, Nicholi's greatest enemy might not be foreign powers or enemy soldiers, or even in the self-serving machinations of his fellow slaves, but himself. (M/M)
http://forbiddenfiction.com/library/story/JAJ-1.000011

Inherent Gifts by Alicia Cameron
Wren was born with a gift that set him apart from others—a gift that dooms him to a life of slavery with no hope of escape, and turns Jere into an unwilling master. When a fiery tragedy brings Jere into Wren's life, it becomes clear that his new master is like nobody else Wren has ever known. How does a slave protect himself from someone so foreign? How does an unexpected master stay true to his egalitarian roots? Can real love exist between master and slave, or will their passion destroy them both? (M/M)
http://forbiddenfiction.com/library/story/AC2-1.000068

Subjection

Demoted
Book One

Alicia Cameron

ForbiddenFiction
www.forbiddenfiction.com

an imprint of

Fantastic Fiction Publishing
www.fantasticfictionpublishing.com

SUBJECTION
A Forbidden Fiction book

Fantastic Fiction Publishing
Hayward, California

© Alicia Cameron, 2015

CREDITS
Editor: James L. Wolf and Kel Draves
Cover Design: D.M. Atkins
Cover Art: Natalya Nesterova
Production Editor: Erika L Firanc
Proofreading: JhP323

SKU: AC2-000202-02 FFP
ISBN: 978-1-62234-225-9

Published in the United States of America

DISCLAIMER

This book is a work of fiction which contains explicit erotic content; it is intended for mature readers. Do not read this if it's not legal for you.

All the characters, locations and events herein are fictional. While elements of existing locations or historical characters or events may be used fictitiously, any resemblance to actual people, places or events is coincidental.

This story depicts fictional BDSM; it is not intended to be used as an instruction manual. It contains descriptions of erotic acts that may be immoral, illegal, or unsafe. The characters are not models for the Safe, Sane and Consensual forms embraced by most current practitioners of BDSM. The author takes license with the use of BDSM for dramatic effect. Do not take the events in this story as proof of the plausibility or safety of any particular practice.

To everyone who begged for Cash's POV: You got it!

Contents

Chapter 1
Peace Day Celebration

My master and I arrive at the Peace Day Celebration looking like the perfect couple. The glitter and paint make me sparkle, but more importantly, they cover the scars.

The Celebration commemorates the end of the fourth World War and the signing of the Peace Declaration. I've never seen it as all that peaceful; the Peace Declaration came at a steep price: the Demoted system was signed into place with that agreement, enslaving approximately fifteen percent of the population, a demographic I would join decades later.

I'm grateful that my master has taken me to a high-end costume designer, who took it upon herself to coordinate me as a shining accessory to my master. The theme of this year's Peace Day Celebration is "Luck," and I'm decorated from head to toe in thin latex paint that fits more like a second skin than clothing itself. Hundreds of painted four-leaf clovers blend together on my skin like glistening camouflage, and peeking out from behind them are carefully painted coins, replicas from ancient history books. Some are outlined with sparkly gold rhinestones, disguising the marks that my previous owners have left on me. I sparkle no matter which direction I am viewed from. The costume designer added some designs along my face and hands as well, not to cover anything, simply to match. The same gold dust that glitters on my body adds highlights to my dark brown hair, and complements my dark green eyes.

To even the best-trained observer, I am a prime specimen, a highly-valued Demoted slave, not the brothel whore I once was.

My dick has been spared the green paint that decorates the rest of my body, and is the only clothed part, covered in what basically amounts to a g-string. The paint blends seamlessly with the fabric, and she's covered most of my ass up to look like I'm actually wearing pants. Strangely, I feel more covered with my ass swathed in paint that I ever did in some of the other outfits I've been forced to wear. Maybe it's because the paint is a lot harder to rip off, or maybe it's just because it was applied with such care and attention to detail, the goal being to make me look valuable, not cheap. She's even painted a tie around my neck, matching the real tie she chose for my master. The dark green suits him quite well, though it is the most color I've seen on him since he purchased me a month ago.

Cashiel Michaud made my heart race from the first time I laid eyes on him. He pulls off the stereotypical "tall, dark, and handsome," while still managing to take my breath away — usually, from fear, but tonight he's simply stunning. His look, as expected, is classic suit and tie, but it's the subtle hints that make him shine; the tie, some cuff links, the costume designer even dabbed some makeup on him while he scowled at her. For once, we look less like a detached master and a used up whore, and more like a businessman and his high-class escort.

I try to hold onto this idea as we arrive at the casino, where my master hands his keys over to the valet to park. As practiced, I am literally holding onto his arm, clinging, really, and I find myself glad, because all of a sudden I'm terrified.

The casino is immaculate. The biggest and most prestigious in the city, if not the state, it features a marble entrance with inlaid diamonds, matching perfectly with the diamond chandeliers that hang low and heavy from the ceiling. Everything shimmers; the gold flecks of paint, the glitter embedded in the glass, the Demoted slaves who are owned by the casino.

The other guests look at home; unlike me, they aren't staring wide-eyed at the decorations or one another. My master must fit into this world as well, but I'm used to him. He doesn't seem so superior, so distant. The attendees continue with conversations as if the extravagance is commonplace, and the slaves remain focused and attentive without looking tense. They move gracefully, fitting under a master's arm, holding a mistress's purse, making everything look so effortless.

This was a stupid idea. I can't do this. I can't pretend to compete with the beautiful men and women here, the real high-class escorts who have trained for years to come to expensive parties on the arms of other beautiful men and women. I'm a goddamned brothel whore who's no good for anything but torturing and fucking!

My master must notice my increased heart rate, or that I'm gasping for breath, or something, because he looks at me with a raised eyebrow. "Doing all right?" he asks, and it's so normal that I forget to be scared for a minute.

"What if I can't do this, master?" I need to know. I need to know how badly he'll hurt me, or if he'll sell me, or what other consequences there might be. I need to know how soon before I get put back in my place.

He shakes his head. "Don't be ridiculous, Sascha, of course you can do it. I wouldn't have bought you if I didn't think you could, and you certainly wouldn't be here if I wasn't completely certain that you would succeed. Stop being so melodramatic."

His words affect me more than he probably knows. He isn't just hopeful, he's confident that I can do this, and it's been an awfully long time since I've had someone believe in me like that. There's no threats, no bribes, just a simple statement of fact. I can do this, and he knows it.

Okay, maybe I am a little melodramatic.

We enter, and I'm soon so swept up that I forget to be nervous. There are people to meet, drinks to fetch, plates from snacks to clear away and hand to the proper attendant, compliments to accept. Because, yes, I do receive compliments on my attire, as does my master, but it seems acceptable for me to directly thank the person paying the compliment, and I fall into it naturally. As if I belong in this world.

Perhaps I do.

The card games and gambling start up quickly, and my master takes me to a table full of wealthy individuals, surrounded by Demoted men and women. Their outfits are perfectly tailored and display the best assets of the slaves, though none are as creative as mine. I watch in amazement as the free people throw down ludicrous amounts of money, cashing in on the opportunity to out-donate their peers. Charity and social causes are big on Peace Day. It doesn't explain the greed that happens during the rest of the year, but it's a nice show.

I perch on my master's lap, as practiced, and I let him play a few hands on his own. He bought me to serve as eye candy, and my skill at counting cards adds the bonus of him being able to appear "lucky" in the gambling games, when the time comes. We've trained for this for weeks, working out subtle hand signals, brushes of hair, and smiles that I can use to guide my master's moves. I don't flinch any more when he touches me, and I don't mind sitting at his feet or on his lap. Whether we're sitting or standing, his arm fits naturally around my waist, pulling me close against the curve of his body, and I don't have to try very hard to lean into him.

I play with his hair and whisper things just for fun, just to make it clear that I'm a handsy, needy boy who's entirely uninterested in the card games my master plays. He smiles indulgently at me, and I fall into the role more easily.

It's nice to lie for something other than sheer physical safety, and it's nice to have him smile at me, even if it is an act.

I help him to win a few hands, here and there, hands where it won't look too obvious to the others playing with him. He rakes in a huge pile of chips, and the wide smile on his face assures me he's pleased. I share his enjoyment.

"Cash, you're having quite a winning streak!" one of his coworkers says, smiling as he loses his chips to my master. "Last week you said you weren't an experienced gambler. Congratulations on your beginner's luck!"

I smile along with everyone else, but it's my master's appreciative look that really reassures me.

He's told me about each of his coworkers, especially his superiors. I can tell that it's Mr. Dean, the head of the company, who's actually doing the worst in the game. He's betting too high, taking too many risks, and while he's passable at bluffing, he just doesn't have the cards to back it up. He's almost out of chips, and on his next turn, he pulls the blonde girl standing next to him directly onto his lap.

"I'll raise you a night with Melinda," he challenges Cashiel, a gleam in his eye as he runs his hands over her most prominent features.

4

I'm appalled. So base, for such a supposedly high-class event, and this wager won't even benefit charity. It's nothing but an excuse to stay in the game, to keep having fun without the bother of getting up to buy more chips. There's silence for half a second, before everyone starts jeering and laughing. Of course, they wouldn't call their boss out for being over the line. Melinda looks scared, but she hides it by turning her face into her master's chest and giggling. That move has never worked for me.

I'm rather stunned when my master's turn comes and I hear his reply.

"I'll see your bet with Sascha," he smiles, winking at his boss. "I'm sure he'd keep you company."

The older man leers at me, and I wish I could hide like his girl is doing. Instead, I force my best sexy smile and lean over to blow him a kiss. In the resulting cheers, the rest of the crowd is distracted enough not to notice all the signals that I slip my master. I've developed excellent card-counting skills, and I watch the game carefully, running a hand through my master's hair when he should bet higher, twisting my legs up with his when he should stay. He doesn't respond, not that anyone else can see, but he makes the moves I want him to.

I've been playing casually up until now, just making my master win a little more than he loses, but now that *I* am at stake, I'm tense, on my game, refusing to lose. I study the cards carefully, even going so far as to peek at the hands of others. Nobody suspects a pretty little slave boy of understanding the game, much less cheating at it. We've been dealt a decent hand; I try to convince myself that my master must have known this before he agreed to place me as a bet. Still, it needs some help, and I hold my breath as I cue my master to draw more cards. The highest are still in the deck — that is, if Mr. Dean isn't holding them.

I try not to appear tense, but I'm more eager to see the cards than my master is. As usual, he is calm and collected, pulling the cards slowly and returning them to his hand without haste. I hold my breath as he does, willing him to go faster, and when he finally turns them so I can see them, it's all I can do to avoid gasping for air.

Mr. Dean isn't holding the two highest cards, because my master has them in his hand. We win the round, and we win the girl, and her master shoos her away with a laugh. She's smiling, but I can see the fear in her eyes as she comes toward us. I'd feel bad for her, if the alternative were something other than me being passed around. My master, to his credit, merely pulls her close with an arm around her waist, his hand locking in place just above her hip and not straying at all. I think at first that it's because he's not attracted to girls, but he surprises me by acting remarkably protective of her. The man sitting next to us tries to feel her leg under the table, and the glare he receives makes him retreat instantly.

We continue to play, and I'm careful now, both for myself and for Melinda. I let us win and lose money steadily, and I let some of the other plays come close, but I don't separate either of us from my master. When the stakes are for money, I throw the game, signaling for my master to make bad plays, especially when it's his boss who's eligible to win large sums.

As the game draws on, I wait for my chance, and when I see it, I lean in and dare to whisper to my master, "her." It's not something we discussed, but he takes the bait, offering Melinda—and *only* Melinda—up for trade. We throw the hand, and Melinda goes back to Mr. Dean, looking honestly relieved and happy.

She can look the way that I feel.

She's not put up for trade again, and neither am I. I don't even know how to express how happy that makes me. I keep my master winning, and he draws quite a crowd—teasing him for his good luck, joking about the "good luck charm" sitting in his lap.

I'm happy to be his good luck charm, then I realize that I don't care that I'm being referred to as some sort of object. The realization bothers me more than anything. When did I let this become my life? But it is still better than any other life I could hope for, so I keep up the act, keep being a perfect slave and making my master win.

The casino would probably have called us on cheating hours ago if we were playing for real, but this is Peace Day, and the proceeds are going to charity, and the house has made plenty of profit just by hosting the event. The fact that my master and I are cheating is ignored by the staff, just like the casual inclusion of slaves and sexual favors into the barter pool. We continue to win and dazzle for the rest of the night.

Finally, it is our time to leave, and the company head comes up to shake my master's hand, making some sort of business small talk and hinting toward a promotion. I'm tired, and let my head rest against my master's shoulder as I sit there, eyes half-closed. Nobody minds a sleepy pet, and if that's the role I'm supposed to play, I figure I may as well take advantage of it. As harsh as he can be at times, right now his shoulder is warm and soft, and I don't want to be anywhere else.

I let their words wash over me, becoming pointless noise until I jerk back as a hand caresses my chest. It's been too long since I've been touched so casually, it shocks me and scares me, and I force myself not to glare. My master's arm tightens around my hips.

"Perhaps some other time, Mr. Dean," my master says to his boss with a smile. "The poor boy seems a little bit tired tonight, doesn't he?"

The other man nods, but his eyes are still roving over my body. I shrink down as much as possible, wishing I could disappear. Melinda glares at me like *she* wishes I would disappear.

"That's true, that's true," the older man says, still leering at me. "I wouldn't want to exhaust him. Perhaps you should stop by sometime for a few drinks; we can talk about the future and get to know one another a little better."

A cheesy business come-on if I've ever heard one, but this man does seem cheesy.

"That would be spectacular, sir," my master replies, smiling and charming.

"Make sure this one gets some rest, hmm? Don't keep him up too late!" the boss teases, actually daring to pinch my cheek.

I want to punch him, but I can guarantee my master would happily beat the shit out of me for trying something so terribly stupid. I turn and hide my face against his chest, instead, wishing I were a cute little girl who could get away with it. But it's better to look stupid or get smacked for being clingy than to be called out on my shitty attitude.

He doesn't smack me, though; he doesn't even push me away. He just stands up, placing me on my feet next to him.

"Most certainly, sir," my master replies, calm as ever. "May peace and prosperity find you."

"You as well!" My master's boss smiles and puts his arm around Melinda, who looks relieved. I'm amazed to realize that she views me as competition.

We take our leave, and I can't help but to be glad that we are away from the crowd and the commotion and the lustful eyes of wealthy businesspeople. I let out a breath I hadn't realized I was holding, and I stumble a few inches. My master puts his arm around me, and I'm more thankful than I probably should be. I know it's still an act, but his touch feels firm and secure.

"You were excellent tonight," he whispers, and the words send almost as much of a thrill through my spine as the soft brush of his lips against my ear.

I start to relax as he leads me to wait for the valet, so I'm surprised when he curses and pulls me off the sidewalk and down a dark alley.

"Sir—"

My protests are cut off by my master's hand wrapping hard around my mouth. "Hush," he orders, keeping his voice low.

I don't fight him, but I look to see what—or who—he's hiding from. A group of people pass us by, chatting and laughing. They are dressed well, obviously out celebrating Peace Day as well, and the focal point of the group seems to be an older woman, comfortably in front, flanked by a pretty slave on either side. There is nothing I recognize about any of them, but my master clearly does. He's tense, nervous, and he doesn't release his grip on me until they are down to the next block.

"Someone I'm trying to avoid talking to," my master explains. He doesn't elaborate, but he does release his grip on me, and we meet our valet to pick up the hov-car as if nothing ever happened.

I fall asleep on the drive home, but my master doesn't seem to mind. He wakes me gently once we get to the house, his hand light on my shoulder. He puts his arm around me again and leads me up the stairs, and I just want to lean into him, let him hold me, pretend...

Just pretend.

But I don't, because pretending would only be fun now, and tomorrow I already have to worry about if he's going to get rid of me or not, now that the Peace Day Celebration is over. That's what he bought me for, after all.

Once we get inside, he looks at his hand, slightly smeared by the paint, which is starting to rub off ever so slightly.

"Make sure you wash up before going to bed," he comments. "I don't want green paint all over the place. I'm sure it would be impossible to get out, and it will track everywhere."

"Yes, master," I mumble, wishing I could just collapse into bed. I head toward the shower instead, surprised when he follows me, stripping off his shirt.

"Master?" I ask, too tired to guess at what he wants. I'd like him to fuck me, right in the doorway to my room, but he hasn't shown any interest in touching me, much less fucking me, since he bought me. That sort of interaction is reserved for my own private fantasy world.

"You won't be able to reach it all," he says, matter-of fact. "I could use a shower, too."

Maybe I am in a fantasy world.

Of course, my fantasy world would involve a lot more kissing and touching and a lot less scraping with the exfoliating brush, and certainly *no* scraping with nails, at least not in the absolutely unsexy way he does it.

I do my best not to whimper from the pain, and I really do my best not to get hard from it. It sucks, having your sexual responses all fucked up from slave training. Really messes with your mind.

But the areas with the most freshly healed scars are sensitive, and those are the areas where the rhinestones seem to be glued on with something stronger than latex body paint. When his nails scratch over one of those just the right way, I can't help but yelp and pull away. I cower, waiting for the smack.

All I hear is a sigh.

"Sascha, for fuck's sake, could you manage to tell me, with actual words, if I'm hurting you?" my master mumbles, placing a firm hand on my shoulder and using the other one to rub gently at the spot he has just hurt, easing the pain at least a little. "I didn't realize I was hurting you — your skin's quite sensitive. I really should have gotten something to remove this, but I didn't think it would be quite *this* difficult."

"Sorry, master," I mumble. I'm focused on squirming as far away from him as I can, trying to will my erection away.

He continues rubbing at my back, much more gently now, and that doesn't help my current state at all. "I'll be more careful with the rest," he says quietly, and he makes good on his promise, peeling the remainder of the paint and glue off with only the slightest irritation and rubbing the places where I'm sure my skin is red and blotchy.

"Turn around," he says, his hand insistent on my shoulder.

I hesitate. Is it worth it? "I can get the front on my own, master, and let you get to bed sooner if you'd like." I wait for his response, praying that he won't just order me to turn around and reveal how excited he's made me.

"You've got a point," he says, as though it's nothing out of the ordinary for me to contradict him. "Hand me the shampoo, then."

I hand it to him, silent, unable to believe my good luck. I work over the paint on the front of my body, a bit gentler than my master had been, and I'm relieved when he finishes and steps out before I do, bidding me good night.

I paint my own dick green as my paint-stained hands rush to work off the burning excitement and energy of the night. I'm thinking of nothing but my master's lips against my ear and the feel of his hands on my skin as I come.

Chapter 2

Opportunity

I saw my master for the first time a month ago.

I was down on my knees, scrubbing the floor and trying to avoid the pain that radiated through my battered body. Mistress Bethel, the owner of the brothel, had turned me into a torture-whore, suitable for little other than beating, fucking, and meeting her demands.

When the two men walked in, the first thing I noticed was that they appeared much wealthier than our usual clientele. I expected them to turn and walk right back out.

"Bobby, I can't believe you brought me to *this* part of town!" one of the men said. His voice was filled with disdain and disgust at the low-class establishment.

"I can't believe that *you* are so unprepared all the time," Bobby replied, laughing and teasing. He sounded like the type that liked to come down from his high-rise and take an e-train to go slumming for "fun."

"I didn't expect Emmett to break things off a month before the Peace Day Celebration, and I wasn't exactly looking to book an escort when I had a boyfriend to bring as a date and conversation piece."

I risked beating to put a face to these voices. Chances were pretty damn good that I would be getting beaten anyway, because that was how every day ended. I studied them as they discussed the difficulty of finding a suitable slave for the Celebration at the last moment.

Even though I didn't know so much as his name at the time, the man who would become my master was stunningly attractive, so much so that I tried to push the thought of him fucking me far out of my mind, focusing on the bucket I was cleaning with. And then I peeked out again, hoping to get a look at his ass.

It was nice.

He was dressed in black, head to toe, except the button down shirt, which was blue. Navy blue, of course, nothing too colorful. He was the picture of a slightly depressed, just-got-dumped, climbing-the-professional-ladder twenty-something. I peeked at his face again and decided that early-thirty-something was more accurate.

Next to him was a blond with scruffy hair, a wide smile, and a trendy jacket thrown ultra-carelessly over an ironic t-shirt that hinted at a very well-maintained physique. I assumed, correctly, that this was Bobby. He looked more like a surfer than a business professional, but the cut of the clothes and communication device built into his wristband suggested the latter. He had an open, friendly face, but I wasn't drawn to him. Bobby kind of reminded me of the strong, athletic guys in school who used to try and beat me up before I arranged for them to get caught with drugs and sent to the "special" school. Clients who were that friendly were the ones who tended to like to disfigure me, or at least threaten to.

The other man seemed calm, relaxed, put together. He was still in comparison to his friend's movement, quiet in response to his noise. His voice was smooth, lulling me into a strange sense of security, and his eyes were so piercing, so blue...

"Is there someone who runs this place who I can talk to?"

He sounded impatient, but his voice was still nice to listen to. "Yes, sir," I said, allowing myself to be smitten with the fact that someone was deigning to speak to me. I only noticed the awkward silence once it had gone on too long.

"Sorry, sir," I muttered, standing and ducking my head away from an imaginary blow. "I'll fetch Mistress Bethel at once."

I got her, and she cuffed me. She enjoyed hitting me so much that there didn't even need to be a reason for it. I followed her back out and resumed cleaning, surreptitiously wiping some of the dirt and blood off myself. I was suddenly aware of how dirty and beaten up I was.

"He waited too long and all the high class hookers sold out," Bobby explained, grinning as he pointed a finger in his friend's direction. "What can you do as far as merchandise?"

Mistress Bethel looked puzzled. I could almost see her greedy pig fingers counting the money she would make from such a transaction; she knew good and goddamned well that she didn't have any such "merchandise" that could reasonably be passed off as anything other than a cheap whore. She had no clue of what I could do. I thought about how nice it would be to see a Peace Day Celebration again, and how much of a respite I would have from being able to leave Bethel's Brothel for even one day.

Mistress Bethel stalled, asking questions and trying to think of some way to rake in some money off of the situation. Trying to figure out a way to dress up a donkey as a steed. A whore as a courtesan. The man wanted a pretty boy to keep him company at one of the nicest casinos in town, in hopes of getting a promotion.

He wanted a party favor, and I was happy to play the role. I even had a trick...

"Sir," I crawled out from behind the counter, heedless of the fact that I was beaten and bloody and scrubbing a floor like the lowly, smelly slave I was. "Sir, please, let me go with you! I'll be the best good luck charm you've ever had!"

Mistress Bethel started beating me instantly; the lazy bitch could move awfully fast when it came to beating me. She grabbed my hair to drag me out of the room, muttering apologies as she did.

I squirmed, desperate. "I can count cards!" I insisted, locking eyes with the man again. "I know how to play all the common casino games and I'm good at it! I'm good, really good, sir! Just let me show you!"

Mistress Bethel smacked me again, still attempting to drag me away.

Bobby gave his friend a look and shrugged. "If the kid can really count cards, that would be a neat trick!"

"He's too stupid for something like that!" Mistress Bethel snapped. "He's just a torture whore. Good for nothing but beating and fucking."

I clawed desperately at the floor, at the reception desk, anything I could to avoid being dragged away. I usually hid from visitors, but I fought to stay on the floor, displayed for all to see. It was my only chance.

The man held up a hand, indicating for Mistress Bethel to stop. I fell to my face.

"Do you have cards, then?" The man asked.

I nodded, my head spinning.

"Go get them so we can stop this foolishness!" Mistress Bethel snapped.

I tried to run, failing pretty damn miserably. I finally located the cards and flipped through them to make sure they were all in the deck. They were.

I returned, walking as boldly as I dared, trying to feel some of the confidence I needed to pull off my trick. Bobby grabbed the cards from my hand and announced that he was going to play dealer for a game of blackjack.

It was as easy to make this man win against the "house" as it had been to make myself win when I played against the other slaves for food or blankets. I had learned traditional card-counting measures when I was in middle school, and could figure out the probability of a given card coming up with near-perfect accuracy. Statistics had always been fun and challenging. I let myself get absorbed in the task, and in a few minutes, Bobby was cheering, and the man I wanted to rent me out went quiet, a slight indication of approval on his face.

"Give him the cards back," he said quietly. He turned to study me. "Have you ever attended any sort of formal event?"

I thought of how I must look, and I could see the doubt in his eyes. "Not since I was a kid, sir," I answered, then added, "but I swear, I'll do whatever you say. I learn fast and I promise I'll make you look lucky, and I'll be obedient and perfect, I promise!"

Bobby laughed. "Come on, Cash, I bet he cleans up all right! Take him home and try him out!"

"He is rather personable," he admitted, scrutinizing me. "A slave might even rectify my image, and he might not look too bad once he's cleaned up."

I wasn't sure whether to stand tall and display my bruises and welts, or shrivel to the floor to hide from his gaze. I stood there, frozen, instead.

As they talked about price, it dawned on me that I would still be stuck at the brothel for the rest of the month. I risked further beating and dropped to my knees. "Sirs, I'm sure you wouldn't want to take me to a nice event looking the way I do—only trash would leave such visible marks on their slave!"

I felt Mistress Bethel glaring at me, probably memorizing the two or three inches of my back that weren't already covered in marks to beat later. "If you rent me out until the Celebration, I can heal and look much better and learn how best to please you. Nobody will ever know that you rented me out from a place like this, it will be like I've been trained specially for you!"

The man frowned. "I'm not sure if I need a slave around for a month..."

"Give me a chance?" I begged. "I can cook, I can clean, I'll beg you to fuck me every night and do everything else you tell me to! Mistress Bethel just uses me for torture—I could be worse off by the time you pick me up for the Peace Day Celebration!"

My Mistress seethed, and I was terrified of what she would do to me if I was left with her. To my surprise, the man relented, and Mistress Bethel quoted him a price to rent me for the month.

"May as well buy him for that price!" Bobby commented. "He could be fun to have around."

"If *you* like him so much, why don't *you* buy him?" the other man retorted.

I was astonished when he went on to discuss the purchase price with Mistress Bethel. They settled on a price, and Mistress Bethel retrieved my ownership paperwork.

I dared to stand up, watching the man sign his name on my ownership papers. "Cashiel Michaud." Cashiel. I rolled it around in my mouth like a cock. Er, like a candy. Or whatever people who aren't whores say. I wanted to try to be a bit more classy, since I was leaving the brothel.

"Keep a firm hand with him," Mistress Bethel sneered at me. "He's a stupid whore. Very difficult to train."

I couldn't resist. I knew she couldn't touch me, and I lost my fucking mind at the momentary freedom. "Difficult for ignorant assholes like you!" I spat out. "You wouldn't know intelligence or potential if it bit you in the ass!"

I felt a rough hand grabbing the back of my neck, and it occurred to me that Mistress Bethel wasn't exactly the person I needed to be worrying about anymore. The grip tightened and my master dragged me outside, ownership papers clutched tightly in his other hand.

Once we got outside, he reached into his pocket, pulled out a set of keys, and tossed them to Bobby. "Bring the hov-car around," he ordered, and Bobby obeyed without question.

I was slammed against a wall by my neck, and I tried to look pathetic.

"I don't deny that she deserved that, but I will not tolerate disrespect!" My master hissed, his face close to mine. At first I thought he was being intimidating, but I realized he didn't want to cause a scene, as if anything could cause a scene in that part of town.

"If I *ever* hear you speak to a free person like that again, you will be beaten and gagged for the remainder of the day, is that clear?"

I didn't move. "Yes, master," I whispered. I was relieved to avoid beating that day, but his threat was real.

He pushed me away and we stood in silence until Bobby returned with the hov-car. We dropped Bobby off at his house, and I stared out the window, amazed that I was never returning to Bethel's Brothel. I dozed off, lulled by the movement of the hov-car and the momentary safety. I was taken by surprise when I heard the door to the hov-car open, revealing my irritated master.

"I'm sorry, master," I mumbled, trying to surreptitiously wipe the drool from my face. "I wasn't able to sleep much when I was with Mistress Bethel."

He gave me wide berth as I exited the hov-car. "Don't mention her again," he ordered, calm, yet threatening. "I wasn't particularly fond of her."

I wanted to agree with him, but that might have been disrespectful, and I didn't want to challenge him. I wanted to be good, to jump through hoops, to earn and keep my place. I wanted to try with him, like I hadn't with anyone else since I had been Demoted.

Chapter 3
Arrival

I followed him into the house in silence. It was meticulously clean, almost to the point of not looking lived in, and I wondered why he bothered to purchase me if he had an adequate cleaning service already. Clearly, he could afford a cleaning service; the house spoke of money, taste, refinement. It wasn't overly large, but it was spacious, and each piece of furniture I could see must have cost more than my parents used to make in a year. The casually displayed rack of vintage wine and massive vidscreen in the living room confirmed my observations.

I tried my best to memorize each room, and I ran into my master because I was too busy trying to remember the layout of the house to realize he had stopped walking. I yelped and cowered away.

"Pay attention," he advised, his tone dry. He opened a door to a room on our right, and I forced myself to stand tall and act like I wasn't terrified to be beaten. When he reached over to turn the light switch on, I flinched away again, whimpering.

"Jesus, is that all she ever did was hit you!" my master exclaimed, grabbing me rather roughly by the arm and pulling me into the room.

I did my best not to disappear, trying hard to stay in my body and not float off like I do sometimes. "Yes, master," I answered.

He sighed. "Well, calm down, I'm not going to waste my time hitting you for no good reason. You were right, only trash would leave their slaves marked up like you are—my god, you're bruised and beaten all over!"

I wanted to hide, which was stupid, because there wasn't even anything to hide behind. I was wearing some hotpants and nothing else, and even those were ripped. My clientele never cared much for costumes.

"This will be your room," my master informed me. "There's a bathroom attached; I don't fancy sharing my shower with you. You'll use this one, and you will keep it clean at all times. Your job right now is to get in there and get yourself cleaned up so I can tolerate being in the same room as you. You'll find shampoo and soap in there and you'd better put them to good use. I'm assuming you can bathe yourself?"

The words stung more than I wanted to admit. I wanted to scream at him that it wasn't my fault, that I hadn't chosen this, that I hadn't made the decision to get hosed off on the back patio instead of being allowed in the shower because the blood stained the tiles. I never chose to have other men's come in my hair and on my skin.

"Yes, master," I replied tonelessly.

"Good," he nodded, satisfied. He turned to walk out.

"Master?" I risked asking. "What should I wear?"

He turned, looking irritated, but not exactly angry. "I'll bring some clothes," he muttered. "Don't walk around naked in my house like a whore."

I had always thought the shame would stop if someone saved me, took me home, but it wasn't stopping. I was torn between screaming and sobbing, but neither was acceptable.

I reminded myself that he was at least bringing me clothes, letting me wear them, letting me shower. He didn't even seem particularly interested in fucking me, which I hoped meant that I would get a chance to heal from the tears left from brutal fisting I had endured a week before. I focused my thoughts on how nice it would be to be able to shit or sit down without pain again.

I went into the bathroom once he left and peeled off the disgusting hotpants, dropping them in a trash bin. I didn't even care if he wanted me to keep them; they were disgusting and they reminded me of what I had been doing and what had been done to me.

I looked at myself in the mirror, the first time I had the chance to look in weeks. My face had mostly been left alone, at Mistress Bethel's request, but there were still some bruises there. The cutting and breaking of skin had been reserved for my back, stomach, and legs. I wondered what the hell I could wear to the Peace Day Celebration to hide the mess.

I looked like a beat up whore, and I was ashamed to realize I was still naked. Like a whore. I was doing exactly what I was ordered not to do.

I turned on the water and stepped in immediately, yelping and pressing against the wall when the warm stream hit the open welts on my skin. The hose on the patio had been miserably, painfully cold, especially in winter, but at least it had somewhat of a numbing effect. The shower just burned, and hurt, and it took me a minute before logic kicked in and I realized I could turn the fucking water down to a cooler temperature. I tried not to cry as I lathered up a washcloth and started to carefully wash away terrible mess on my skin. I had to stop three or four times to rinse the blood, dirt and come from the washcloth.

I was sobbing by the time I finished.

Washing my hair was a little more pleasant, which was why I saved it for last. There was minimal damage done to my head. It hurt to lift my arms above my head, but I figured that would go away. A few days before, one of the brothel clients had tied my arms together and hung me from them for hours while they beat me. I had felt far worse pain.

I finally got clean, and I felt a little bit better. I even forced my-self to wash my ass, which made me cry some more, and my dick, which miraculously got hard. I took advantage of it, jerking off into the shower drain like I used to when I was growing up at home. My master hadn't told me not to jerk off, and besides, he didn't look like he wanted to fuck me. Maybe de-louse me, but not fuck me. I didn't think of much of anything while I jerked off. It was barely sexual for me anymore; it released tension, it killed some pain, it gave me an endorphin rush that was better than the drugs I had tried a few times as a teenager.

I came out and took another look at myself in the mirror. I looked better clean. I hoped my master would like me better, too. I desperately wanted him to like me, at least a little, at least enough that he wouldn't hurt me too bad or sell me back to Bethel's Brothel.

I found a towel and clothes on the counter; my master must have brought them in while I was showering. I dried off quickly, hoping I wouldn't get in trouble for getting blood on the towel. He had to have known, right? He saw me. He had to have known what would happen when I went under a stream of water. He had to have known that all of the scabs and fresh wounds would open up. He had money; I knew he shouldn't be too upset about a towel, even if it was a plush, high-quality towel, not just a scrap of old sheets like I had gotten used to. I trembled at the thought, anyway.

I stood there, dabbing at the cuts with the towel, waiting for them to stop bleeding before getting dressed. I heard a loud knock, which must have been from the entrance to the bedroom, not the bathroom, because it was muffled.

"Yes, master?" I called out, wishing I would hurry up and stop bleeding already.

"What's taking so long?"

I winced, afraid that I had angered him with my slowness, not to mention the bloodstains he had yet to discover. "I'm sorry, master." I tried my best to sound pathetic. "I have to wait until I stop bleeding. I don't want to damage the clothes you brought me."

I expected him to go away, but I heard his footsteps drawing closer. Suddenly, he was standing in the doorway. He looked at me, his nose turned up in disgust, and he raised an eyebrow as he saw the towel. "Yes, it would be best if you weren't bleeding. You've ruined the towel, and you've managed to bleed on the floor as well. Turn around and lean against the wall."

I panicked, unable to make sense of why he would have me turn for whipping if he wanted me to stop bleeding. It made no sense. "Master, please," I whimpered, turning around anyway. I expected to hear an angry reproach.

I heard a cabinet opening.

"Calm down, boy, I'm going to bandage you up before you bleed all over everything!" My master snapped at me. I noticed him taking out a first aid kit, and I calmed a little.

He wasn't particularly gentle as he wiped away blood and bandaged the worst of the cuts, but he wasn't trying to hurt me, either. He sprayed something on that burned, and I struggled not to cry out.

I failed, just like I failed to stop crying.

He just kept taping bandages over the wounds. When he finished with my back, he turned me around with a hand on my shoulder and took care of the ones in front as well. I could have reached those ones, but it felt good to have someone take care of me, even if he was doing it as methodically as humanly possible.

"Do you need to see a doctor?" he asked, his voice quiet.

"No, master," I replied, without even thinking of it. I didn't want to inconvenience him with complaints. Besides, I figured the pain in my shoulders would subside soon enough.

My master nodded, satisfied. "Clean up, get dressed, and meet me in the study."

"Yes, master," I replied. I did as he ordered, dressing myself quickly. The clothes hurt as they brushed against my skin, but at least the worst of it was bandaged. The clothes were soft and a few sizes larger than what I usually wore, even when I had been at a healthy weight. I glanced at the spray my master used on me, unsurprised to see that it was an antibiotic and disinfectant spray.

I found the study without too much difficulty. My master was sitting at a big, mahogany desk that matched his appearance and personality perfectly. Dark. Stately. Intimidating. It just needed to be black, to match his clothes. It was rather handsome, too, the desk.

"You may kneel," he said, interrupting my musings.

He said it like an invitation, but it was an order. I obeyed, regardless, and waited for his next demand.

"You're emaciated," he pointed out.

I bit my tongue to keep from screaming at him. I hated him for making it sound like it was my fault

"Do you have some sort of eating disorder, or did she just not feed you?"

"She didn't feed me," I muttered. "Master."

"Cut the attitude," he warned. "I won't put up with it."

I didn't say anything, because I was still irrationally seething. He continued just as calmly.

"You'll have free access to the kitchen and all the food. I want you to eat, get back up to a normal weight. Eat whatever you'd like, and I'll show you later how to order supplies and groceries. You can order what you'd like. You said you can cook?"

I hesitated. I had said that, hadn't I? "I can learn, master."

He went silent. "That wasn't how you described it earlier," he reminded me.

"I meant—"

"Don't lie to me again," he cut me off. "And you'd better learn quickly, if you want to eat. I go out for meals more often than not, and you'll be sorely disappointed if you think I'm bringing you home something."

My face burned with shame. I stayed silent, waiting for more blame, maybe punishment. He was interrogating me like a common criminal.

"Lying, hiding, and any number of other vices may have kept you safe in the past," he said, his voice a little softer. "You would have said anything to get out of there, understandably. But no more."

I nodded, unable to speak. I knew how to handle cruelty; the fact that he was trying to be understanding was unfamiliar and terrifying.

"Can you actually clean?"

Either he was taunting me, or he thought I was that stupid. Either way, I couldn't reply at first. I bit down on my lip until I tasted blood before I spoke. "Yes, master. I can clean just fine."

"Good," he continued, as if there was nothing the matter. As if I wasn't trying to rub tears off my face. "I'll cancel the housecleaning service. Nice to see you'll be good for something until the party."

I was struck with the irrational desire to tell him all the other things I could do. All the ambitions I once had. I wanted to tell him that I could help him with account management, whatever research he did at work, mod his tablet and wristband, do all sorts of cool shit, but I didn't, because slaves aren't supposed to do cool shit like that. "I'll try, master," I mumbled.

"I'm sure," he said dryly. "You may move freely around the house. Make sure things are cleaned. Don't pry or look through my belongings; that will be very unpleasant for you. Let me know at once if there's something you need, whether that's medical treatment or cleaning supplies or anything else. If you're sore, you should rest for a few days; I don't want you any more damaged, is that clear?"

"Yes, master."

"I work from home quite often. Stay out of my way while I'm working, I don't want a needy slave around," he ordered. "If you have a question, figure it out yourself or ask me later. I assume you can make simple decisions on your own, don't come bothering me all the time. That's why I don't have a slave. Pesky things, really, always underfoot."

I seethed at being compared to a child or an unwanted pet. "I'll stay out of your way, master."

"Good," he nodded, frowning at me anyway. "We'll start next week working on training you to act like something more than a common brothel whore. For now, take care of yourself and keep up around the house. Are there any questions?"

I wanted to ask him if he hated me so much, or if he was always this cold. I wanted to ask why he bought me in the first place. "Just one, master. Are there any food allergies, dislikes, or preferences that I should be aware of?"

He looked at me for a moment, and I thought he might get up and hit me. That would have been better than the scrutiny. Suddenly, he smiled, ever-so-slightly, the first he had directed at me. "I *detest* olives," he replied. "But anything else is fair game."

"Thank you, master." I waited for his next command.

"Go find the kitchen and then get some sleep," he relented, after staring at me for a while longer. He waved his hand, dismissing me.

I ate like a starved animal that night, pausing only to notice the quality of food in his refrigerator. Expensive sodas, high-quality restaurant leftovers that had been left untouched, supplies of foods bought from international imports. I tried to notice what I could, but I was starving, just like he said, and once I ate my fill, I made my way to my new bedroom. I stripped off my clothes and crawled into bed, thrilled at the soft, cushiony mattress and pillows. Even if my new master hated me, I was in love with the bed, and nothing else mattered.

Chapter 4
Expectations

I never wanted a slave, and the more I think about it, the last one I would possibly want would be one like Sascha. When Bobby told me he had a lead on a slave for the Peace Day Celebration, I never expected him to drag me to a sleazy whorehouse. I thought he had a legitimate lead, maybe a new escort service, preferably one with free persons instead of property. I swore I was done with slaves. I made up my mind years ago to avoid live subjects, only dealing with the research and financing aspects of the whole Demoted system, and yet... the way he looked up at me, there was something more. That desperation, that ruthless desire to survive. I haven't seen it in years, but I recognized it. At least, I thought I did.

Sascha is difficult. He amazed me at the Peace Day Celebration last night, making me wonder how such a damaged individual can put on such a convincing act. Any other time we're together, he ignores what I say in favor of staring at me in fear. The look on his face when he does something wrong, or thinks he's done something wrong, is terrible. He's appropriate and grateful, something the years of abuse will naturally create, but he doesn't seem to have many other original thoughts in his head. Was I wrong? Did I see something that wasn't there?

I do my best to leave him be. He seems so uncomfortable around me. I have my own work to do anyway. My own indentured servitude.

Dean & Chanu Associates, the soulless investment firm I've been with for seven years, demands an excessive amount of time. Playing with numbers, calculating financial possibilities, researching trends and comparing the best investments and returns in every profitable industry. It's busy work, something the damn slave could probably do if he's as bright as I thought. But he doesn't speak, or ask, or do anything. I thought I saw a little spark from him when he demanded to know my food preferences, but it didn't pan out to much more than safe, boring dishes. He looks at me in terror when he prepares something for me to eat, taking any enjoyment out of the meals. He cooks and cleans and follows orders, but aside from that, he hides in his room most of the time.

The abuse he has endured is horrible. I knew it at the brothel, but the full extent didn't become apparent until I was bandaging him up once I brought him home. He wasn't just beaten and starved, he was purposefully used as a torture victim. He is covered in scars, old and new, some with patterns and initials visible. It was intentional. No matter how severe re-education center training is, there is never the intentional, pointless infliction of pain that my new slave has endured. It sickens me to see it. Pain can be fun at times, but what has been done to this boy is just wrong. Disturbing. The panicked look he gets in his eyes when I move too quickly or speak too loudly unnerves me, so I avoid moving or speaking around him. I'm not sure if he can be rehabilitated.

He leaves me alone as well, although I guess he's following my orders. I wonder sometimes if he's even alive, but then he shows up, cowering and nervous, and I remember why I've avoided him.

But the show he put on at the Peace Day Celebration makes me think that perhaps he's not so damaged as he seems. My boss found him attractive, which he is, even in spite of the condition I bought him in. I got many approving nods for having such a pretty, well-trained slave, although I found his training to be distinctly lacking. Still, he may prove to be more of an asset than a liability.

I hear a knock on the door to my office, very light, like he's trying not to make a sound. It irks me—if he's going to knock, he can at least do so with some force! But at least he's not loitering around until I notice him. Proper as it may be, it's annoying in one's own house. I wait for him to come in, and when he doesn't, I call "what?" through the door.

If he wants to speak with me, he can come in here.

He does, and he looks even more terrified.

"Master, I was wondering..."

He stands there trembling, ducking his head down and allowing his hair to fall over his eyes, shielding him. He looks ridiculously young, like he should still be in school. Of course, that would put me in the position of the principal or something of the sort, which is the exact opposite of what I want. I scowl and wait for him to get to the point.

Finally, he takes a deep breath, steadying himself before he speaks. "May I look at a tablet, master, for some recipes?"

I roll my eyes and look back down at the work I have on my desk. He finally interacts with me, and it's to borrow a damn tablet? "I'll see what I have around. Go. Don't bother me."

I wave him off, hoping he'll leave me to my work. I've asked him plenty of times if he needs anything, but he's always so quiet. I hope it's a good sign.

I resume my work, but not before doing a little research on the boy. There's little that I can find; most of the accessible information on children is destroyed once they are Demoted. What's left is school newspapers, community announcements, things like that. Not very useful, but they give me a picture of who this slave is, or, rather, who he was. Average family, no connections to anyone particularly important, no outstanding achievements from anyone. I can barely tell him apart from any other slave, the banal existence of the typical slaves blending together as I continue to read.

Sascha's reports from the re-education center are far more interesting, and probably far more relevant to his life as it is now. He's been marked as a problem, nominated for research and medical testing, but spared, perhaps by a favorite guard or instructor. As much as the re-education centers are standardized, there is always room to play, especially when one takes a liking to a slave.

Before he was so damaged, I could see Sascha being likable.

I finish my work for the day and dig through a drawer full of old electronics; last year's wristband model, some com devices, and finally, an older tablet. It's a little used, but it will suffice for the slave, at least until I decide whether I'm going to keep him much longer. I bring it to him in his room, obviously surprising him.

"Older generation. Probably the model you're familiar with," I explain. "Let me know if you need help working it."

"Thank you, master," he replies, staring up at me in shock and awe.

The way he looks at me is unnerving. I haven't hurt him and I don't intend to. But the worshipful look on his face is over the top. All this, for a used tablet?

"I would like you to learn to cook," I say calmly, hoping I can get him to relax. "I'd also like you to brush up on some more formal training. I'll be flashing over some training manuals and videos that will review some of the basics of posture, movement, and conduct."

Sascha goes pale, looking up at me with wide eyes.

"I'm sorry, master," he mumbles. "I didn't realize I wasn't pleasing you. Please, I promise, I can do better."

I try not to scowl. He's not exactly begging me to keep him, but it's what he wants, and the desperation puts me off. "You haven't done anything wrong," I assure him. "Your performance at the Peace Day Celebration was wonderful. You far surpassed my expectations, and you impressed my colleagues. I'd just like to invest more time in working with you."

He looks up at me, hopeful once more. "Thank you, sir. You won't regret it."

"Get to work," I order. The gratitude is as unnerving as the desperation.

My master hasn't given me any indication of what my future will be, now that the Peace Day Celebration is over, but the tablet gives me hope. Even more, the fact that he is specifically choosing to invest in my training makes me think that he really might keep me instead of selling me or giving me away.

But then, he might just be investing in me as a product for sale.

Over the next few days, he flashes a few instructional booklets over to my tablet, which I review carefully, in addition to watching videos of how to cook and looking up recipes.

I sigh when I first see the training materials, because they are so

fucking basic and elementary, but then I realize that he must be mis-
taking my fear for a lack of training. As it is, I have forgotten so much
of the training I was supposed to have learned at the re-education
center, having spent far too much time being used for nothing but
pain. I can't blame my master for the insulting level of materials; after
all, I sometimes still forget to speak or that I can move around without
permission. It's amazing how quickly one can turn from a human into
an animal, and I'm rather dismayed to realize that I've turned into a
rather pathetic sort of animal. Maybe a goldfish. No. Goldfish swim
around freely.

I'm experimenting in the kitchen when I hear him attempting to
place a com call, then hanging up when he receives the alert that the
number is no longer in service. I hear him curse, and despite my desire to avoid him when he's angry, I step out to where he's sitting in
the dining room.

"Sir, is there anything I can do for you?" I want so badly to prove
to him that I can be useful.

He shakes his head. "I was just trying to order Thai food," he explains. "It seems they've closed down."

Thai food does sound delicious, and I found a recipe a few days
ago that I've tested a few times. "I could make some, master?" It's
supposed to be an offer, but it comes out as a question, because I'm
debating whether it's a good idea to suggest it or not.

"Don't bother," he dismisses me. "Find me the brochure for the
place on the East side of town."

"You said last time that they overcook their noodles and use too
much salt in their sauce," I point out, recalling what I had overheard
him complaining to Bobby about. "Although, I'm pretty sure it wasn't
salt, it was the fish sauce that made it salty."

He raises an eyebrow at me. "Eavesdropping is your new way of
getting into trouble?"

He seems to be in a decent mood, but I press against the wall anyway, clenching my teeth when I put too much pressure on my injured
shoulder. I don't know why I pull away, it's not like I'd run away
from him or anything, and he's never even hit me. "Uh, no, master,
I just... I overheard, and so when I tried to make the recipe myself, I
made sure that it was better. You put the leftovers in the fridge and

never ate them, so I tried them a few times and I found a recipe and I've tried making it, except I made sure to make it a little different than the one you had. We have the ingredients; I can make it."

He laughs, which stings a little, but then he says, "Hell, why not. That place was pretty awful, and they took forever to deliver, too."

"I'll be quick, master."

He waves me off, and I head straight to the kitchen. I have actually been learning how to cook since I got the tablet, usually when my master goes out to do whatever he does all day. It was a challenge, at first, because it was something I had never tried, but cooking reminds me a lot of chemistry: you just follow the instructions, so I took to it pretty quickly. I can't help enjoying myself when I'm learning something new, and this is interesting and challenging enough to keep me on my toes, especially with dishes I'm not particularly familiar with. For the first time in my life I can order whatever groceries I'd like to be delivered regardless of cost or rarity, and that alone is inspiring enough for me to want to experiment.

But it's not my mouth I want to feed, because after three years of eating terrible shit or nothing at all, I would be content eating bread every day. It's my master I want to feed, because pleasing him is certainly in my best interest. Even if he still chooses to go out to eat all the time, I hope that showing him I can learn to cook will somehow convince him that he should keep me. Not only that, but a part of me just wants to prove to him that I can do it, that I'm not too stupid to learn how to cook a goddamned meal.

I'm pretty confident in my Pad Thai recipe, because I've made it multiple times in the past few days, changing and refining the flavors a little bit at a time. The other good thing about starving for years is you don't get bored very quickly, which allows you to try all sorts of tiny changes back to back. I just got the tamarind paste in yesterday, as it was on some sort of special import list, and I feel like it really brings the dish together.

My master never told me I had a budget for groceries, after all.

So I soak the noodles, and prepare the shrimp, because I know that he likes shrimp better than chicken, and I wash the vegetables and I make the sauce, and I forget to be afraid for a few minutes as I become absorbed in my task.

I finish, placing the food into two bowls, which I carry out without a thought. I realize, about halfway across the dining room, that I probably shouldn't eat at the table with my master, but it's where I usually sit to eat, because I usually eat while he's not home. I hesitate, and only the burning of the hot bowls in my hands gets me to move, depositing his in front of him before setting mine down and standing there awkwardly.

He ignores me, like the bastard he is, and pokes around at his dish critically for a moment before trying some. I tense up, like this is the most important thing in the world, which maybe it is. He tries some more before looking at me, and the fact that he's even looking at me is shocking.

"I'm actually quite impressed," he says, calmly, like he compliments me all the time or something. "You put that takeout place to shame."

It takes me a moment to process it, because I'm expecting some sort of criticism or dismissal, but the words finally sink in and I smile, daring to let the tiniest bit of hope cross my mind. "Thank you, master."

"Perhaps I'll stay in for dinner on occasion," he comments, and I think I might die, I'm so elated.

Okay, it's overdramatic, but it's how I'm feeling. I figure it's a side effect of feeling like an absolute fuck up for so long.

"I can learn to make other things, master," I rush to say, before the moment is spoiled, before he forgets or I forget or something is bad. "Anything you want, you can tell me, and I'll learn, I like to learn, and I'm getting good at basic things, and I could make whatever you'd like." It occurs to me that I've crossed the line from "eager" to "desperate," but I can't seem to stop myself.

He rolls his eyes at me. "Sit down and eat before it gets cold." He kicks out the chair a little bit, pointing. "Not that you should probably be sitting at the table with me, but I'm not particularly inclined to care at the moment. I suppose it's what I get for being gone so much; you pick up bad habits."

I sit, feeling smug, and ignoring the "bad habits" comment. I am inclined to believe that if he were really bothered by it, he would order me to sit on the floor or in the kitchen or something.

We eat in peace, and I look over at him for just a moment, enjoying how happy he is with something I made, and I feel this painful longing to stay with him. To belong to him. To be safe and valued, even if only because I make noodles better than the takeout place on the East side.

"It means a lot to you that I keep you, doesn't it?" he asks, like he's read my goddamn mind.

I turn away, look at my food. "Yes, master." I can't bring myself to say anymore, because if I start to speak, I'll end up begging, and if I beg and he turns me down, I might kill myself. I can't take the thought of going back to a brothel again.

"I *had* planned on selling you, when I bought you," he states, still calm. I guess he can be calm; he's not the one whose life gets passed around like a used hov-car. "I even thought I might give you to Bobby or something, he certainly seemed interested enough, and I have no idea what to get him for his birthday."

I force myself to remember it's not that bad, Bobby seems friendly, and it's not a brothel. Hell, my master isn't even *nice* to me, I just want to stay with him because I'm comfortable and he hasn't hurt me, yet. "Yes, master," I force the words out of my mouth. Nothing more. No begging.

"We'll see what happens," he says, and I'm strangely comforted. "Like I said, you need to brush up on your training, but you made a good impression. Besides, I'm keeping you at least until I find out what kind of curry you make."

Chapter 5
Re-Education

I wasn't always so desperate to be owned. There was a time when I was sure I would succeed in life, when I thought there was no chance I would ever be a slave.

That all changed so quickly.

From the time I was little, it was clear that I was the one who was going to succeed. The first to walk, the first to talk, the first to take the trip out the birth canal, although I fortunately don't remember that. I was always able to one-up my twin brother, Abriel, even when we were born, even if only by eight minutes.

The differences grew as quickly as we did. By our first birthday, I was starting to get a grasp on language. My twin's name was the first word I ever spoke, while crawling around the living room and demanding my mom's help whenever Abriel started crying. As the stories and videos show, I seemed almost unable to be content when my little brother was upset. By three, when our parents bought our way into one of the most competitive preschools in town, I had learned how to write my name, and Abriel's, and was eager to get a better understanding of the mysterious world of letters and numbers.

We didn't know it at the time, but this sort of success would determine our futures. At night, our parents watched the news while we played, and the stories of the world's dangerous overpopulation and the new diseases that were defeating even the most cutting-edge technology faded into mere background noise. We had no idea that we were part of the next generation of children who would be thrust into a system designed to curb that population and solve those problems, selecting the brightest of the population and pushing them toward even higher levels of critical thinking and achievement.

Abriel, to put it nicely, was "below average." That was the term the psychologist used, anyway, when she had the conference with my parents and Abriel and me, after trying to chase me out of the room. Bri-Bri and I were only eight, and there was no way I was letting that woman talk to Abriel alone, not after she made him cry the first time with blocks and pictures and things that were too hard for him. Anyone who messed with my brother messed with me, and I considered myself quite a force to be reckoned with. My parents always did say that I excelled in temper tantrums and defiance along with everything else.

The scary psychologist, who was actually quite nice to me, explained that "below average" was why Abriel didn't talk until he was almost two, why he still read the books with more pictures than words, and why he preferred to color and play with our puppy more than read books and solve puzzles like I did. She explained that Abriel would continue to struggle in school, and that it might get harder as he got older. She explained to my devastated parents that Abriel would have to study a lot and have tutors and take remedial classes to catch him up for the Assessment.

When I was eight, all I really knew about the Assessment was that it was the last thing you did as a child. I understood, vaguely, that it was like a test, but I didn't know what it was about, and it bothered me more that nobody would tell me. I considered it a personal offense to not be told things. All I had learned about the Assessment was that you had to be "good" on it, and that people who weren't were Demoted, but I didn't know much about what Demoted was either, just that you didn't want it to happen to you.

After the psychologist told us about "below average," our parents spent a lot of time looking worried around Abriel and having "adult conversations" that they wouldn't let me listen to. I heard the word "Demoted" whispered so many times that I finally snuck into their room one night, snatched my dad's tablet, and looked up what it meant, and what the Assessment was all about. Some of the words were too big for me, and others just didn't make sense, but I got the general idea, and I had never been more worried about anything.

That was the night I started waking Abriel up and teaching him.

Our parents found out, weeks later, and they tried to dissuade me, but my wails and shrieks and temper tantrums convinced them otherwise. Instead, they appealed to my quickly growing logical side and set up an hour before bed every night for me to teach my brother everything I possibly could. I started by teaching him exactly what the Assessment was and what being Demoted meant.

Sadly, I think I learned more from those sessions than he did, and my parents must have realized that, which is why they let it continue for so long. Looking back, it horrifies me that they used one son to further the development of the other, but it was just the way things were done. Even the play dates that our parents arranged for us were focused on learning and achievement; both our parents and the parents of other children seemed eager to use each other as stepping-stones to get a competitive edge. I was the child they had hoped for, my quest for knowledge and new skills never ending, but I wouldn't leave my brother behind.

I read fluently by age seven, started accelerated track courses at age ten, and spent most of the day dozing or pissing off teachers by the time I got to high school. I was a bit of a jerk back then, but what teenage boy isn't a bit of a jerk? The truth was, my life had always been easy. I didn't study, I didn't try, I didn't even care most days, preferring to ditch class. Still, I managed to get mostly A grades, with a B here and there because some teacher felt like going on a power trip and marking me down for my "attitude."

Could I help it if my tenth grade English teacher didn't appreciate my term paper on the subject of "Assholes in Academia?" I had a full bibliography and everything.

Abriel struggled his way through middle and high school. He started dating his girlfriend during our freshman year, and between her and I, we forced him to keep up his good grades. I didn't mind that he had someone and I didn't, just like I never minded when he fit in better with the other kids than I did, but it made me feel left out. I had always assumed that we'd find a set of twin girls, or, preferably, a brother and sister, because I liked boys a lot more than girls, and we'd each date one of them, and it would always be the four of us, just like it had always been the two of us. Instead, Abriel spent free periods and lunch with Maggie, enjoying the success he had in his relationship as much as I enjoyed my success in education. I was placed in advanced track classes, and my guidance counselor threatened me with extra gym classes if I didn't comply.

Abriel struggled to keep his grades up while I tried my hand at computer hacking and college-level math just to keep myself from causing even more trouble. Our report cards came out as mirror images of each other—mine always talking about my intellect and academic ability, along with my "oppositionality" and "defiance" and "difficulty cooperating with peers." Abriel's always mentioned his wonderful social skills and friendliness and politeness, but actively avoided talking about his academic struggles. Unless a rare good grade occurred, that wasn't the sort of thing that got mentioned.

I always wanted to protect my brother, but as we grew older and our differences grew stronger, I knew I had to do something to help him. My decision should have been difficult, but it wasn't. I focused on the strategy, I made my plan, and I executed it flawlessly. The day that we took our Assessments passed quickly, but I never doubted my plan or my intentions.

We sat there, silent, as the results were calculated. You could almost hear the nervousness in the room as the answer sheets were scanned through a machine, which scored the sheets right on the spot instead of sending it wirelessly to another system. All my research had indicated that they used this system for security, just like they had used paper forms for the tests themselves. So much technology, yet the best and brightest can always outsmart it. The creators of the Assessment thought they had the system beat by reverting back to the anachronistic paper forms, but I had exploited that.

Finally, the machine made an innocuous beeping sound, and I felt my pulse race as I realized that the results were in. A sheet of paper printed off, and I scanned the proctor's face for any sign of a problem. She looked calm, unsurprised. My deception went undetected.

The proctor read the names off of a sheet. Abriel and I were on different lists, sealing my fate as Demoted, and his as passing. Those on the first list were instructed to go to the gym, those on the second were instructed to go to the cafeteria. The makeup of the groups seemed to be puzzling most of the kids. Mostly because I was in the one headed to go to the room where you get Demoted, and even the many kids whom I had alienated over the years knew I should have passed the Assessment with flying colors. I couldn't bring myself to look at anyone, too afraid that I would give away my secret and ruin the whole thing.

We were instructed not to speak or exchange anything on the way out, but I tackled Abriel and gave him a hug and told him I loved him before joining my group. I was certain that I would never see him again. The proctor glared at me, but she gave the same confused look that Abriel did. I ignored it like I ignored the stares of my former classmates.

I was herded with my not-peers into the gym, where the lower echelons of our fine academy had been gathered. Nice enough kids, most of them, from what I knew, but I hadn't had classes with most of them since we were in elementary school. They knew me, and a few of them glanced around hopefully upon seeing me, perhaps thinking that they had been placed in the non-Demoted group. I felt guilty to disappoint them. We were lined up according to our SID numbers — Statewide Identification. I had always hated that acronym, but it was unsettling to be rid of it. Once a person is Demoted, their SID is stripped and they are assigned a property number instead. Nobody has ever thought to make a corny acronym for that.

We were kept standing, and when people complained, they were immediately shouted at by a man with a taser. I thought of how petty it seemed to threaten to tase high school kids for talking. I suddenly realized that we weren't kids anymore, not protected as youth or innocent in the eye of the law. Neither was the other group, but they had achieved free adult status. It struck me as comical that my little brother was an adult.

I went along with the orders, and a few minutes later, about one tenth of the graduating class was standing in the gym, lined up in nice little rows. The doors closed, and I started to get a little alarmed when I heard them lock.

A man in the front of the room, dressed in standard government enforcement teal, picked up a microphone and started speaking into it.

"I'm sorry to inform you, but you've been Demoted. From this day on, you will take your place in society as a Demoted human. You will be considered an adult minor under the law, under the protection of your trainers or masters. You will be considered property for tax purposes. We understand that you are of the lower range of mental functioning, and this shall be taken into account."

It sounded easy, if dreadfully boring.

"You will spend the next two years in one of the state-approved re-education facilities. You will be taken there immediately after the sterilization procedure is completed and all shots are made up-to-date. From this point on, you will cease speaking, making unnecessary noise, or causing disruption. The guards will escort you to the transportation modules of their choice."

A small girl who I remembered from the art class I took in tenth grade piped up, in tears. "What about my family? When do I get to say goodbye!"

The man who just finished addressing us turned his nose up as though he smelled a skunk. "You are property. You have no families." He turned to exit the stage.

The girl darted toward him, yelling something that I couldn't quite make out from where I stood. Before she could reach him, her words were cut off by screams as she was tased simultaneously by two of the guards who flanked the man who had spoken to us. She fell to the ground, twitching and sobbing.

It hit me just how real it was.

Nobody else tried anything sudden or impulsive, which was good, because the smell of singed flesh made me a little nauseous. Any other day, it would have been lunchtime. I wondered if they planned on feeding us.

We were herded into hover-vans, which were decidedly unappealing. Vans of all sorts had gone out of style decades earlier, since most people drove alone or with one passenger, two at most. People didn't tend to have more than one or two kids due to the population growth and the escalating cost of education. Hover-buses caught on briefly, before the e-rail system caught on in most areas. Vans fell into use only for prisons and the like. Being Demoted wasn't much different.

We weren't fed until we arrived at the re-education facility. A big, brick building stood four stories tall, and electrified gates surrounded the perimeter. It seemed like a bit much to me, but for all I knew, maybe people tried to flee from a government-imposed life of servitude on a regular basis. It didn't seem like the brightest idea in my book, but then, the place supposedly housed people who weren't so bright. I discarded any hope of running anyway on the sheer logical realization that it wouldn't work, no matter what I tried. Even if I was to get past the guards and the gates and the distance, there would be no place to go. I realized I'd rather live as a Demoted person than die of starvation or an animal attack or something. I had spent my whole life in a small city; my idea of wildlife was squirrels and pigeons. The trees and vast expanses of space were unnerving. Not only that, but Demoted don't do well outside their usual status as pets — without a wristband or identification, there is no way to buy anything, nowhere to go, and no way to hide. The thing about Demoted trying to escape is that there is nowhere to escape to. To survive, a Demoted person must have a master.

After our uninspired but filling dinner of some sort of oatmeal-mash-thing and water, we were taken to dormitory-style rooms, mostly separated from our schoolmates. I ended up in a room with approximately twenty other boys, none of whom were familiar to me. The guards who escorted us one by one pointed to a bed for each of us, and there were sheets and clothes waiting. I stood beside my bed, awkward and bored, much like the rest of the boys. It was obvious what we were supposed to do, but we all waited for orders anyway. It seemed safer.

"You have five minutes to make your beds, change into regulation clothing, and get to sleep. There will be no talking, no leaving beds, and no contact between any of you."

I hesitated for a moment, watching the other boys scurry to follow the orders. As if they had been doing it all their lives, they stripped naked in front of a room of dudes. I wasn't a prude by any means, but I didn't even know their names! I fiddled with the hem of my shirt for a few moments before trying to stall.

"Um, excuse me, what do I do with *my* clothes?"

The guard slapped me in the face before I even registered him walking toward me, and I cried out as I stumbled aside. Nobody had ever hit me like that before, and it hurt!

"Your job is to do as you're told," the guard growled, seeming pleased when I cowered a little. "Don't waste time asking stupid questions about things you're too ignorant to understand."

"Yes, sir," I mumbled, deciding that perhaps my unquestioning peers were right about it. I eyed up the pajama shirt and decided it was long enough to offer me some modesty, so I changed into that first, then the pants.

I was halfway through putting the sheets on my bed when a guard announces that it was lights out. The beast towered over me, smiled sadistically, and ripped the bedding from my hands.

"You sleep on the floor," he ordered. "Maybe next time you'll move faster."

I sighed, figuring he was enjoying his little power play. I was about to retort something sarcastic, but my cheek still hurt where he slapped me earlier, so I held my tongue. I lay down on the floor and looked hopefully at the bedding that he took from me.

He dropped it back on the bed.

"Touch it tonight and I'll beat you within an inch of your life," he warned. I didn't doubt him, although the urge to touch it was strong. I resisted.

The floor was cold. Not intolerably cold, but maybe five degrees above intolerably cold. The pajamas were thin and scratchy, and I longed for blankets to curl up with more than I longed for the mattress. Even the regulation-grade pillow sounded pretty damn good. But I was afraid to fuck up so soon. Not before my first full day. I couldn't handle that much. I could barely handle the situation as it was.

If the sounds were any indication, the other boys weren't handling it much better. There were muffled cries and sobs, and the sounds of lots of people tossing and turning in what must have been uncomfortable beds. I was surprised the guards didn't come and yell at them for making noise, but maybe they did have some sort of compassion. That, or they just didn't care. As far as anyone else was concerned, we were no longer people, no longer worthy of compassion. Like animals, we had been sterilized earlier, our "inadequate" genes removed from the gene pool. My dick hurt, well, my balls, more accurately, but it seemed to spread to the whole thing. As I lay there in the dark, I reached down and gingerly ran a finger along the small line of stitches from the vasectomy. It was such a little thing, but it changed me forever, just like the Assessment, just like the choice that I had made.

I thought about my brother, who got to go home, who got to go to the graduation ceremony and see mom and dad. I knew it would be hard for him to go on alone, and I knew it would be hard for our parents as well, but I knew I made the right decision. Mom and dad would have eventually grown bored of my "selfishness," as they called it so often, my tendency to look out for nobody but myself.

I did always look out for Abriel. I had always considered him an extension of myself, and I wouldn't have done it for just anyone. My sacrifice was for my brother, my twin, my genetic pair. I had always thought we did best when we were together, when we could both use our own strengths to compensate for the other's weaknesses, but I knew I did the right thing by saving him. He could go on to do so much.

I tried to be happy about that fact, but I couldn't help but realize that I had a whole life in front of me as well. A life of loneliness and humiliation. It washed over me all at once, and I tried to stay strong. I squeezed my eyes shut against the tears and tried to pretend I was just going to sleep, blocking out the dim light from the hallway. I got exactly what I wanted, I had just never considered the consequences.

Chapter 6
Training

I've only had the training materials for a few days when my master breaks his usual pattern of ignoring me and stops by my room.

"Show me what you've learned," he orders, standing there expectantly.

I stare at him, silent and confused.

"That was an order, as if it wasn't entirely clear," he says, curt and cold. I tremble.

Slowly, I stand, unable to take my eyes off of him. I know it won't stop him from hurting me if he wants to, but at least I'll be able to see it coming. He doesn't move, though, and after a moment, I try to focus on what I've read in the training manuals. It's easy to forget, when I'm alone, when there aren't many demands placed on me. But when my master speaks to me, when he makes demands, I realize how lost I am. Every interaction is a terrifying challenge, as is figuring out when to walk and when to sit and where. I used to take all this for granted, but now it just leaves me terrified.

"You did fine at the Peace Day Celebration," he reminds me. "But I don't want you clinging to me at the next event we attend. That sort of show only works once without raising questions. Show me that you can pull off an event where there's more than a few inches between us without looking like a kicked dog."

I turn away from him and close my eyes, trying to recall the positions and movements I read about in the training manuals, and I pretend I'm just practicing by myself as I demonstrate them for him. I show him how I can walk, the smooth, graceful, restrained gait that is valued above regular walking. I kneel for him, in a variety of positions, demonstrating how I would wait, unobtrusive, or how I would sink low to the ground, begging forgiveness.

The training manuals explained it in so much detail, telling me how and when I should move, and speak, and laugh. It's not how I would have moved before. At least, I think it isn't. I wonder if I could even step back into my old life now if it was an option. I throw myself into moving like a slave with the same enthusiasm as most people studied for the Assessment. I've studied the positions for days, tried them out on my own even, because I *want* to look right. I *want* to say the key phrases that all good slaves should say. I want to succeed, just this once, and I want him to keep me.

I show him how I can crouch low to pick up a fallen item, ensuring that I present myself properly, in a pleasing manner, even when it's not quite functional. I do all the things that slaves do that nobody really notices, but that take practice and work, anyway. I show him everything I can think of, and when I've exhausted myself, I go to my knees next to him again, and my heart soars when he nods at me.

"You could use some practice so you aren't so stiff, but you've come a long way on your own," he tells me. "We'll work on postures and positions for a while, and then you can continue on your own."

I try not to draw away as he walks toward me, but his face doesn't give me any indication that he notices. Then again, he seems to notice everything else, so maybe he's just letting this slip.

He guides me through some positions, referring to them by name or reason to assume them, and when I move, he watches carefully, guiding me into more proper stances. I have no idea how he knows so much about slaves, but he does, and he points out little corrections here and there that I need to change.

"Put your hands a little higher," he orders, and I tentatively raise my arms.

"A little more," he demands.

My shoulders still hurt, remnants of the abuse I suffered at the brothel. I pray there's no permanent damage, that I've just pulled a muscle or a tendon or something, but the longer it lasts, the more afraid I get. I doubt my master would want a permanently damaged slave. I used to be able to diagram all the parts of the human anatomy, but now all I know is that my arms and shoulders hurt a fuckton.

"I can't put my arms above my head without being in a lot of pain, master," I confess. "I'm hoping it will heal on its own."

"You should have seen a doctor when I first bought you," he comments. "Do you need to see one now?"

I consider the lingering pain in my arms. "Well... maybe. I'm not sure."

He looks at me and I expect to see pity. I don't. All I see is irritation, presumably at me, presumably because I can't even make the decision of whether I need to see a goddamn doctor or not.

"What happened?" he asks.

I'm surprised he cares, but it still seems so impersonal. "I was tied and hung by my arms for a few hours, master." I was beaten and raped and taunted throughout the process as well, but I spare my master these details. A part of me doesn't want him to get any ideas of how to use me; another part of me doesn't want to admit what has been done. He seemed disgusted enough with my condition when he brought me home.

"Are your arms or hands numb at all?" he asks.

"No, master, not anymore."

He nods. "You'll tell me if it gets worse or if it doesn't go away in a few days. My doctor can get you in immediately."

I'm relieved. When I told Mistress Bethel about it, she hit me and told me to stop whining about it. "Thank you, master."

I'm elated that my master hasn't sold me, yet. I know it can happen at any time, and I know that I can go back to a brothel, or to someone who hurts me. He doesn't seem to like me, at least, not in a way that I've ever seen a master act when he likes a slave, but he also doesn't seem to be as disgusted as he was when he first brought me home. I do my best to please him, hoping for a kind word, and acknowledgement, something to tell me that I'm doing the right thing. But I know better than to ever hope for something like that. It's all business with him; I'm his property, he's training me to serve better. It's all I can do to keep myself from begging him not to sell me off once I'm trained to his specifications.

"It won't do to have you immobile," he replies. "Let's focus on some lower body moves."

I bite down on my tongue, because the idea of working on my

lower body makes me think of something far more exciting than slave postures. The fact that he's been touching me, just barely, but still enough to feel the soft strength in his hands, doesn't help that matter at all.

"Kneel," he orders, when I stand there like a statue. "Like you're waiting for orders."

I'm relieved by the order, just as I'm relieved by his brusque manner. He poses me like a mannequin, guiding my body parts to the proper location without saying more than a few words. Hands a little higher. Legs wider apart. Back straight. Head up. In between, he stops and nods. I can't tell if he's approving of my work or his.

There's one thing in particular that I'm supposed to do while kneeling, that I'm apparently doing all wrong, and his pointers just aren't cutting it. He comes up behind me, after ordering me to keep facing forward, and nudges my legs apart a little with his foot. He doesn't kick, which is nice. Once he does that, he stays, standing between my legs, and he leans over to position my arms from above.

I try my best not to think about the fact that my head is at the exact level of his cock.

"You need to relax, you're far too stiff for this to work."

His words only increase the tension, and the warmth of his body against my back makes me aware of how close we are, how easy it would be for him to grab me and throw me to the floor and take me. I should be afraid, but I'm not. He's being gentle with me, despite my thick-headedness, and it's been so long since anyone has touched me.

"Try and focus on what I'm telling you," he demands, increasing his efforts and moving me a little more forcefully. He moves in closer, almost straddling me to get the effect he's looking for.

I try really, really hard not to think about what it would feel like to turn and feel his thighs brush against the sides of my head. I hear his voice, a distant hum, and I try not to think of how much nicer it would be if he was whispering my name, claiming me with his words and his body. I *especially* try not to think about what it would feel like if he were in front of me instead of behind me, and how he would smell, and taste, and feel...

"Sascha, are you even paying attention, anymore?"

My master's voice is exasperated, but not quite angry. His grip on my arms becomes a bit firmer, as he all but drags them into place. I attempt an answer, but all I get is some sort of muted consonant sounds that make me sound like I'm drowning. The forcefulness as he moves me pushes me past the point of no return, and I'm just thankful that I avoid moaning.

"Christ," he mutters, and I can feel him moving away from me. I hear him pause by the doorway to my bedroom. "Well, get up, then," he says. "Maybe we've done enough for one day."

I hear him, this time, but I don't want to get up, I don't even want to turn and face him, because there's an uncomfortable bulge in my pants. I failed miserably at not thinking of all those things that I was trying to not think about. I try to tell myself that it's just habit, that it's just because he's attractive, but I can't help wondering what it says about me. If I wasn't so afraid of disobeying him, I would refuse to move from this spot until it receded.

I get up, and I sort of shuffle around, wishing for a tree or a chair or something to hide myself behind. I settle for clasping my hands in front of me, trying to hide it.

"Sascha, what—" he stops, looking at my hands. A look of realization crosses his face, and I realize I probably made the problem more apparent, instead of less. "Oh."

I can feel myself going red, and my face is burning in shame. It's not my fault. I've been trained to view anything as a source of sex, and to expect that anyone and everyone is going to be fucking me. I want to take it back, to see the pride that was starting to show on his face when I was pleasing him, but all I see is the discomfort. All my hard work, and I can't even keep my own body in control.

The fact that he's annoyingly attractive doesn't help matters any.

"We were finished for the day anyway," my master says, clearly uncomfortable. He's doing a terrible job of hiding it. "You're free to go, and in the future... take care of that beforehand, please. I may have neglected to tell you, but you have my full permission."

"Yes, master," I mumble, the heat running through my body mixing with the blush on my face. I want to cry, but I can't draw more attention to myself.

He nods, looking unsettled for another moment before turning and walking out of my room, leaving me with my hard-on and my shame.

The shame doesn't stop, although it helped a little to notice that he wasn't comfortable, either. The fucking truth of it is, I have been taking care of it, pretty regularly, but it's apparently not enough. Maybe I am just a whore.

Chapter 7

Impressions

I blaze through another training book and allow myself some quality time with the tablet. It's been a *long* time since I've touched a tablet, but it's like riding a bike, except I've always been rather clumsy on bikes, unlike tablets, which I've been able to master since the time I had adequate fine motor control to work the screen. I don't even think about doing anything untoward with it until I want another training manual, which says something about my frame of mind, but once I start down the road of hacking and modding, it's like it all comes back to me, and I can't stop, and I look forward to it every day.

It's only an hour or two before I've destroyed the content blocker that limits my searches to dull topics, and from there I manage to mod it to work with voice commands, steal media, function in all sorts of ways it was never intended to. I sneak in my own reverse content blocker, so anyone peeking in on my connection will be unable to see what I'm working on. I break into a few small sites, just for fun, just to see if I can.

I remember, and it's glorious.

I look up my family to see how they're doing. I can't visit them or anything, but I can't just ignore it. I find their address is still the same, still the house we grew up in, but the last census data indicates two married adults living there without anyone else. Abriel?

I know he passed the Assessment, but what he did after that... I never really thought about it, just like I never really thought about what *my* life would be like. Is he okay? Did my plan work? I comb through registries of college after college, desperate to find his name among the registrants. I can live through him, right?

I'm engrossed, hunting for Abriel when I finally become aware of the feeling of eyes watching me. I glance up and see my master, and I quickly tap out the combination that will clear my screen except for the training manual I am supposed to be viewing and a page of recipes I was looking at before I started on this new task. I glance up at him, trying my best to look innocent.

He stares at me for another moment or two, long enough to make me want to squirm and hide. I resist the urge to cower, because I know he doesn't like it when I cower.

"The reverse content blocker needs to go," he says, matter-of-fact. "Do you really think I gave you a tablet so you could sneak around and do illegal things on it?"

I blush furiously and try not to tremble. "No, master." Simple is better.

"It won't happen again." His words aren't threatening, nor are they a question. It's like he's stating that the sky is blue, he knows it with that much certainty.

And he's right. "No, master."

He nods. He's not angry, which is good, because I don't even know what I'd do if he was angry. He just nods at me and keeps standing there.

"You obviously need more to do with your time," he states. "Meet me in the dining room in twenty minutes. The content blocker will be removed by then."

"Yes, master," I mumble, as he strides away. I disable the content blocker immediately. He hasn't told me to take away anything else, so I don't, not yet.

He doesn't seem angry, but he wasn't particularly pleased, either. I hadn't expected him to check, I figured he would have assumed I was just a stupid slave and never thought of it.

I wonder how long he knew before he told me.

With that taken care of, I have a few minutes to ponder his request to meet him. More to do with my time, he said, what does that even mean? I clean when he asks, I try to cook...

I wonder whether he's going to fuck me or beat me.

I have myself in a blind panic by the time I arrive in the dining room, and I rush to drop to my knees at my master's feet the second I get there. I don't wrap myself around his legs, because I'm terrified he might kick me in the face if I try it.

He looks at me critically. "Is there a problem?" It sounds like an accusation.

I stare up at him, silent and stupid. Wait for him to hurt me. He raises an eyebrow, and it's like I'm afraid he's going to hit me with it, because I cower away.

"Go get me a soda, calm yourself down, and when you come back, show me some of the things you've learned in the training manuals. The ones I sent you and the ones you stole."

I continue to stare at him, his words landing on my ears like an alien language. The meaning sinks in bit by bit, in little pieces. He knows I stole training manuals. Soda. He knows how terrified I am. He *wants* a soda. And for me to get it. Calm down. My heart is racing and I can't breathe, and I realize I'm having a panic attack, which must be why he told me to calm down.

I nod, unable to speak because my chest is too tight and my tongue is too big and my mouth is too dry. My master looks on calmly, through me almost.

I finally manage to force my legs to cooperate, and I get up and walk into the kitchen. I start crying, even though I know I'm being ridiculous, and I go to my knees in there, too, just for a minute, just long enough to catch my breath. Get a soda. Calm down. Show off what I've learned.

It shouldn't be this fucking hard.

I stand up, shaky, and run some water over my hands and face, hoping my eyes won't be so red. I take a few deep breaths, dry off with a towel I've left hanging off the stove, and take a soda from the fridge. I've never seen him use a glass for his soda before, so I don't bring one, I just carry the can out and crack it open before handing it to him, still silent.

He doesn't say anything, which I'm glad for, because I've apparently gone non-verbal for the moment. A thousand thoughts inside my head, and I can't even manage a "yes, master" out loud.

We spend the better part of two hours with me serving him, or bringing him things, or showing things off. Unlike the position training, this doesn't require me to move my arms into any painful positions, and I can perform as expected. He is pleased, and while he isn't overly congratulatory, he shows his approval. I'm elated to be smart and successful again, even if it is just fetching drinks.

He sends me to retrieve my tablet, and I take notes while he rattles off his preferences for drinks and food in various settings. As a brothel whore, I never had to worry about things like that. At some point, I remembered what my clients liked, but that was going above and beyond my duties. If I hadn't recalled, or didn't bother to try to recall, they'd tell me, quickly, and correct me for doing it wrong.

As a personal slave, I realize it's important for me to know that if my master says "get me a drink" at home when we're alone, he probably means a soda, and if he says it in the casual bar he goes to with Bobby, it probably means a vodka martini, no olives, and if he says it in a place where his superiors will be, like at the Peace Day Celebration, it probably means a classic, sophisticated cocktail, like an old-fashioned. It's important because it makes me look attentive and obedient, and it's important because my master doesn't have to waste any more time than necessary ordering me around.

He drills the preferences into me, and orders me to memorize them.

"Think that will be enough to keep you busy?" he asks.

If it was anyone else, I would think he was joking, but he's always so serious. "I'm sorry, sir," I mumble. I want to tell him how I could help with his business, how I could learn and join like a real person, but I don't. I consider offering to let him fuck me, but what purpose would that serve? He can do anything he wants, and he doesn't. He lets me sit around like a spoiled house pet, and I repay him by sneaking around behind his back. I'm lucky he hasn't sold me, yet. "I'll do anything you want."

I was impressed with Sascha's demonstration, not to mention his quick learning, although it's not proper to tell him that. Just like it isn't proper to ask how he had so flawlessly installed the software on his tablet, a feat I doubt I would have been able to accomplish, much less a slave. Every slave trainer I've ever met would have suggested I punish him for that, but I saw it for what it was; exploration, a desire to learn. I have that same desire, and I admire it in the slave.

"How are your arms?" I ask, hoping to change the subject.

I watch him go stiff and still.

"Fine, master."

Nobody who is fine goes pale at the mention of a potentially injured body part. "Arms above your head," I order, keeping it short and simple in hopes of cutting through his panic.

He obeys, partially. I can see the way he sets his jaw, gritting against the pain, and I notice the careful way he stops when his arms get to a certain point. He can function, I'm sure, shower and clean and dress himself, but he should have a far wider range of motion. I wait for him to lift them higher, to tell me it hurts, but he doesn't. He just looks at me, questioning.

I frown, place one hand on either arm, and push them higher up.

The yelping and whimpering catch me by surprise, and I pull my hands away instantly. He lets his arms drop, looking terrified.

Does he really think I'll be angry because he's injured? Hell, I was part of the institution that caused these injuries! I remember when my mother took over the very re-education center that Sascha spent his years at. The merger had been cause for celebration, although I was too young to attend the grand opening party she threw.

"I told you to let me know if they didn't stop hurting," I remind him. It's been a week, and he's allowed himself to hurt this whole time? I'm angry at him for not mentioning it, but far more angry at myself for not noticing.

Sascha gives me a stupid, scared look. "Yes, master."

I smack him in the chest without even thinking about it. Years of training have primed my movements for violence, and he's annoying me. I don't hit him hard; I can't, knowing what's been done to him. Still, he yelps and recoils. I regret it. I didn't mean to scare him further, but it's far easier to fall back on the training methods I was raised with than to figure out something new.

"When I give you an order, I expect you to follow it," I snap. It's far more comfortable to give him orders. Despite the fact that I didn't hit him that hard, he still appears terrified.

"I'm taking you to the doctor."

I walk out, unable to figure out what else to do. He doesn't seem to want comfort, and I've never been good at providing it. I call ahead and make sure my doctor can get me in. I wish I could call him over to the house so I don't have to take the slave out, but I suppose the doctor's time is valuable, too. I indicate that Sascha sit in the passenger seat and the act of pointing seems to terrify him. I stay quiet as we drive.

I lead the slave into my own doctor's office without a word. There are slave doctors, under-qualified medical students looking to make some side money, but I would never take my property to one of those. We wait in the reception area, and the slave even glances over the magazines and loaner tablets scattered on the counter. It's not long before the doctor comes through the door with a smile on his face. He's been my doctor since I was a child, and his hair had already started to whiten by then. He's always claimed to be too old to care about politics, but as I age as well, I realize it's little more than a convenient cover. He cares about health and well-being; he knows that the Demoted are no different from anyone else.

"Cashiel, what brings you here in such a hurry?" he asks. "Naleen said you told her it was urgent."

I walk over to the door, looking back at Sascha when he doesn't follow. The order seems unnecessary, so I wait until he finally jumps to his feet and makes his way to us. I can see the doctor's eyes taking in my slave, and me.

"And just who is this?" the doctor asks, his voice holding a hint of judgment.

I wait until the door is closed and we are on our way to the exam room before replying. "Slave," I mutter, just now wondering if slaves are accepted here. I know the doctor is friendly to slaves, too friendly, some would say, but even the friendly ones don't want to risk contaminating their offices by treating slaves in them.

"Your mother would shake her finger at you for bringing him in here," the doctor teases as we enter the exam room. "I didn't realize you were back in the business, anyway. Tell me what's going on?"

I glance at Sascha and nod at him. "Lift your arms."

He does, getting them about as high as he did earlier, and then he gives me that nervous look again.

I turn to the doctor. "He can't lift them any higher without being in pain. It's been that way for a little over a month, hasn't it?"

I glance at Sascha, but it takes him a moment to come out of his panic.

Finally, he nods. "Yes, master."

The doctor frowns. "Cash, what's gotten into you? I've known you and your family for years; you're not the type of people to bring down the value of a slave like this! Especially not a personal slave."

I scowl. "It wasn't me; I just bought him a few weeks ago. It was an interesting situation... Anyway, I want him taken care of. I would have brought him in sooner, but he didn't mention that he was in pain. When I bought him, he was all beaten up, bruised and cut and burned all over, but I took care of that. I suppose you could look him over, though, while he's here."

The doctor doesn't seem exactly pleased with the answer, and he focuses his attention on Sascha. "Be that as it may... what's your name, my boy?"

The slave freezes, as if the simple request to say his name is about to destroy him. "It, um, sir, I... Sascha, sir."

The doctor nods. "All right, Sascha, go ahead and take your shirt off and sit up on that table for me."

I stand to the side of the room, trying to look bored. I've never taken anyone else to a doctor before, much less a slave. I watch as the doctor leans over runs his hand over Sascha's skin, where the scars shine on his flesh, making Sascha wince.

"Someone got him bad," the doctor comments. He goes on to peek at a few of the other ones before looking back at me. "Well, you've done a good job patching him up. I'm surprised none of them got infected. They were very deep."

I just nod. I'd rather move onto other things.

"Now, Sascha," the doctor says, his voice calm and professional. "What happened to your arms?"

"Sir, at the last place I was owned... someone... they tied me up, with my arms above my head, and they hung me like that, from my arms." Sascha squirms and fidgets; clearly, the conversation is more painful than his arms at the moment.

The doctor's eyebrows narrow, but he nods. "Did anything happen to put strain on them?"

I watch my slave struggle to answer, barely getting the words out as the doctor continues to probe.

"Um, they hit me, sir," he manages. "Hard, a lot of times, uh, with a lot of things, and I probably struggled. I think they wanted me to struggle, sir. I don't really remember much. And then, uh... well, there was probably some strain when..."

It's too degrading for me to watch. I cut in with my version of what I'm sure happened. "He was a brothel whore. They tied him up and tortured him and raped him for hours, and this is what it does to a person!"

"Ahh, all right," the doctor says. He seems bothered by the information.

The doctor puts Sascha through a variety of diagnostic movements, pushing to see where things hurt. Sascha is surprisingly quiet. It takes me a moment, but I see the distress on the boy's face and realize that he's flinching away every time the doctor goes to touch him.

"For god's sake, Sascha, tell him if he's hurting you!" I snap.

He does, although with quite a bit of hesitation. The doctor is more gentle, and Sascha no longer looks like he's going to pass out. The doctor finishes his tests, then he puts a little radiation-scanner on Sascha's shoulders for the x-ray. While we wait for the results, the doctor glances at me.

"Cash, why don't you give Sascha and me a moment alone?"

I hear the order in his voice. He wants me out. It irks me to be ordered about. "It wasn't me who did this to him. I'm disgusted. It's why I dragged him in here as soon as I found out it wasn't healing right. Besides, he's a slave. You don't need to treat him like a child."

The doctor just gives me a pleasant smile, the same one he gave me when I protested things as a child. "That may be, but this is my policy, and I'd appreciate it if you'd respect it. I just want a few minutes alone to talk to the boy, nothing major. Be a good boy now, Cashi, run along."

There is something about being seen by the doctor who delivered you that makes you feel like an eternal child. I roll my eyes and storm out, equally mortified by the nickname as I am at my behavior.

I take my place in the waiting area, pawing at the outdated magazines and wondering if they arrive outdated and irrelevant. So many people grace the covers; how many will be forgotten in a year? Five years? I fell from the public eye in just months, but I had some encouragement.

My eye catches a flier for a slavery protest rally that happened last week. I'm inspired enough to pull my tablet out and look it up. The results are not surprising. The peaceful rally took a "sudden violent twist," requiring heavy police intervention. Eighteen dead, over a hundred wounded, almost all the attendees imprisoned. The preservation of the Demoted system is considered vital for the functioning of our peaceful society. Everything about it, the selection criteria, the Assessment, the re-education centers, the slave placement... it's all so carefully constructed.

I should know. My family has restructured almost every re-education center in the country, and many across the world.

Chapter 8
Games

As my master leaves me with the doctor, I repress a giggle at the nickname. It's nice to see evidence of a real human life with a childhood and twee nicknames, although I'm sure I'd be just as embarrassed if anyone ever used the nicknames that Abriel and I had for each other.

It hurts to think of him, of our happy childhood.

The doctor stands in front of me, looking serious. "Tell me, son, does Cashiel hurt you? Is he the one who did this?"

I shake my head, vehemently denying it. "No, sir, my master is very kind to me." I'm surprised just how defensive I am, after all, it's not like we have any sort of special bond. Compared to what I'm used to, my life now is paradise, and I suppose he deserves some credit for that. "It's true, what he said about the brothel."

"I've been seeing Cashiel since he was a little boy," the doctor reveals, looking sad at my comment about the brothel. "I've known his family for years now, and they don't leave their slaves with injuries like this. I would be very concerned to hear that Cashiel had lost his temper so violently."

The familiar setting of the office and friendly nature of the doctor loosens my tongue. "The people who did this to me didn't lose their tempers, sir. They did it on purpose."

The doctor looks surprised, and I can't tell if it's because of what I said or the fact that I said it. "Well, I suppose that's true," he says quietly. "I'd be even more concerned to hear that Cashiel did anything of that nature. I know he's been in a rough place for a while now, but he was never cruel, not even as a boy."

I don't know what to say to this, not sure if my master wants me to hear anything about him, and not wanting to speak out of turn again and risk getting into trouble. I sit quietly instead.

The moment passes. "Well, I doubt you'll be coming into more injuries now."

I nod, unable to say anything. I hope he's right.

He gets me to drop my pants so he can check me there, too. I guess I'm glad he asked my master to leave. It's already awkward enough between us without him watching his childhood doctor stick his finger up my ass while I try not to scream.

"You should have had stitches at some point," he mentions, tossing away the glove.

I say nothing, just sit up. Medical treatment wasn't exactly something that was allowed or accounted for in the brothel.

"Make sure your master knows, you must always, *always* use lubrication," he advises.

I blush. I've been fisted, with and without lube, hell, I've wrestled in a fucking *pool* of lube before, but something about hearing the full word, "lubrication," coming out of a doctor's mouth... it's fucking embarrassing. I mumble, "Yes, sir," before I die.

He smiles at me and pats me on the leg, too high, like doctors always do after they stick their finger up your ass. Like we're buddies now. He tells me to get dressed and I do, quickly, and he calls my master in.

The doctor explains how I've torn the tendons around my rotator cuff, which sounds familiar, and he goes on to describe some exercises I should do daily, maybe forever, how I should rest, and prescribes me some anti-inflammatories. He glares at my master and orders him never, *ever* to tie me with my arms above my head, and my master just nods, saying he wasn't planning on doing it anyway. Finally, the doctor tells us that my chances for recovery are good, because I'm young, and I'll likely be fine without surgery.

I've only been a slave for a little more than three years; already, I'm facing lifetime limitations. How much worse would it have been if I hadn't been purchased when I was? I understand why slaves don't live very long.

I am shocked when my master walks up to the counter and pays the exorbitant bill like it is pocket change. The doctor's visit alone is nearly a third of what he paid for me. I can't imagine this added expense will endear me to him. The last surprise is that he also stops off at a pharmacy and picks up the anti-inflammatories that were prescribed, tossing them to me casually as if it's normal to care that a slave is in pain.

"Don't overdose or anything stupid," he warns. "You'd be miserable if you tried that with these, anyway."

I read the label and swallow down two pills, the maximum I'm supposed to take at once. It seems too good to be true, and I want them in my system before my master has a chance to change his mind. The doctor has given me hope, for once, that I won't be in pain. They are wonderful, and even though the exercises and stretches sound like they'll be uncomfortable, I trust that they'll help, and that I'll once again be able to wash my hair or grab items off of high shelves without wincing.

I assumed I would never see a real doctor again, unless that's how slaves get put down. My time at the brothel had pretty much confirmed that theory. Being taken not only to a doctor, but apparently my master's personal doctor, blows my mind. The last time I saw a real doctor, it was for a far less pleasant procedure.

Our first day at the re-education center, we were taken to the local hospital. I felt about two seconds of relief before remembering what they were going to do. It didn't matter that this was where all of my childhood injuries had been treated; that day, I was to be neutered like a dog. Well, not exactly; thankfully, some officials had determined that vasectomies were just as effective, less risky, and less expensive than complete castration.

A team of doctors and nurses waited for us. They started with a medical records scan, updating a few shots here and there. I was up to date, fortunately, so I spared myself the embarrassment of yelping and shedding a few tears like I always did when I got shots. I was always sensitive to pain.

We were ordered to strip from the waist down and lie on the cots they rolled out. It wasn't too different from the state mandated yearly physicals, except the physicals never included being shaved with a straight razor by one of the nurses. I tried to pretend I was just visiting an aesthetician, like I did once before a date with a cute boy from the uppity private school. It was one of the only dates I ever went on, and it struck me as sad that I would never go on one again. Of all the things to miss, it seemed trivial.

Next came the cold, wet feeling of disinfectant. The moment it dried, a nurse gave me a shot, and I yelped and cried, and the nurse actually patted my head like I was a little kid again.

The shot was a local anesthetic, and I tried not to think of the fact that I was about to get my nuts operated on while I was conscious. I looked up at the ceiling, but the too-bright glare of the industrial strength eco-lights hurt my eyes. I closed them and tried to block out the panicked screams from the others who were being sterilized before me, mixed with the buzz of tasers from those who tried to escape. A doctor came by, and I sort of felt the hand that touched me, squeezing around for the right place, locating the tubes that were about to be severed. It was numb, but there was still a sense of pressure, and I felt the gloves brushing against the inside of my leg. I heard the doctor demanding tools, a scalpel, a clamp, someone to wipe away the blood. I couldn't bring myself to look, but the smell of burning flesh suddenly wafted up, and I realized that I had been cauterized. The scar tissue would make sure that nothing regrew, that the little tubes that used to transport my sperm would never open again.

I heard the doctor call for stitches, and felt a light tugging sensation. The curious part of me would have liked to watch, just to see what I looked like on the inside. The whole ordeal was so unreal that the fact that my dick got snipped wouldn't really set in until later. We were transported back to the re-education center, where our training began for real.

"Being Demoted means taking your place in society. Since the end of the fourth World War, the world has enjoyed peace and prosperity as a result of Demoting a small segment of the population," a vidscreen presentation informed us. In reality, the world traded uneasy freedom for totalitarian control and government-sponsored terror. As that wasn't enough to inspire a false sense of "Peace," the forced sterilization and mass killings of protesters that erupted during the first few years did. Everyone was able to focus on one thing—not being Demoted.

"The re-education centers are vital to the functioning of the Demoted system. A properly trained slave can be a valuable asset to any individual or business, and nobody knows this better than Kristine Miller, the woman who revolutionized Demoted training worldwide!"

The bright colors and smiling presenters may well have been selling the newest wristband or tablet. After a dull history of the re-education centers, the "revolutionary" herself was shown.

Ms. Miller could have been anyone's mother; she smiled brightly, wore a conservative business suit, and laughed at her own jokes. The only clues toward the horror she created were the rather severe hairstyle and the look of utter disgust on her face when she discussed the Demoted.

"The Demoted were one of the most underutilized resources for decades. But the Miller System has transformed you into one of the top trade and development industries in the world. Redeem your place in society by reciting our mottos, obeying your guards, and following the standardized training protocols. Our system ensures that you will become a fully functional product. Remember, your superiors know what's best!"

As the last line was spoken, a loud buzzer went off, and the words flashed on another screen. "Say it!" a guard ordered, and we repeated the first of many standardized lines that Ms. Miller had developed to keep us subservient.

She was the one we could all thank for the routine beatings, starvation, and uncomfortable beds. I wondered what kind of monster spent her life thinking of newer and better ways to torture, ensuring that the "functionality of the product" was never compromised by beating it too much or starving it to death. If only the best and brightest work on the Demoted training projects, maybe society was all backward. Maybe they were the ones who should have been Demoted to keep the rest of the population safe.

We sat through many presentations that week, allowing us to heal from our sterilization surgeries with a minimum of disfigurement and infection risk. The presentations reminded me of school, which I figured was why so many accepted it. We were forbidden from talking to one another, and I got strange looks from the others when I whispered to them when we were alone. I had never been content to follow unquestioningly. I still wanted to learn, to find out if we were being taught the same things, if we all had the same fates planned. I wished I could read the research behind our training. Instead, we were given pointless tasks which could just as easily have been done by robots.

The guard who made me sleep on the floor my first night was a regular on our unit, and he took a particular dislike to me. I learned that his name was Devlin, and promptly started "accidentally" referring to him as Devil. I had to do something to amuse myself; I could feel my brain rotting away from lack of use. It never seemed worth it when he was hitting me, but the rest of the time, I knew I was winning.

"Clean this silverware," the Devil Man grunted at me during one of our training sessions, dropping a box in front of me as I knelt before him.

There were plenty of machines and chemicals that could have done the task far more quickly, but I assumed that one of the hotels nearby had some sort of contract agreement with the re-education center. I wondered how many times I had been the beneficiary of slave labor in the past without realizing it.

He must have seen the skeptical look on my face, because he pulled me to my feet by my hair and yelled in my face. "You have two hours! Leave one spot and I'll whip you bloody and make sure you don't see the inside of the cafeteria for the rest of the week."

There had only been one whipping on our unit so far, a slave who attacked his guard, so I assumed he was bluffing. Still, I started polishing. Once I completed a dozen, I realized that this was one of the impossible tasks that could never be completed. The pieces I polished took ten minutes, and there were hundreds in the box. In two hours, I would be nowhere near finished, and then the Devil Man would win.

They used impossible tasks to break us down and make us feel worthless, giving them a reason to punish us. The fact that the tasks were easy made it worse, because it hurt more to fail at an easy task than it would have to fail at a clearly difficult one. Most people actually believed they were doing poor jobs, and tried harder to do better, not seeing the futility. I got strange looks from the others when I tried explaining that, and some even asked why I thought our trainers were trying to be so cruel.

Everything at the re-education center was a lie.

I started looking around for an alternative method, recalling the chemistry classes I had breezed through just weeks before. I snuck off to the cleaning supply closet, where I found a few chemicals and a bucket. A bit of trial and error later, I mixed up a solution that would de-tarnish the silver in about five minutes, and I dropped a fork in and waited.

I was successful.

The rest of the silverware got dropped in at once, and I swished the bucket around a few times to make sure none were sticking together. I rinsed it thoroughly with water, dried the water spots and carried them back to the Devil Man, who was chatting with the other guards.

I stood silently, waiting to be noticed. They insisted that this was the "proper" way for a slave to get attention. Having my mouth taped shut once was enough for me to learn never to say "excuse me" again.

"What is it, slave?" the guard sneered.

I kept looking at the ground so they couldn't see me roll my eyes. "I finished, sir."

I expected him to be surprised, maybe irritated, but a naïve part of me wanted him to be pleased that the task was complete. While he would have to come up with something else for me to do, at least the task was done well.

He cuffed me, and I barely managed to avoid dropping the box.

"Quit lying!" he snapped, turning back to the other guards.

I felt my face turning red and I fought to keep my tone of voice quiet, calm, and submissive.

"I *finished*, sir."

He turned and yanked the box out of my hands, causing me to stumble before I realized I should let go. I didn't breathe as he pawed through the box, eyeing up the perfect, sparkly silver.

He glared at me. "How did you do this, boy?"

"I created a chemical mixture that removed the tarnish, sir," I explained, forgetting for a moment that I wasn't supposed to be bright or capable. "I got some cleaning supplies, and I combined — "

My words were cut off as I felt myself land on the floor, the strength of his blow knocking me off my feet. I curled up in a ball to protect my stomach as he kicked me a few times. Pain exploded as he grazed my kidneys.

"Get up!" I heard him shout over my head. When I didn't move, he grabbed me by the hair and dragged me where he wanted me. "I'm gonna whip the defiance out of you!"

I tried to run along with his larger strides to keep him from jerking on my hair so much. He dragged me into the punishment room and clamped my hands into a set of manacles hanging from the wall.

I started to shake, realizing he was actually serious about his threat to whip me.

He yelled at me and told me what a terrible slave I was, but I barely heard him. I was too busy in my head, being disillusioned and jerked back to reality. For the first time in my life, my creative problem solving skills and verbal acuity and all the other things that I had been praised for in the last eighteen years were not assets anymore. They were problems, hindrances, signs that I was a dangerous, rebellious slave. I had stupidly hoped that my guard would be proud of me for finishing my task, that someone would give me a goddamn cookie for being clever.

The whip cut into my skin for the first time and I screamed, I wailed in agony, both at the searing pain on my back and at the loss of the person I used to be. Without my intellect to fall back on, I had nothing. I was nothing. As the blood ran down, my hopes for holding onto some part of myself seemed to pour down with it. I retreated from my body and disappeared into some sort of safe space inside my head. It was something I had always been capable of; I could avoid boring classes or nagging adults, but I had never needed it so much, nor had I ever disappeared this effectively. I detached from everything around me, pretending I was just evaluating the situation, not feeing it at all.

I was given twenty-five lashes, even though I only remembered the first one and then a lot of blurry pain. The thought crossed my mind that it would have been more efficient for my guard to stop after the first few lashes, when I was subdued but not damaged. I would have gotten the point of the punishment without dissociating, and I wouldn't have spent the next day healing. I realized nobody cared about efficiency, or healing, or anything else but breaking us. In a way, that very logical error was what pulled me back, made me start to think and criticize and analyze everything around me again instead of just giving in.

It was bad, very bad of them to give me a whole day to do nothing but think and lie in the infirmary.

I thought of the historical torture methods I was briefly obsessed with in the ninth grade, when most of my peers were reading about world history and political structures. I had completed additional projects on the Nazi holocaust, the Spanish Inquisition, the American torture at Guantanamo Bay. I had been equally horrified and amazed at the atrocities people could commit against one another. I never really understood it until I experienced it firsthand.

I recognized the repetition of history when the guards treated us as less than human. Demoted. I could hear it in their voices, when they referred to us as "slave" or "girl" or "boy," sometimes even "it" or "beast" or some other offensive term. Never by our names.

I was barely healed from my first whipping when the Devil Man offered me an "opportunity" after lunch one day.

"You and that scrawny boy over there, the one with the black eye," he said, pointing at the other slave. "Fight for us. There's some extra food in it for the winner."

"No, thank you, sir," I replied, keeping my eyes down. I didn't want him to see the repulsion.

"Wasn't a request." He jerked me to the center of the room, while another guard dragged out my opponent. I had no desire to hit him. I didn't need to reduce myself to fighting for food. If we starved to death, the re-education center would lose profits.

"Well, get moving!" The guards shoved us toward each other.

I watched my opponent warily. I would rather have been beaten than participate.

My opponent seemed to think otherwise. He looked as scared as I felt, but he came at me, landing a punch to my stomach. I winced at the pain, but stayed still, refusing.

"Put him on the floor!" one of the guards cheered. "Get him down for three seconds and you win!"

I smelled food, and I saw them waving a sandwich in front of us. I wanted it, but not as much as I wanted to retain my dignity. My opponent slapped and punched at me a few times, and I considered the rules. I could end it.

Without waiting for another hit, I dropped to the floor, lying on my stomach and covering my face. I heard the guards ordering him to kick me, and he did, his bare feet hurting more than I expected. I didn't count, but I knew it went on longer than three seconds, and once he stopped, heavy boots replaced his feet, kicking harder. I didn't look up until the pain stopped, and I saw my opponent looking hopefully at the guards.

"I did it, sir. Can I have the sandwich? Please? I'll kick him more if you want." He was desperate, nearly drooling at the sight of the sandwich like a dog for a bone. A word from the guards and he would have danced on his back legs.

I was sure he was a nice kid before.

He didn't get the prize, and the look on his face when they ordered him to bed was one of pure shock. He looked at me, and I saw hatred. He didn't hate them for making him play the game; he hated me for ruining it.

The next time they tried to make me fight, I hit the floor and started counting out loud, ending the game in seconds. I was surprised when the guards didn't beat me for it, but that night, I was pinned to my bed by two people while my opponent punched me until I passed out. One of the last things I saw was the faces of the guards smiling from the hallway.

Just because we didn't score as high on the Assessment, we were reduced to less than animals. Maybe we were having a bad day. Maybe we swapped tests to save our loved ones. Maybe Assessment results don't fucking matter, or shouldn't, and I couldn't help but think that most of these people would have been a hell of a lot better off as free people.

The only thing that separated the Demoted from the rest of the world was the treatment. Degradation. Refusal to treat us as human beings. We were all raised in a society where the Demoted were viewed as less than human, and the only way most of us could reconcile that fact with our experience was to believe that we were, in fact, less than. Except I knew it was a lie.

Chapter 9

Borrowed

It's while I'm serving my master another gourmet meal that he springs the next piece of information on me.

"My boss took quite a liking to you."

He says it like it's unfathomable, like someone had just expressed their undying love for cheap convenience store foods. Like someone had just expressed their undying love for an overpriced whore.

"Yes, master," I mumble. What else am I supposed to say? I'm already thinking the worst, praying that he isn't thinking of selling me to the man, giving me to him as some sort of friendly gift. I hadn't gotten much of a read off of Mr. Dean at the Peace Day Celebration, but what I did didn't exactly endear him to me. Besides, I finally feel like I know what to expect from my master, and it's a comfortable feeling, if not a very warm one.

"He's requested my company for dinner tomorrow night," my master informs me, not looking at me for once. "As well as yours."

"Yes, master." My voice is stiff and I know it, but I try to remind myself that he just said for the night, not forever, and that means I might not be given away, I might stay with my master. After all, they had mentioned this before we left the casino after the Peace Day Celebration.

"You understand, then..."

"Yes, master." I feel my face reddening as I anticipate his question. Of course I understand. I understand that I'm a slave, a whore, a hole to be fucked, and if his boss wants to fuck me, I am to do it and not complain, because it could be worse. I could be in a brothel again. He doesn't have to remind me. "I'll do it without complaint, master."

He nods, still looking uncomfortable. "Well, it will be something to do, at least."

It's the closest I've heard him come to making small talk. My stupid response of "yes, master" doesn't do much to further the conversation, though.

We go to his boss's house the next day, and my master and I don't exchange words. This doesn't make me any less nervous, unlike the carefully selected outfit he had handed me after breakfast. I'm glad I don't have to pick out what to wear. All I want is for him to tell me what's going on, but I know I won't get that. I shouldn't even think that I deserve it, but I have to bite my tongue to keep from asking him.

I try not to think of anything as we're escorted through the house, and I've gone completely away by the time we are seated, my master in a chair, me on the floor at his feet. I see the girl, Melinda, who the boss had at the Peace Day Celebration with him, and I smile at her hopefully.

She pretends I don't exist.

I wait as the masters eat and chat about a promotion, wishing I'd be hand-fed by my master like Melinda is by hers, but no such luck. To be fair, my master hadn't told me not to eat dinner, which probably meant I should have, but I would have been too nervous anyway. I almost miss the cue to stand, but a light kick at my back has me scrambling to my place next to my master.

"I would *love* to sign the final documents to finalize the promotion, Cashiel," the boss says, his voice soft and content, lulled by the wine he's been drinking all night. "I'll have my staff draw them up and you can pick them up tomorrow."

"Of course, Mr. Dean, that would be lovely," my master replies, all smiles and business-appropriate happiness. "I'll pick them up when I pick the boy up."

I realize he's talking about me and my stomach churns. It's not that I didn't know this was the plan, it's just that I was trying to forget, trying to deny, and I was actually doing a pretty damn good job.

"Perfect," Mr. Dean replies. He beckons me closer with a smile and I take one step, maybe two, before glancing back at my master hopefully.

"He's a little shy," my master says quickly, shooting me a glare that cuts through my entire being. "You know, takes a few minutes to warm up."

"Well, I doubt you let him out of your sight," Mr. Dean leers at me, holding an arm out.

I can't ignore the glare I still feel from my master, so I force myself to go to the other man. He pulls me tight against his body and smells my hair. I try not to be sick and I look at my master, pleading, hoping. Don't leave me here. Don't leave me with him.

"I'll be back tomorrow morning, Sascha," he says. His voice is even, but the look on his face is a little irritated. On anyone else, I'd say a little worried. He squints at me for a few more seconds before addressing his boss. "Feel free to com me if there are any problems at all, sir."

"Oh, I'm sure there won't be."

His hand tightens on my hip and I force myself not to shudder as my master nods and walks out without another word.

I want to run after him. Want to apologize for whatever I did wrong, beg him to take me back, beg him to keep me safe, like he has been.

"Sascha. That's a pretty name, for a pretty boy."

I barely hear the man's voice, but his lips at my neck clue me in. "Yes, sir," I mumble, my voice barely above a whisper. Maybe if he can't hear me he'll forget I'm here?

"I like girls, but I enjoy a pretty boy now and again, too," Mr. Dean informs me, rubbing his hands across my legs and ass, pulling my body closer to his as we stand there. "Let's move someplace a bit more comfortable."

I do as he asks without a word, because there's nothing I can say or do that would make me feel better, and if I protest, I'll only anger my master. I let Mr. Dean lead me down a hallway and up a flight of stairs, where we come to a huge, ornately decorated room with an equally impressive bed. I'm like molding clay in his hands as he leads me toward the bed and sits down, pulling me to lie next to him and awkwardly cuddling me. I feel his lips brushing my collarbone and neck and cheek, and I realize he's one of *those* guys. To think I used to appreciate this. The gentle, cuddly ones used to be my favorite.

His slobbery kisses make their way to my mouth and I fight to keep from pressing my lips into a tight line to keep him out. But I can't resist. I can't offend him, and even though I feel like slugs are crawling across my face, I let him kiss me.

It's not as bad as all that. He's gentle, at least, none of the bruising that I had almost gotten used to at the brothel. He certainly wouldn't split my lips.

I still hate it.

He molests my mouth with his tongue for a while and then pulls back, a smile on his face. I try to return it, knowing I'm probably mostly unsuccessful.

"You are a little shy," he smiles at me, his tone encouraging. "Not too shy to show off that beautiful body, are you?"

My body isn't beautiful, and I'm not shy. But shy is more attractive than disinterested. I look down and try to force myself to blush by holding my breath. When I feel my face redden, I look up and shrug. "If it would please you, sir."

He smiles at me and runs his hand over my leg. "It would," he says, but there's no order to it. He pets my leg for a few more seconds. "Perhaps it would make you more comfortable if I took my clothes off, too?"

It wouldn't, actually, but I don't say that, I just look down and nod. It's going to happen anyway.

I hear him undressing, and I'm bold enough to look up, curious as to what I'll see there. I'm not surprised. He's let his body go, which I suppose he's entitled to, the head of a successful company, an older man. He's not flabby, but he's not toned by any means, and he has hair in all the places I wax. He looks almost nervous when he realizes I'm appraising him, which I would expect anyone else to smack me for.

"I'm past my prime, but I'm considerate and I'll be gentle with you," he says softly, actually looking into my eyes.

It's the sadness that does it. He wins me by being pathetic, and I can't say anything, so I strip my own clothing off, wondering what his response is going to be to the scars on my body.

He reaches out and touches them, very lightly.

"Cashiel told me about this," he says softly. "What a terrible shame, that anyone would do this to such a beautiful creature."

I'm not a creature.

"Yes, sir," I mumble.

He eases me down on my back softly, and I comply, becoming uncomfortable only when I feel his lips graze over the worst of the scars on my stomach.

"It's terrible, like defacing fine art," he comments, running his hands over my skin like he owns it.

He doesn't, and I'm also not fine art.

"Yes, sir," I repeat.

"Cashiel doesn't hurt you like this, does he?" he asks, his eyes suddenly hard as they stare at me. "I wouldn't want someone working for me who could be so cruel."

"No, sir," I answer quickly. "My master doesn't hurt me." I don't mention that he doesn't fuck me, either, and that he hates the very sight of me without clothes. And sometimes with clothes.

"Good." He seems to relax.

He alternates between stroking along my skin with his hands and his tongue for a while, and I'm damned because my body responds, my cock hardening at once even though I don't want this. He doesn't comment, but he's touching that part soon, and I hate it, but it feels good. When he wraps his lips around it, I can't fight back the tears that are pooling behind my closed eyes.

He doesn't suck cock expertly, but I can tell he enjoys it, and he takes his time, and I'm trained to respond to stimulation.

It's wrong, and I wish he wasn't doing it, even though it feels good. I wish it was someone else.

I'm just about to come, holding back because I doubt it's allowed, and I feel him change positions and I hear him gasp. He pulls off my cock and comes up next to me immediately, brushing his hand through my hair.

"Sascha, darling, are you all right?" he asks, his tone conveying his distress.

It takes me a moment to realize that I'm crying, and he noticed, and he cares. While the first thing happens often, the second one rarely does, and the third almost never.

"I'm fine, sir," I mumble.

"Sascha, what's wrong? Am I hurting you? Am I going too fast? Tell me what's wrong, beautiful boy, I'll fix it! You shouldn't have a bad time!"

He's so concerned that I feel guilty. I'm a whore, doing my job, and he's treating me really well, and I'm crying and scaring him. I can't keep doing it; I can't make him feel like this.

I lie, instead.

"I'm fine sir, it's just..." I force myself to smile. "It's just that it feels so good, and I'm so happy, and it's been so long since someone's made me feel this good. I'm sorry I get emotional!"

He kisses me, soft, like he might break me. His lips are papery and clammy all at the same time. "It's okay," he whispers. "It feels good, then?"

No. "Yes, sir. Very good, sir."

"Good." He breathes a sigh of relief. "You want me to keep going?"

Not in a million fucking years. "That would be wonderful, sir."

He holds me for a few more minutes, petting me and I suppose trying to soothe me. I wish he'd just fuck me already, so I can stop pretending. One more minute of this twisted kindness and I might start crying for real, and I worry that I might never stop.

He goes back to giving me head, and it does feel good, and I don't think he minds that I'm still crying a little, now that he has a nice lie about why I'm doing it. I suppose I appreciate the fact that he doesn't *like* that I'm crying. I guess I'm pretty fucked up, if I have to appreciate that.

After another eternity, he gets up, and I wonder if he's going to leave me all horny and hard like this. I can't decide whether that would be a good or a bad thing.

He doesn't, though, he comes back with a bottle of lube and kneels between my legs. He prepares me more slowly and thoroughly than I've ever been prepared before, and I admit that it does feel good. He hits a sensitive spot and I moan, mortified by my response.

He laughs. "It's okay, dear, you can show me if you like what I'm doing. I was worried you'd gone to sleep there for a minute."

"No, sir, I'm certainly awake," I mumble. "You're... very talented. You make me feel wonderful." It's not a lie. He *is* making me feel wonderful. I just hate it. I hate that he's using me, and I hate that he's being allowed use me, and I hate that I'm enjoying it.

"You're very tight," he comments. "Your master must be very careful with you."

My master would rather fuck a cheese Danish than me. "He's a very careful man, sir."

"I'll go slow," he promises, leaning over me.

He does. It's some of the most considerate, gentle sex I've ever had, and despite not having been fucked for over a month, he doesn't even hurt me in the slightest. He keeps going, thrusting in and out with utmost care, and he starts to stroke my cock as he does. I can't help whimpering, just like I can't help moving along with him, but I keep my eyes closed, and I try to pretend it's someone else.

I wish I could pretend it's my master, but I can't imagine him having sex like this, ever. I can imagine him forcing into me as I scream and claw at his skin, both of us biting and kissing and hurting each other. I can imagine him making me beg and me enjoying the begging even more. I can imagine us passionate.

One of my hands rests near my hip, and I pinch my skin between my fingers until the pain blossoms through my body, until I know I've drawn blood, until I feel myself coming. I don't remember the last time I came with another person when I wasn't in pain, and I guess it won't be tonight, even if I have to be the one to bring the pain.

It's not long after this that I feel Mr. Dean coming on top of me, inside of me. I grit my teeth at the familiar, unpleasant sensation of his come inside of my ass, and I take a deep breath just before he collapses on top of me, crushing my delicate frame for a minute.

To his credit, he rolls off quickly and even apologizes. He reaches over me to grab some tissues from next to the bed, and he wipes away the evidence of both our pleasure, still gentle. Damn him for being such a nice guy. I can't even hate him.

"Did you have fun?" he whispers in my ear, provocative.

I squirm and stretch, trying not to make it too obvious that I'm moving away from him. "Yes, sir," I reply, forcing a smile again. "It's been a long time since someone's treated me like that." There. The last part wasn't a lie, at least.

"Cashiel doesn't make you feel this good?" he asks, surprised.

Right, I *am* supposed to be my master's loyal fucktoy. "It's... different, sir. With my master." Yeah, if "different" is the same as "not-fucking."

"I'm sure," he says, smiling. He gives me a few more minutes before pulling me close, all possessive and needy, though still gentle. "Do you like to be the little spoon or the big spoon?"

I don't have the heart to tell him that I'd rather be the teakettle, sitting on the stove all by myself. "Whichever, sir, it feels very nice when you touch me."

He grabs me and pulls me close, wrapping his body around mine like he's protecting me from an earthquake that's making the building collapse. He kisses me, lightly, and I hope he'll end it here. I guess it wasn't that bad; it's true that he is the most considerate person I've been fucked by in a while, and he really did seem concerned with my pleasure. I can't blame him for my being a slave, and I can't blame him for passing me around like a whore. I only have myself and my master to blame for these things.

Chapter 10
Service

I spent two years in the re-education center, learning how to be a slave, and unlearning how to be human.

The only area in which I excelled was sexual training. Our unit was the first to advance to this "secondary" skill, one that they taught us after we had been effectively broken and beaten into compliance. Plenty of us were uninitiated to the world of sex, and the guards stood by during the first few days not only to assist in raping us, but to hurt those who refused.

The trainer was a dull, slight woman in her mid-forties, who introduced herself to us as "Mistress Rae." She started by pairing us up with other Demoted, ordering us to strip and explore each other's bodies. My partner that first day was a stocky young man, one who hadn't bothered me too much, and who turned pale at the order. I moved quickly, obeying before I could be hurt again, and I touched him gently. We hadn't been told to speak, but I did, quietly assuring him and myself at the same time. He stood still until I took his hands and placed them on my body.

"Please, don't," he whispered. "I don't even like guys."

I preferred guys, but not unwilling ones. I could hear the screams and the sound of leather striking flesh from the other side of the room. "Just close your eyes," I whispered. "I'd rather do this without being whipped on top of it."

He let me move his hands over my body, tolerated my hands on his, and by the time Mistress Rae came over to us, we had been ordered to start using our tongues as well. I was on my knees, being a show-off, putting my barely developed skills to use on the cock of my fellow Demoted. I half-expected to be reprimanded for taking it farther than ordered, but I managed to convince myself that I wasn't really being raped if I initiated it.

"So eager," Mistress Rae observed, her voice soft and appreciative.

I paused, waiting for correction.

"Keep going," she encouraged. "Bring him off."

I didn't hesitate. I tried everything I had seen in dirty videos, everything I had experienced in my own limited sexual encounters. I had never really learned much about sex, just a few awkward make-out sessions and a single, fumbling sexual experience in a dingy motel room after another school's prom. I had no idea what would work, because my partner seemed disinterested. Still, my partner was a teenage boy who was getting his dick sucked. I made him come, and when I finished, I looked up at our trainer, desperate for approval.

"That was very nice," she told me, reaching down to pet my head.

I was desperate for the praise, and shifted toward her without thinking about it. "Thank you, ma'am," I said softly, cherishing the soft touch.

"What's your name?" she asked, surprising me. Most didn't bother to ask, or to refer to us by anything other than degrading terms. She made the question sound friendly, and I was happy to play along.

"Sascha, ma'am."

She smiled and kept petting me. "I see potential in you, Sascha," she told me. "You're good at this, if untrained. We'll have you perfect in no time."

The little bits of praise she gave me during my time at the re-education center were like a drug. It didn't matter that she had me put things in my ass, around my cock, and down my throat, it didn't matter that she let the guards use me and took her turns as well. It didn't even matter that she used me as a shining example of perfection while degrading and criticizing the others, because I was doing good, I was succeeding. I convinced myself that I wasn't being raped if I enjoyed what was being done to me, and I convinced myself to enjoy it. It was a lie, and I knew it, but it made it easier. I had to succeed at something. I pretended that my partners were people I was attracted to and I even forced myself to smile. I had read somewhere that the physical act of smiling could make you enjoy things. I got some satisfaction out of being one of the only slaves who wasn't sobbing in bed every night during our first week of sexual instruction.

Learning something new was enjoyable enough to let me ignore the violations that were committed against my body on a regular basis. Mistress Rae bought my big eyes and pathetic tears, and kept me after class for "additional instruction" on more than one occasion when I knew my guard would be beating the shit out of me after class.

She even found a way to deal with that, the pain and physical abuse I suffered. More than anyone else, she saw the evidence on my body, the way it hurt to move or breathe or be touched. As much as I tried for her, some days I just failed to do more than whimper at even the lightest touch.

"Sascha," she said, running the back of her hand over a set of fresh welts against my ass. "You keep getting yourself hurt."

I nodded, unwilling to correct her and point out that it was other people who were hurting me.

"Would you like to learn to cultivate that pain?"

I didn't understand what she was asking, but I took offense at being compared to a plant. Still, she was never cruel to me like she was to the others. I trusted her, in a way. "If you wish it, ma'am."

"I think it will serve you well," she explained. "You need a special skill, anyway."

She taught me to respond to pain instead of shying away from it. She started light, a slap or a pinch while one of the other Demoted got me off, then increased it, mixing the pain and the pleasure until I lost the ability to separate one from the other. It didn't make the whippings better, but it allowed me to continue responding to sexual touch no matter how battered I was. She cultivated me like an heirloom vegetable, tending to me carefully and clipping away what she didn't like. I bloomed for her every time she demanded it, letting her help me channel my pain and fear and frustration into something different, something valuable. We were both surprised when she tried to reward me with "normal" sex and I couldn't bring myself to come. I was not only addicted to praise, but to pain.

It shouldn't have been such a surprise when our job postings were revealed and we found out which sector of service we had been chosen for.

One of the trainers had explained how some of the Demoted were selected as bodyguards, others as personal attendants for the wealthy, some as human companions for spoiled dogs and cats, a position so degrading I would want to kill myself, and a good hearty portion as "sexual servants." Every service usually included meeting the baser needs of society, but at least those of us with legitimate jobs might not end up on our knees all day. We all dreaded finding out that we would be among the portion of us who were selected for work as escorts and courtesans and brothel workers.

I wasn't surprised when I saw my name on that list on the vidscreen. After all, I had been labeled as "defiant," "uncooperative," "resistant," "rude," and "lazy," but good in sexual skills. I figured Mistress Rae had put in a good word for me, and I hoped to end up as some spoiled courtesan pleasuring a wealthy senator or something. I figured I could make cute, politically correct comments and show off my "trivial" knowledge of classic literature and arts. It wasn't exactly the kind of hopes and dreams I had when I was a kid, but I thought it would be a pretty tolerable life. I looked across to the specific job postings and saw that I was listed for service at a notoriously low-class brothel, the kind of place that was joked about in fear. I traced the line with my finger, to be sure, and when it didn't change, I turned to the person next to me with a shaky voice and asked him to look for me.

The asshole laughed as he told me I was indeed registered for service at "Bethel's Brothel," a name so unoriginal it made me cringe. I didn't say anything, I just walked away, numb.

I sat on the floor at the edge of the room, not speaking or moving until the Devil Man came up, smiling at my misery, and smacked me on the shoulder in a poor imitation of the gesture meant to bring me to my feet. I stood, because I didn't have the will to fight. If he beat me, then, I knew I might start crying and never stop.

"Looking a little down, slave," he snickered, his stupid glee obvious on his face. "I knew from the first day I saw your scrawny ass that you'd be no good for anything but a hole to fuck! Just glad I got to stick it to you before the general population had a chance!"

I hated him more than I had ever hated anything else in my life, and I wanted to leap out, strangle him, bash his face against the floor until blood spewed out and bones cracked. I wanted to rip his arms off and use the bones to bash his eyes in and stab through his throat until he suffocated and drowned in his own blood.

I stared at him, expressionless.

"You always thought you were smarter than everyone else, didn't you?" he taunted, grabbing one of my ears and twisting it until I squirmed. "Thought you were clever and cute—all I see is a defiant, untrainable pile of shit who likes to cause trouble!"

His words hit home, and I felt my stomach twist. Two years, and that was the impression I gave off? Even after all that time? I had realized early on that I should play their games, that they didn't appreciate intelligence or independence or individuality, but I had done this poorly at hiding it? Untrainable? Had I learned nothing? I had never failed so badly at anything in my life. The truth hit harder than any blow he ever gave me.

"At least I'm through with you now," my guard said, shoving me away. "You're Rae's problem until the transport next week. Special training."

The words barely sank in. I was glad to be rid of the man who had single-handedly made my life hell for the past two years, but that didn't cut the misery I felt at the moment. I failed. I ruined everything, every chance I had at any sort of comfort or decency. I fought back tears, willing them not to fall, not yet, and I ran down the corridor to the sexual service training room where I displayed at least some skill in the past.

It was empty, none of the other slaves too eager to come here to accept their new life as sexual servants. Heedless of punishment or reprimand or anything but my own misery, I rushed into Mistress Rae's office, where I knew I wasn't allowed to go, and I saw the only person who had been remotely kind to me at the re-education center. I threw myself to the floor at her feet and started sobbing.

I heard her gasp in surprise, but her hand was light in my hair.

"Sascha, Sascha," she said softly, and I could hear the regret in her voice. "Shh, it's okay. You'll do fine there. You're a good boy, you'll please the clients and you'll do well."

I couldn't say anything, in part because I was crying too hard, in part because I didn't want to tell her she was wrong. I knew I was a failure, a useless fuck up who couldn't even lie his way through re-education, and I knew I would never please anyone.

She let me cry for a few more minutes before cupping my chin gently in her fingertips and tipping my face up to look at her. Her voice was barely above a whisper, and I had to stop crying to hear it. "Listen, there are worse things than brothel work—they don't tell any of you, but there is a blacklist for slaves who can't conform, and it was all I could do to get your name off of it. The blacklist is where they get human subjects for experiments, or organ transplants, or other ter-rible things, and I just... you're far too capable to go there. I saw a different slave than anyone else, and the clients at Bethel's won't care about your history. I've prepared you the best way I know how, and I know you're strong enough to make it. Start fresh, and put your skills to your advantage."

I nodded, nuzzling up against her hand and her legs like she had taught me to. I half-expected her to order me to pleasure her, because that was how slaves usually paid for comfort. I didn't mind. But she didn't, she just held me close against her legs and petted my hair until I calmed down.

"Sascha," she said, sadly. "You could have done so much more. You still can. Keep an eye open and remember to put your best fea-tures forward."

I let her words flow over me. She was always spewing out mes-sages of hope and happiness; I guess it was expected for someone who had fifty goddamn orgasms a day and wanted all of them. She let me cry in her office until I calmed down, and she allowed me to sleep in the small room next to it instead of returning to the regular dorm. Just avoiding the guards was enough of a reprieve.

I was fortunate to have "special training" with her for the next week until the transport. Any other trainer would have beaten the sulkiness out of me, and Mistress Rae even threatened to, once, before my pathetic sobbing won her over again. Instead, she had me help with the new batch of slaves, getting them to relax and accept that their bodies were not their own anymore. The work itself wasn't hard, but it didn't mean I liked it, either. I touched them when they begged me not to, made them touch me, kissed them and sucked them and told them how to do it in return, how to make it feel good. It was hard for me to enjoy even the best sexual touches when the person touching me was in tears, but I knew they would be punished if they failed to please me. The fear added enough excitement that I could force myself to get hard, to stay that way, even to fuck them when ordered.

I was complicit in their abuse, but at least I was kinder than the others, and I tied to remember to be patient. I hated having anything to do with the re-education process, but at least teaching others something new was a challenge. It comforted me as I prepared to leave the terrible, familiar life I had become accustomed to.

I was taken with another boy and two girls, and the hover-van dropped us off unceremoniously in front of a garish purple building with red lights in the window. Ironically, I found myself eager to go inside, if only to escape the fucking eyesore that stood in front of me.

Even two years in the re-education center hadn't beaten the good taste out of me.

A heavyset woman wearing an unfortunate-looking corset came storming out with a riding crop in her hands, and she looked like every cliché dominatrix I ever saw back when I modded Abriel's tablet so he could watch porn and see tits. At least it was me here, and not him.

The woman raised her riding crop and gestured with it as she spoke, and I was struck with the ridiculous image of her conducting a marching band with it.

"My name is Mistress Bethel, and you'll be answering to me and this crop for the rest of your foreseeable future," she announced, her voice excessively loud and overdone considering there were only four of us, and we were all on our knees a few feet in front of her.

She pointed toward the door with the crop. "Get inside."

The others crawled, but I felt stupid and daring as usual, so I got up and walked, holding the door for the other three like some sort of valet. Mistress Bethel glared at me, but said nothing. Still, I dropped to my knees again once we got inside. I didn't actually *enjoy* being beaten, at least, not outside of the bedroom.

Somehow it took her nearly an hour to tell us we were going to fuck for money and that we better damn well be good at it. I tried to count the varicose veins that were visible on her legs, which earned me a smack with the riding crop when I failed to respond to her question.

"Um, I don't know, Mistress?" I played dumb. The fucking crop hurt, the Demoted are expected to be stupid.

"Always!" she hit me with the crop. "Get the money!" another smack. "Before the service!" A final smack, and there were tears in my eyes.

"Yes, Mistress," I answered, my shoulders stinging.

We were put to work instantly, Mistress Bethel half-leading, half-dragging each of us to the room that we were going to "occupy" for the night. I expected them to be gross, but exactly how gross they were startled me. The sheets were stiff with dried come and probably a variety of other bodily fluids I didn't even want to think about, and the walls were splattered with something as well. You couldn't really tell, because they were painted a sort of mottled greenish brown, and the lights were dimmed. I thought it might have been better if the lights were off entirely, but our "customers" probably wanted to see us going down on them or something.

My first few customers were pretty standard. They came in, handed over money, and rammed their cocks into me. It was unpleasant, but it didn't exactly hurt, especially not after the first one was finished. One had me suck him off, which I actually found more tedious than being fucked, because I had to put some effort into it. The asshole insisted on grabbing my hair and jerking me up and down on his cock until he came, but he didn't seem to mind my teeth grazing him, so I let them. Better his dick getting scraped up than my lips.

After what seemed like an eternity, but what was really probably only five or six hours, we were told that it was our "shift" to sleep. Another slave came to collect us, a little redheaded girl whose ribs showed and who had welts over all the visible parts of her skin, which there was a lot of. She half-dragged us up some stairs to an attic, where I figured we would be sleeping. "Half-drag" seemed to be synonymous with "walk" around here, which was rather unpleasant, but I didn't complain. I wanted to avoid being "half-beaten-to-death."

The attic did contain a place for sleeping, although calling it a "room" was quite an exaggeration. Actually, calling it an attic was a bit of an exaggeration—the floor wasn't even finished, it was just a series of boards over top of a layer of insulation. The girl warned that if we fell through, we would come through the ceiling of the brothel. I could imagine the kinds of punishments we would get from that. Here and there, I saw sheets tied around the boards, making a sort of tiny hammock between them. I wondered if I would ever get any sleep.

"They're actually pretty comfortable," our battered tour guide whispered next to me. "Better than downstairs was."

I didn't ask about downstairs, because I had enough nightmare fuel already.

The girl introduced herself to us as Raven, pointed out empty sheet hammocks, and showed us how to tighten the knots around the beams before darting back downstairs in response to Mistress Bethel's scream. I lay down, starting to feel exhaustion setting in. I wondered when we would be allowed to shower, and I tried to ignore the smell of come and sweat and dirt that permeated the place. I rejoiced in the almost trivial fact that I managed to avoid a beating that day, which two of the others hadn't, and I tried to ignore the hunger I felt. I simply assumed we would get fed enough not to starve to death. After all, dead whores didn't bring in money.

Chapter 11
Fallout

Leaving Sascha with my boss is surprisingly difficult. I spend the night vacillating between feeling guilty and feeling ridiculous. He's a sex slave. He's had plenty of experience being used for sex, plenty who have hurt him. I know Mr. Dean will treat him well, but it's hard to get the look Sascha gave me out of my mind. I wonder if I'm becoming possessive over him, a jealous master, but it doesn't sit right. Why should I be possessive? It's not as though I'm interested in him like that. While I do find him catching my eye on occasion, it's always spoiled by his fear, his anxiety, and sometimes his annoying defiance. In different circumstances, there might have been something between us, but as far as I can tell, he has no interest in ever being touched by me. I won't push the issue.

I try to put the thought out of my mind, think about the promotion I'm earning. It will earn me more money, but more importantly, it will give me access to the accounts I've been interested in. It wasn't my original plan, back when everything went to hell and I had to erase that part of my life, but some of the financial partners whom Dean & Chanu Associates work with are directly relevant to the research I used to do, the research I want to do again, one day. It's this thought that captures my attention more than anything, and I'm still engrossed in it by the time I go to pick up Sascha.

He looks drawn and pale; I ask him whether he's been hurt at all. He mumbles, "No, master," while looking out the window. I frown, but say nothing else. I wonder if he's angry that I lent him out, or that I came back for him.

He retreats to his room the moment we get home, and he avoids me after that. I give him his space. I have no demands for him, and I assume he can keep himself busy. After all, there are still illegal activities to fill his time with. He's more careful with his tablet now, but I know he's still exploring with it. It surprised me when I first found out, especially when I realized how advanced and elegant his codes were. He's far brighter than he lets on, and if he wants to keep his secrets, I'll let him.

After all, I have my own.

Sascha cooks, although he doesn't seem to like to eat when I'm around. Grocery bills come and food disappears from the fridge, so I assume he's enjoying his creations. I wonder if it's my presence that ruins his appetite. I start to eat out more, which works well. I have meetings set up with investors on a regular basis, both for work, and for my research project. The re-education centers may have been revolutionized by my mother, but I want my generation to be better. I want it overthrown, and to do that, I have to be more careful than I was last time. It makes me smile to think of Sascha and his adventures on his tablet; trouble finds both of us. I only hope that I complete my project this time.

In between meetings, I try to have at least a little social time. I invite Bobby over and suggest that Sascha prepare something spicy for us. I do like his food, and I want to see how he interacts. He amazed me at the Peace Day Celebration, Mr. Dean still raves about the night he spent with him; I want to see him in a less formal setting.

The smell of spices and browning meat fills the air by the time Bobby arrives, and I'm amazed by the ease with which Sascha manages it. He serves us, not well, but he tries. It's a good skill to have; I keep in mind that he might be a valuable asset to bring to meetings and negotiations. To play in a world of slave-owners and stakeholders, owning a slave makes one far less suspicious.

Bobby and I engage in banal, light conversation, as always. We've been friends since we were children, and we've gone through plenty of periods of growth and change with one another. Bobby compliments the food; he has such an easy manner, even if Sascha seems to flinch away from it. I attempt to praise Sascha, and he turns away from me as well.

"Cash, the kid cooks quite well, but don't you ever let him eat it?"

Bobby asks, shoveling food into his mouth as he does.

"Of course," I reply, offended at the suggestion. I'm not some sort of monster. Sascha is fed better than the majority of free population. "What, would you like him to pull up a chair next to you? I'm sure he has a dish back in the kitchen, or maybe he's eaten already. He's capable of feeding himself, I'm sure."

Bobby laughs. "It's not that, man, he's just so damn skinny! I can't believe he hasn't put on any weight since you bought him!"

I turn my glare toward Sascha, who seems to shrink before my eyes. His clothes are baggy, loose, not the well-sized garments I purchased for him. He seems to curl into himself, and when I catch his gaze, he glances away.

"He did," I answer evenly. "It just seems to have disappeared again."

"Maybe he's sick," Bobby comments. "I probably couldn't pinch anything but skin on that little ass!"

The comment gets me a little ruffled, but I don't want to offend Bobby. I keep glaring at the slave, who is trembling now that he's the center of attention. "I'll look into it."

I steer the conversation toward more appropriate topics — work, movies, anything but my slave and his lack of body weight. I can see Bobby eyeing Sascha up throughout the night and it irks me. Health is important. I didn't buy the slave so he could starve himself. Sascha keeps bringing us more and more drinks, as if I'm stupid enough to get drunk and pass out without dealing with him.

"I think we've had enough drinks, Sascha," I tell him, fixing my glare at him. He pales, but nods. "I have an early morning. Clear the table and bring Bobby his coat."

We finish talking as Sascha cleans up, and I wave Bobby out the door. Sascha is cleaning up by the time Bobby leaves, and I come out to see him standing nervously in the dining room.

I pull out a chair and point him toward it. "Sit there and don't move until I get back," I order. I storm out of the house, intent on finding a solution to this weight loss problem. Sascha can be a valuable asset to me in the slave trade, but not if he's starving. It contradicts all of my research.

My master leaves me in a state of panic, imagining all the terrible things he might come back with. I think of all the torture devices that have been used on me in the past, and what if he finds one of those, what if he takes my refusal to eat as defiance, and he wants to punish me for it? Or what if he doesn't come back at all? What if he leaves me here, forever, and I starve and pee on myself and die?

I remind myself that even if he doesn't come back, eventually, I could get up and use the bathroom or eat or whatever; it's not like I'm chained by anything other than sheer terror. Worrying about him not coming back shouldn't even be my biggest concern; I should really focus on worrying what exactly he might bring back with him when he returns. All the options make me sick to my stomach.

It turns out I don't have to wait that long; he's back in about twenty minutes with a bag. I cringe as I look at it, wondering what sorts of torture devices he might take out of it and hurt me with.

It's an understatement to say I'm surprised when he pulls out a scale.

He drops it on the floor and points to it.

"Get on."

I obey, and he looks at the reading. He glares at me.

"I'll weigh you daily," he says, scowling. "You lose another pound and I'll tie you down and force feed you."

"Yes, master." I can feel the tears starting again. Fuck. I can't even stay alive right. It's not good enough for him. Nothing is, and nothing will be, and I was stupid for ever even trying.

"I thought you said you didn't have an eating problem!" he snaps. The sudden emotion in his voice makes me jump.

"I don't, master," I protest, fully aware of how weak and pathetic it sounds. I never did before, when I was a real human instead of a piece of meat to be sampled by everyone who wants a bite. Even now, it's not about the food, but I can't tell him that. "I just forget."

"Forget?" His tone is incredulous. "You don't *forget* to eat at all. Those clothes hang on you, and they used to fit. Quit lying this instant!"

I stand there trembling, waiting to feel him hit me.

His face grows darker. "Still doing the physical therapy exercises you're supposed to?"

Of course not. "I'll start tonight, master."

I feel him take a step closer, and I realize my eyes are closed when he grabs me by the shirt and jerks me toward him. The motion jars my shoulder, shooting pain through my left side and emphasizing his point. "This is the reason I didn't want a slave," he hisses. "Keep this bullshit up and I'll sell you to the first interested party."

I want to drop to my knees, but he's still holding me. "Please, no!" I whimper anyway, looking up at him. "Please, master." It's all I can to do keep standing, but I think he might let me hang myself from my shirt if I don't.

He pushes me away, a look of disgust on his face. "Get your act together," he warns. "I'm not asking all that much of you."

He walks away and I let myself crumple to the floor, holding back my cries until I hear him slam the door to his office. He's keeping me. He's still keeping me. I've fucked up now, though, too much, too bad, and he's angry, and I'm a problem for him, and if I don't stop fucking up he'll sell me. I don't even want to take care of myself properly anymore. But I will. I'll try. Any other master would have beaten me for letting myself go so much, and he isn't going to do that, and I want to stay with him. I would rather stay with a person who ignores me and weighs me to make sure I'm healthy than someone who starves me and goes out of their way to be cruel. I realize how good I really have it, and I suddenly have the will to fight to keep it.

I force myself to eat. I don't care much about what it is, or even if it's healthy, although the healthy foods seem to make my stomach feel less sick. I read the labels and eat whatever has the most calories. I remind myself that I was stupid to think that I was special, that my master valued me and wouldn't pass me around. I remind myself that my concern now is pleasing my master, not making his life more difficult.

I don't know how all the Demoted don't just commit mass suicide every day.

Then again, I don't actually want to die, which is annoying. It would be easier if I wanted to die. I want to live, and I want to stay with my asshole of a master. I don't know whether to worship him or hate him. Realistically, he's the best I'm going to get. Probably better than I deserve. I'm a slave; I have to stop thinking of myself as a person who deserves things like respect, no matter how much it hurts when I don't get it. I'm being treated far better than I thought I would when he more or less rescued me from the brothel. As soon as I start thinking about that, all I can think of is how much I want to avoid going back there, or to a place like that. It makes me even more desperate to please the bastard. I wish the logical part of my brain would come out of hibernation and communicate with the panicky prey-animal part.

It's the panicky prey-animal part that tends to come out around my master, though, when he weighs me daily and my heart almost stops and I wonder if I've stuffed enough bread and cheese and butter and water into myself to satisfy him.

He doesn't even tell me what the scale says, he just looks and grunts at me. I guess grunt means I did well, maybe if I didn't he would bark or something. Sometimes I can't tell if he's the animal or if I am.

Aside from stuffing myself and doing the physical therapy exercises, I brood, curled up in bed or sometimes on the floor, if getting onto the bed seems too difficult. I shower only because I'm afraid of the repercussions if I don't. I clean the house while my master's out, but I do a pretty terrible job of that, anymore. My master ignores me, and some days, I'd rather have him beat me. I feel myself disappearing, my face drawn and dead looking. I hope it makes me look distinguished.

My master must not think so, though, because when I'm submitting to the embarrassing ordeal of being weighed again one night, he frowns at me.

"Maybe Bobby's right. Maybe you are sick," he mumbles. "Just what I'd like to do, take you to the doctor again."

"I'm not sick, master," I say, surprised that I'm actually speaking to him, much less contradicting him. Maybe I am sick. Mentally. Contradicting him is crazy.

He raises an eyebrow at me.

"I mean, I, I feel fine, master," I mumble, feeling ridiculous. "I'm not trying to argue or anything, and I'll go and see the doctor if you want me to, but I don't feel sick and I don't think anything's wrong."

"Then what the hell is your problem?" he asks, and he doesn't actually sound too angry, he sounds genuinely curious, despite his phrasing. I'm shocked enough that he's inquiring as it is; if he sounded compassionate I'd probably die on the spot.

I'm stumped for a minute. I'm a slave. I'm miserable. Isn't it obvious? "I feel fine, master," I mumble again, useless.

"You don't eat. You mope around this goddamn house like someone just killed your puppy. You do a shitty job at cleaning, and you do an even shittier job of lying to me."

Dammit, I hate how observant he can be.

"So *what*. The hell. Is your problem?" He glares at me, and I wish I had somewhere to hide. He rubs his hand along the side of his face. "You've been strange since I left you at my boss's house — did he hurt you or something?"

"No, master," I rush to correct him. "He was perfectly kind." Too kind, actually, I almost feel guilty about how miserable he made me when he was just trying to have a good time.

"Was he sick? Did you catch something from him?" My master presses, glaring at me still.

"No, master, nothing like that." I want to run out of the room.

He's silent for a few moments, appraising me, glaring at my too-thin frame and drawn look and dark eyes and every other flaw that I know he can see.

"What if I were to tell you that he's requested you for a while?" he says, his face a mask.

My heart drops, and I bite back tears. I'm standing next to the scale that he uses to weigh me, but I drop to my knees. "Please, master, please don't make me!"

He sighs, like he's relieved about something. I don't understand.

"Please, master, I won't be a problem anymore!" A while? How long is that? Is it a trial of some sort, so Mr. Dean can see if he really wants to own me? I should want him to own me, but I don't. At least this master is familiar, and he doesn't touch me. Will I be able to keep up the façade with Mr. Dean for a while?

"Get up!" he snaps, and when I do I see his eyes roll.

He lets me stand there, uncomfortable for a few moments.

"You didn't want to go over there in the first place, did you?" he asks.

How am I supposed to answer? Of course not! But I can't say that. I let a stock slave answer slip through my lips. "It was your decision, master."

"Bullshit." His dismissal is cold. "You didn't want to do it, and I dragged you over there, and I left you there, and I made you do it, and now you're pouting and moping and giving up on life because you're upset."

I stand there and tremble, because denying it would be a flat-out lie, and confirming it doesn't sound much better.

"Dammit, Sascha, I thought you said you wouldn't mind!" he snaps, getting up and walking across the room, away from me.

The distance makes me a little bit more comfortable, even though I doubt that this is why he does it. I don't remember saying anything of the sort, though; I said that I would do it, and that I wouldn't complain. Perhaps I had failed a little bit on the last part, but I'm not complaining, not really, I'm just giving up on life and trying to die. There's a difference, right? I think there's a difference.

"He didn't request you again, by the way."

I can't feel anything but utter relief at those words.

He finally turns and looks at me, and his face has the same tight expression that it did when he left me with his boss. "I really didn't think you'd mind."

What is this? An apology? It sounds more like an observation. I'm probably supposed to respond, but I don't. If he can't offer a real apology, I guess I don't have to offer a real response. I just stare at him.

"He told me he would treat you kindly."

"He did," I admit. But that's not what matters. "He treated me very kindly, master. He didn't force me. I went willingly."

"But you still object to being used like a whore," my master speaks my thoughts like he can read them.

I say nothing. It's true. It's stupid, but it's true.

"Years of brothel work, and you object to being used like a whore," he shakes his head.

Right. That's all I am. So why does it burn so much to hear him say it? "It's not my place to object—"

"Stop."

One word and a glare freeze me solid.

"I'm sorry I made you do that when you didn't want to," he says, calm and assured. It takes a few seconds for the apology to sink in. "If I knew you'd mind I never would have forced you to do it. Hell, Mr. Dean would never have forced you to do it. In the future, you will tell me if something is going to make you this uncomfortable, understood?"

From anyone else, I would feel like I was being blamed, but with him it's just a statement of fact. It was a mistake, on his part and on mine, and he's not just apologizing, he's making sure it won't happen again. I can't expect him to read my mind, and I can't be that angry that he didn't. "Yes, master," I reply, quiet, grateful that he's giving me this opportunity. A part of me knows I should be beaten for being so fucking difficult, if not passed around to hundreds of other people until I remember my place, but he shows no interest in either of those things.

He looks at me for a while longer, making me feel uncomfortable, before walking out of the room. He hesitates in the doorway. "Start eating and drop the attitude," he mutters, facing away from me.

Nothing like getting back to business, after all.

Chapter 12

Inevitable

I hear the distinct, melodic announcement of a com call, and I'm surprised to realize that my master has left his device at home while he went to work. I frown, wishing it would stop, but I don't bother to move from where I'm sitting. After all, he's never told me to answer his calls, and I don't want to displease him.

Things have gotten better since I realized that my master *doesn't* actually want to whore me out. I find myself starting to become more comfortable, now that I know he will keep me. I take care of myself and the house better, because all he asks is that I clean some toilets and wash some dishes. I might just be the most fortunate slave in the world.

I've fallen back into the habit of eating regularly, and I feel better. A part of me wonders if my point was getting him to notice me, but that seems so fucking pathetic that I can't think about it. I can do just fine without him noticing me, and I can do just fine without his approval. I try not to feel proud when he stops weighing me, because it was ridiculous that he had to do it. Could I really forget so quickly what starvation felt like?

My master leads a very comfortable life, and I benefit from it almost enough to forget that it's not really my life at all. I pretend that I'm just a pampered homebody, maybe a college student living with wealthy grandparents, or a young entrepreneur who has "people" to take care of the business all day. My childhood was nothing like that, but I saw it enough on the vidscreen programs that my mother used to watch, and I draw out the fantasies to fit my situation. It helps to pass the time, coming up with these elaborate scenarios.

The device stops ringing, and I settle back into my comfortable spot on the couch, reading a new book on my tablet and contemplating my good fortune. Only seconds later, the device blares again, and I get up, finding it with a stack of papers that my master likely meant to take with him. It's so rare that I hear the sound anymore; my master often places his devices on silent when he's home, no wanting anything to interrupt his preferred silence. But it's such a common sound, one I heard so frequently as a child, and it prompts me to pick up the device. I tell myself I'm not prying, I'm just... okay, I'm prying. I figure it might be Bobby or someone, and I figure I can set it to silent without my master noticing when he comes home.

The screen doesn't display a contact name, it simply reads "Unknown" and displays a contact number. As the device goes silent again, I try to think of who it might be, but I have no clue. I pick it up, looking for the button to silence it, and when I do, "Unknown" calls a third time, just as my finger is glancing over the "answer" sensor.

I stare at it in horror for a moment before habit kicks in. "Hello?" I mumble, realizing just how long it's been since I've answered a com call, much less one that wasn't my own.

"Cashiel?" A man's voice questions from the other end.

"Um..." I stall, seeming to have forgotten everything about polite conversation. "He's not here."

"And who is this?" the voice demands.

I'm confused, but I'm also irritated by the demanding tone. For all this unknown caller knows, I'm not a slave, I'm a guest, a friend, someone who should be treated better than the slave I really am. "Who the hell is this?" I snap in return.

"What did you say to me?"

The illusion of anonymity loosens my tongue. "I asked who the hell you were," I retort, feeling a rush of excitement at pretending, just for a moment, that I'm not a slave. "You're the one who called here, remember? Cashiel isn't here, and even if he was, he wasn't picking up. Maybe you should have left a message, that's what the message system is for."

"Sascha!" My master's voice thunders out from nowhere, and I feel myself paralyzed with horror. He's supposed to be at work! There is absolutely no room in my spoiled pet fantasy for my master to be *home*!

He's not a figment of my imagination, and he's also not very pleased with me as he storms into the room. I'm stupid enough to meet his eyes, and the rage I see there terrifies me. I'm too terrified to even flinch away as his hand approaches my face, I just stand there with my mouth open.

He grabs the phone away from me as I stand there in shock, jabbing at the button that ends the call. He continues looking at the phone, seeing who called, and looking through the list of missed calls, while I tremble beside him.

"What the hell were you thinking?" he growls.

"I—I'm sorry, sir," I mumble, fighting back tears. "I just... it was ringing, and I went to silence it, and I answered it and—"

"Do you have any idea what you have just done?" he hisses. "It's bad enough that you answered *my* call, but how dare you speak that way to the caller?"

"I'm sorry I was rude, sir," I try, but my words only make his face darken. "I was disrespectful and, and inappropriate, and I shouldn't have answered it, even if it wasn't anybody important."

"Wasn't anybody important? Dammit, Sascha, that was—" before finishing, he stops himself. "That was a free person, and it doesn't matter who he is to me or whether he is important or not. You have no idea who may be calling me, and you have no idea the damage you might have caused."

"It won't happen again, sir." I try to think of something to say to make this go away, but I can't.

With a furious look on his face, my master's hand shoots out toward my face again, and this time, I feel rough pressure on my ear. I cry out as my master drags me out of the kitchen.

In a few moments, he's pulled me to the living room, where he forces me to lean over the arm of the couch by tugging at my ear. I don't fight, because I know I won't win.

I feel arms around my waist, and I'm confused for half a second before I realize my pants have just been undone and are now being pulled down, along with my boxers, and left around my ankles. An embarrassing position, certainly, but I don't dare to squirm to try and move them at all. I contemplate the fact that this is the first and only time my master has ever undressed me, and I wish I could be looking forward to what he is going to do next.

I hear the sound of a buckle being unfastened, and I *really* wish I could be looking forward to what he is going to do next.

The sound of leather sliding through fabric isn't unfamiliar, and while it makes me shudder in fear, I know it's not as bad as some other things he could use to hurt me with. I've been hurt with much worse, so much worse, in fact, that I'm almost relieved that he's just going to beat me with a belt.

I still jump when his hand rests lightly on my lower back.

"Don't move and keep your hands where they are," he orders, curt and businesslike. "Can you do that, or should I tie you?"

"I can do it, master." My voice is tiny and afraid. It matches how I feel. But I'm amazed that he doesn't want to tie me, just to make it worse. I'm amazed that he trusts me.

He says nothing, just steps back and starts beating me.

It hurts.

I've met slaves who like to play tough, who act like and pretend and say that whippings don't hurt, or that "just" a belt doesn't hurt, but it does, and I'm crying by the fifth time the thick leather snaps across my skin. Just my fucking luck, this isn't one of the days that he's wearing a lightweight belt.

I dig my fingers into the arm of the couch, clutching the fabric as if I can squeeze the pain away. I can't. It just makes my fingers hurt, too. I don't dare move, because I know my master will make good on his threat to tie me, and I definitely don't want that. I brought this on myself, and I'll be damned if I give him the satisfaction of tying me up, too.

I estimate that he's hit me maybe ten or twelve times before I start crying out, my whimpers creating a melody with the sound of leather striking flesh. I want to wipe at my eyes, but I don't dare move my hands. I sob through the physical pain as well as the emotional blows. I was so stupid to think I could get away with it.

He pauses. "If you think your pathetic crying is going to make me go easy on you, you'd better think again," he snaps, bringing the belt down where my ass meets my legs with increasing force.

"I'm crying because it *hurts*, master!" I protest, almost without realizing it. It doesn't matter anymore that I'm contradicting him. What's he going to do, beat me more? He's probably already going to beat me half to death. Let him. I'll go numb if he hurts me enough.

When he doesn't say anything, I close my eyes, still crying, and try to focus on blocking the pain, on stepping out of my body like I used to. It's hard, it's been so long since I've had the practice. I feel him pause again, and I fight not to tense up, waiting for him to berate me again, or maybe to go and find something more brutal to beat me with. He's hit me two, maybe three dozen times, and I'm sure he's just beginning. I'm checking out, and he's just beginning. This is how it always starts.

"You have a very low pain tolerance," he observes, quiet, like he's commenting on a goddamn statue or something.

I want to say "no shit," but I don't. "Yes, master," I whimper. I should win an award for being pathetic. I hear him putting his belt back into his pants.

"Stay," he orders.

I wonder what the hell else he expects me to do.

I lie there, feeling my ass burn and ache. I want nothing more than to reach back and rub it, maybe put some ice on it in a while. As though I'd ever be allowed to do that. At least he's not yelling at me, or worse, asking me to speak. I'm too angry to speak, both at him and at myself, and I'd be too terrified to make sense anyway.

He returns and I start to taste bitter fear again, metallic in my mouth and heavy in my stomach. I wait for the pain.

It comes, but not as expected. I am expecting another blow, but instead I feel my pants being jerked up, not roughly on purpose, but not with any particular care. I fail when I try not to whimper.

He pulls me to my feet, still facing away from him, and says "open."

It takes me a second to understand, but I see something in front of my mouth and I obey quickly. I think it's a dishtowel, and he secures it in my mouth before wrapping it around my head and tying it tightly. I can't help but try to close my mouth around it.

"Is it hurting you?" he asks, his face blank.

I shake my head, hoping he doesn't change that.

"Good." He glares at me. "I warned you, Sascha. I told you, if you spoke like that to a free person again, you would be beaten and gagged, and here we are. You'll wear the gag for the rest of the day, and *I* will remove it this evening, is that understood?"

I nod. Shit. He really had warned me.

"Do *not* remove it," he glares some more.

I don't know whether to nod or shake my head, so I just stare at him.

"And I want this place clean when I get back," he adds. "I doubt you'll want to be sitting around all day anyway."

He's right. My ass is still on fire, and I have no desire to sit. I watch as he picks up his keys and his briefcase and strides out, as if nothing happened. I don't even know what he came home for. He either took care of it while I was crying over the couch, or he forgot; too put off by my deplorable behavior.

I lie on the couch on my stomach and cry for a few more minutes, only partially because of the pain. I cry because my master beat me, and I had deluded myself into believing he might not, even though he had always made it perfectly clear that he would. I cry because I know it's my own damn fault, and if the situation was reversed, hell, I'd beat me too, and I wouldn't have stopped as quickly as he did. I cry because he *didn't* beat me too badly, which is fucked up, because that should make me happy, not sad. But he's the first person who's ever really noticed when I start to check out, when the pain doesn't matter as much. It's him, so I can't believe it's a coincidence, because he notices everything. I cry because he wasn't even all that angry when he beat me, he was more inconvenienced. All I have ever been to him is an inconvenience.

But mostly, I cry because I've fucked up, again, with him, when I thought I was trying. It was inevitable. I fuck up everything.

Chapter 13
Capable

I'm halfway down the street when I realize I've forgotten the very paperwork I went back to the house to get, before my defiant slave decided to test me. I don't go back for it, though, I don't want to see the aftermath. I didn't beat him too severely, I know that. He's taken far worse before. I was surprised that he broke that quickly. It makes me wonder why others in the past have felt the need to brutalize him so much.

Then I think of the standardized training initiatives my mother's re-education centers implemented, and it starts to make sense. Such a waste of so much potential. No wonder he panics whenever he so much as thinks of doing anything wrong.

I know he didn't try to mess anything up today, but the way he spoke to my colleague placed me at risk. The research I'm conducting on the side requires subtlety, and the less anyone involved knows about my life, the better. I return the call, joke about an "overnight guest," and try to pretend that I don't even own a slave. It's so much safer for both me and Sascha to keep him out of this.

I'm trying to enjoy my lunch break when my com device begins playing the theme from a series of horror films, and I shove my food aside as the name "Kristine Miller" flashes across the screen, demanding my attention and docility. I don't say hello, I just wave my hand across the answering sensor, feeling a cold chill at the prospect of talking to my mother.

"I hear you got a slave, Cashiel," she says, her voice thick and taunting.

"Yes." I don't care if I'm sullen. My mother has ruined my life once, I don't care for her to do it again. The less she knows about Sascha, the safer we both are.

"You know, it's important to keep up appearances in your new life," she advises, as if she were ever the type of mother to give advice instead of orders. "I think it's good that you're starting to come along, giving up all those ridiculous ideas you used to have."

"Why?" I ask. "It's not like I'm your son anymore. You disowned me, remember?"

She laughs, the taunting sound from my childhood that haunts me to this day. "Cashi, you'll always be mine. And you should be grateful. I pulled some strings to get you cleared of the treason charges."

My mother was the one who exposed my research and had the charges brought up in the first place.

"Thank you," I say anyway, because it's what she wants to hear.

"I was thinking we should visit sometime," she suggests. "I miss my little boy. There are still so many things I'd like to teach you, now that you're trying to be all on your own."

It's funny, because she never referred to me by any sort of pet name when I was a child. She would degrade me, humiliate me, terrify me, but my mother never nurtured me like she seems to think she did. I don't understand how she can possibly think that I'm just now "on my own" when I've been struggling to break free from her clutches since I passed the Assessment.

"It was unfortunate that you couldn't continue the family business," she comments, ignoring the fact that I have yet to respond to her last statement.

"You had me arrested for continuing in the family business," I remind her. The three weeks I spent in federal prison had been enough of a reminder of the power of the Demoted system, not to mention the power of the woman who birthed me and bought slaves to raise me.

"I don't know where your father and I went wrong with you," she muses.

I don't reply. My father did nothing; my entire life, he was merely a stock figure who backed up my mother's every wish, including when she had me arrested. I used to try to defend him, but when the courtesy wasn't returned, I washed my hands of him. At least he had the decency to leave me alone.

My mother would never back down so easily. Part of our agreement after I tried to overthrow her re-education system was that we would stay in contact. What I thought that meant when we made the agreement so many years ago was that she would drop the restraining order against me and invite me to family dinners on occasion. What it means to her is that she coms me at least once a month, and if I don't answer and bow to her wishes, she harasses me, often going so far as to hire private investigators to keep me in line.

"Tell me about the slave, Cashi," my mother prods. "Was he well-trained? Did he come from a talent agency? Does he have special skills? I do hope you're putting him to better use than you did the last ones."

The last ones weren't actually mine; they were my mother's. I used them for research that damned me as much as them. I won't make the same mistake with Sascha. Not just because of the research; the fear I felt when I heard him on the phone today made me realize that I actually want to see him safe. "He's a brothel whore," I reply, smiling at the expression I know will be on my mother's face. "I bought him for less than the cost of a nice suit, and I love the filthy things he knows."

The silence from the other end confirms my suspicions.

"Cashiel, I don't know why you try to hurt me so much," my mother says, her voice cold instead of hurt. "After all I've done for you."

She continues to tell me what a great asset I could have made to her business, how I should appreciate the corporate finance job she got for me, how she wishes I could let go of my "youthful rebelliousness" and become a valuable member of society. I wish my words had hurt her, but all I hear is disappointment. I disappointed her by challenging the status quo she set before I was even born.

I tolerate the lecture because I have to, and I listen carefully for any hint that she is aware of the reboot of the research I had to abandon so long ago. She's brilliant; for years I could never outsmart her, but I feel like we are pretty evenly matched these days. What she's lost to age and overconfidence, I've gained in caution and experience. One day I will expose her work for the sham it is, but until then, I play the contrite son, or the spiteful brat, depending on my mood. It's always a risk to antagonize her in return, but she is more likely to slip up when she's emotionally challenged. We play each other like a card game, each hiding so much more than we show.

I leave work a little earlier than usual, on the pretense that I need to get home to meet with guests. In all honesty, I want to make sure Sascha is all right.

I find him in his room, and watch him wince when he rolls onto his backside before getting up. I suppose he deserves it; the attitude he displayed earlier was utterly unacceptable. I don't ask to see the marks I left on him, but I know they are there.

"Bobby's coming by tonight," I inform him. "I'd like you to start dinner."

He starts to nod, then makes a terrible gagging noise. His eyes fill with tears, and I quickly discern the source of his disgust. The dishtowel gag is all covered in drool; no matter how he tries to hold his head or swallow, the soggy, squishy fabric is there. He gags a few more times and I can see him struggling to breathe through his nose.

"Come here," I order. I'm ashamed of myself. I know better than this, or at least, I should. The dishtowel could have been dirty, could have caused him to choke. A proper slave-owner should always have appropriate training tools.

"Turn around," I order impatiently. He's far too busy trembling and worrying to respond quickly. Still, he obeys, and I deftly untie the dishtowel.

I'm surprised when he turns, his eyes wide as he searches my face for the answer to some sort of question.

"That must have been incredibly unpleasant," I comment, hoping to downplay my mistake.

I fail, miserably, because he just shrugs and mumbles something. The look on his face says far more. He must think I did it on purpose.

"That was not my intention when I did it," I inform him. "I intended it only as a reminder not to speak. I should have realized..."

I stop, equally appalled at my choice of punishment as I am at the thought of apologizing to the slave. What am I supposed to do, explain why I should have realized how uncomfortable it was? It was a stupid beginner's mistake, and for all public purposes, I am a beginner in the slave-owner world. I don't know that I can trust him, or that

I want to.

"I apologize," I say instead, changing the subject. "That was an error on my part. You may be released from the punishment early."

He stares at me in shock.

"I'll buy something more appropriate for the future," I decide. "If you think it will be necessary to repeat this in the future."

He struggles, but he finally nods. "Yes, master, it might be necessary. I'll try, but..."

It's amazing to see such strength in a slave. Raw honesty won't serve him well in life, but I respect it. "Thank you for your honesty. Now, wash up and start dinner."

I leave Sascha looking shocked, and I can't help but smile as I walk away. So often, he seems like he's just done, finished, checked out of everything, but now and again I see the brightness that he displayed when I met him in the brothel, when I took him to the Peace Day Celebration. I continue to be reminded of the best subjects of my early research. More and more, I am reminded of myself. The problem is, I never knew what I wanted others to do for me and I don't know what to do for him. Leaving him alone seems to be the best option.

I've put aside the morning's conflict by the time Bobby arrives, and I relieve some stress as I chat and joke with him. Sascha plays the part of the perfect slave, attending as he should be. Bobby is far more interested in the boy than I am, calling him closer and hand-feeding him.

I can tell that Sascha isn't enjoying it. He has probably already eaten, and even if he hasn't, it's insulting. But I don't know how to tell Bobby to stop. He thinks it's cute, and it's not like he's hurting the boy. I just try to avoid paying attention to it.

Sascha starts squirming as he kneels on the floor, and makes a little gasp when he sits carelessly. I suppose the beating left at least somewhat of an effect.

"Not comfortable down there, little one?" Bobby asks, interrupting our conversation.

Sascha blushes. "Um... no. Sir. I'm sorry if I interrupted you."

"Come up here, you can get a little more comfortable, I think."

Bobby is always so forward with slaves. I've never really noticed it until having one of my own. He pats his leg, indicating for Sascha to sit on his lap. To his credit, Sascha does as requested, although he's stiff and clearly uncomfortable.

Bobby misses it, though, pulling Sascha off-balance until the boy is forced to fall into his arms, clutching at him for support.

"See?" Bobby teases, starting to rub his back. Sascha's thinly veiled whimper doesn't suggest to me that he's enjoying himself, but Bobby doesn't stop. I'm not sure whether I want to tell off Bobby for groping my slave in the middle of dinner, or Sascha for being rude again. I check my communication device for updates, hoping they'll both stop being themselves by the time I look up again.

Unfortunately, by the time I do, Sascha is squirming and clenching his teeth as Bobby proceeds to fondle him.

"Knock it off," I snap, glaring at Bobby. "You're hurting him. Stop."

Bobby stops immediately, settling his arms around Sascha's waist. Sascha looks relieved, if still uncomfortable. He gives me a grateful and surprised look. I think I should have stopped it far sooner.

"This sweet ass getting a little too much action, lately?" Bobby teases.

Sascha blushes and I feel myself growing increasingly irritated. "Hardly," I reply. "He was being disrespectful earlier and was punished."

Sascha looks ready to cry, and I'm almost relieved when Bobby turns him away from me. I hadn't intended to embarrass him; I want this entire conversation to be put to rest.

"Aw, did Cash punish you for being naughty?" Bobby asks, petting my slave gently.

Sascha looks like he'd rather bite his hands than answer. "Yes, sir," he grinds out.

"Poor thing," Bobby coos. "You just sit right here where it's soft and comfortable, then." He nuzzles his cheek against Sascha's head in a disgusting display of false affection.

"Yes, sir." Sascha replies, looking no less pleased than I am.

"Cash, I'm surprised at you!" Bobby chastises. "Beating the poor boy — you know how they are. They're simple, delicate. You shouldn't beat him!"

"I dealt with him as necessary, Bobby," I say quietly. I'm getting more and more irritated. "I haven't brutalized him or anything."

"You can't expect him to be perfect!" Bobby protests, continuing to cuddle my slave against his will. "You have to train them, guide them, make sure they don't have opportunities to fail. Beating him? It's inhumane. He probably didn't even understand what he did wrong; you probably just scared the poor little thing. Right, Sascha? Cash is just a big, mean man, isn't he?"

Sascha looks ready to mouth off again. I probably wouldn't even correct him if he did, at this point. He surprises me with the safe answer.

"I respect my master's decision, sir." Sascha is lying, but he's doing it well. I'm impressed.

"As you should," I agree. "The rules are clear and the consequences are efficient. I don't have time for games, and I will not discuss it further."

"Ah, yes, the busy man," Bobby replies, deferring to my wishes. We move on to discussing work, leaving Sascha alone for a while. I can see that Bobby is letting his hands stray somewhere, and I remind myself not to have Sascha attend us in the future. He doesn't need to be fondled for no reason.

As the night finally draws to an end, I can see Sascha's relief at being able to get up and away from Bobby. Sascha has tuned out of the conversation, otherwise he would have heard Bobby suggesting that I lend Sascha to him for a vacation he is supposed to be taking.

"What do you think, Sascha, would you like to get away from this big mean brute of a master you have?" Bobby says, petting Sascha with familiarity.

"What—excuse me? Sir?" Sascha looks terrified.

Bobby continues to touch Sascha's hair as he answers. "I could show you what it's like to be spoiled a bit, maybe have a little fun. Not like Mr. Serious over here, all rules and expectations and efficiency."

Sascha looks more terrified than he did when I beat him this morning. It throws me off. I expected that he would welcome such an offer; after all, I do nothing with him. I don't hurt him, except when he deserves it, but I have neglected him in ways that I am not proud of. I would have thought that he would have been thrilled with the opportunity to get some adventure. Instead, he looks over at me for help, pleading almost.

"Please, sir," he says, and for a moment, I can't tell if he's talking to me or Bobby. "That's not my decision to make, sir. You'd have to ask my master if you want to borrow me."

I study Sascha for a moment. Perhaps I underestimated him. Bobby offers fun, but only at the price of dignity.

"Bobby, as dear as you are to me, I like Sascha around for myself," I say firmly. "Who knows what the future holds. Right now, he stays with me. He's probably not well-behaved enough for your sorts of activities anyway."

The little smile I see on Sascha's face tells me that he knows I'm bluffing. I wouldn't have tolerated misbehavior for this long, and I most certainly wouldn't have taken him to the Peace Day Celebration if that was true. I'm pleased to see that Sascha understands what I'm doing.

"All right, all right," Bobby laughs. "Have it your way. But be nice to him! He's a good boy."

I don't reply. Sascha is not a "good boy." I'd refer to a dog that way, but not a human. But to disagree would suggest that he has failed, which he hasn't.

"Start cleaning up," I order Sascha instead, sending him out of the room.

I lead Bobby to the door and outside, where he tries to convince me further that I should let Sascha have some fun with him. I play possessive, trying to downplay the fact that I highly doubt that Sascha would enjoy any part of his fun. But Bobby is convincing, talking about his beach house, and the other slaves, and how much fun everyone has. I tell him I'll let him know if anything changes, and I go to find Sascha in the kitchen.

He's content to be cleaning, working efficiently and quickly. If he resents the beating he earned earlier, he's not showing it. More than anything, I think he was just happy to have something to do tonight, something to succeed at. The slaves that I used in my original research did so well in gentle environments. Am I providing the right environment for Sascha? I don't know why I care; he's not part of my research. I wonder why it even matters, and I realize that I want to find a place for him in my life. He's like nobody I've ever met before, slave or free, and relegating him to washing dishes and whoring for my promotions seems like a waste. I wonder exactly what I could make him a part of.

He turns and sees me, going instantly from confident and efficient to mumbling and scared. Maybe he would be better off with Bobby.

"Would you like to?" I ask. Sascha looks utterly confused. "Go with Bobby, I mean. He would treat you well; he's not lying about that. He doesn't have slaves of his own, but he likes to borrow them and spoil them. He'd never hurt you as long as you at least tried to please him, or begged his forgiveness if you slipped up."

Sascha looks torn. He takes forever to answer, studying his feet and the floor as he squirms. "I'd rather stay with you, master."

He seems to resent the words, which is understandable. He has sacrificed so much to keep himself safe, and I am not safe in the way that Bobby is. "I thought so," I say quietly. "You didn't seem too thrilled about his attentions tonight."

I consider the interactions, and realize that Sascha had been extremely uncomfortable. But then, I would have been, if I was in his place. While I'm pondering, I realize that Sascha's all but stopped breathing, going pale and staring at me, waiting.

"Relax, Sascha, I'm not giving you to him," I say, shaking his head. "I'm not even lending you to him, is that clear? I told you I wouldn't do that again if it made you uncomfortable."

He stands there, speechless, like he didn't believe me when I told him that before. I've carried through on every promise and threat I've made to him, but I suppose I can still surprise him.

"You don't have to be so formal about it," I add. "If I ask you if you'd like to go with someone else, you can answer yes or no. Don't try to be vague, and perhaps we can avoid the angst we had last time."

He nods, silent, like he doesn't want to trust me. It's unnerving. I haven't been that cruel to him, especially not when he tries to behave.

"Go to bed," I order, dismissing him. I turn and leave, suddenly uncomfortable. I beat him this morning; that was easy. He deserved it. I had warned him, all the pieces were in place. I've been trained for years to deal with slaves in that manner. But tonight, I wanted to protect him, to find out what he really wanted and hoped for.

Those are things that nobody ever learns how to give a slave. Few learn how to give things to free people, friends, lovers... Sascha is none of these things to me, and even entertaining the idea makes me uncomfortable. It's ridiculous to start a relationship like that with a slave, and yet, I find myself wondering how I can accomplish exactly that.

Chapter 14
Purpose

I focus on being a good slave over the next few weeks, the kind that doesn't answer his master's com calls disrespectfully and get his ass beat more than once. I try to be what my master wants, and tonight, that's a waiter, bringing him dinner in his office so he can continue to work. He gets up to wash his hands before he starts eating.

While he's gone, I peek at the papers on his desk and the files that he's left open on his tablet. His company handles financial investments for major corporations, and I know he's been having considerable difficulty getting the numbers on his most recent project to work out. It's probably wrong of me, but I tend to listen to his conversations when he coms the office, as much for entertainment as self-preservation. I don't mean to pry, or maybe I do, but it only takes a few glances at what he's working on before I catch his error.

"Sascha, if you've brought everything, you can go," he says as he walks back into the office, drying his hands on his pants and effectively eliminating any cleaning he just did. "I didn't ask for dinner in here so you could bother me."

It stings, and I recoil and respond automatically. "Yes, master." I take a few steps toward the door as he seats himself and stabs at his food while glancing over the papers and tablet.

A good slave wouldn't even *consider* mentioning it and embarrassing his master, but then, a good slave wouldn't have been prying into his master's business in the first place.

"Um, master?" I ask, tentative. He's only beat me the one time, but I don't doubt that I could irritate him enough to beat me again when he's in this bad a mood already.

"What!"

"I just..." I feel my hands start to sweat. Bad idea. I should have just left and let him struggle. "I just noticed something, master, with what you're working on, and I thought I could help—"

"Don't be ridiculous, you have no idea what I'm doing. I've told you I don't like needy slaves."

The dismissal burns, and it's the burn that gives me the stupid courage to walk toward his desk. "I apologize if I'm being too forward, master, but I think I am perfectly aware of what you're doing *and* I know what's been holding you up."

He looks at me, something he rarely does, and I feel myself start to tremble. Fuck. If he *looks* this angry, what will he do?

"You *are* too forward," he says, threatening. His expression is cold.

I move closer, figuring I'm screwed anyway, I may as well at least have the satisfaction of proving myself right. "I can help you, master." He can beat me, but he can't deny me this. It's in his best interest, and I've never seen him act against his interests.

"Fine." His voice is flat. He pushes himself back from the desk and glares at me.

I force my hands to stay steady as I grab the papers I had looked at while he was gone. I stare at them, not at him, while I explain what had happened and where there was an error and why this is what has been messing him up for days. I point to the details that he overlooked on the papers and on his tablet, and I point to the chain of errors that it caused, feeling the tiniest rush of excitement as I am finally doing something worthwhile, no matter the consequences. I finish and take a step back, bowing my head and waiting for my punishment.

He's silent as he reviews the forms and makes a few notes, correcting things here and there. I know I'm right, but my heart still pounds. I don't know whether he'll be more or less angry that I'm right, and that he was wrong. Is his pride more important, or his work?

"You're right," he says, glancing at me and looking irritated. "Next time, you will ask before looking through my things."

"Yes, master," I nod, relieved to be getting off the hook. I start to walk away.

"Where the hell do you think you're going?"

He doesn't sound particularly angry, but he's hard to read. I freeze, wondering what my punishment will be. Prying into his business, looking through his things, correcting him... I was stupid to think he would let me get away with it. I try to disappear, to go somewhere else where it won't hurt so much.

"You're not getting off that easy," he says, and I flinch as I hear him stand. "I want these finished by the end of the week."

I focus my eyes again and he's handed me a stack of papers and forms, most of which I recognize from the piles I had just pawed through on his desk. There are some new ones as well, but they seem to have similar data.

"I'll flash some other files to your tablet tonight," he continues, as if nothing is unusual. "I wish you would have mentioned this earlier—I hate this part of my job."

I look at the papers, then at him. "You... you'd trust me to do this, master? You'd trust someone who's Demoted to do something this important?" I know better to question him, but my worldview just got thrown off balance again, and I kind of want to hear his condescending tone to prove I'm not dreaming.

"Quit that passive-aggressive bullshit," he snaps, and it takes me a minute to understand what he's talking about. "I know as well as you do that you aren't some mindless slave, and you've been terrible at pretending it from the first moment I met you at the brothel."

I say nothing, stunned.

He shakes his head. "I'm sure you were one of those bright, cocky little bastards that got caught doing something stupid and got Demoted before even getting a chance to take the Assessment."

"Something like that, master," I mumble, not wanting to correct him. Let him think I cheated on it, or got caught with drugs or something. Nobody ever needs to know the real reason I let myself get Demoted.

"Too bad, really," he shakes his head, and looks like he's about to say something else.

I wait, wondering. So few people are opposed to the Demoted system; it's almost heretical to criticize any part of it. Those who do are frowned upon, and those who do more than criticize it are accused of treason.

"It's nice to have you able to help with something relevant," he declares. "I'm enjoying the food, but you must be bored to tears."

I'm amazed that he noticed. How much does he really notice about me, and why doesn't he ever say anything? I never imagined he would care, but then, I never imagined he would think I was anything less than happy with my lot in life.

"Make the corrections and let me know if you have any questions," he orders. "I'll have something else for you when that's finished. I'm about to become the most productive member of our team, thanks to you."

I don't answer; I just walk out the door in shock. He must think I'm selectively mute for as often as I don't answer him.

I have the data finished for him by the end of the week, and he says "thank you" when he takes it from me, which nearly makes my heart stop. This long, and he finally says something normal? Something he'd say to a coworker? I can't believe my good fortune, and I'm even more glad when he seems to overlook the fact that I gape at him instead of replying. He does overlook it, though, or maybe he really does think I'm selectively mute, because he moves on and gives me something else to do, a new set of financial projections that are just as complicated. He explains it thoroughly and carefully, but not in simplistic terms. I even force myself to ask him a question when he's unclear. If he's bothered, he doesn't let it show, he just explains it in more detail until I understand. It's not that the work is so complicated I don't understand it, it's just that I'm unfamiliar with a lot of the procedures and forms that his company uses. He seems to accept this, as though I am a new intern or something.

For the first time in three and a half years, I'm being used for something that interests me, something that challenges me on occasion, and I feel a new sense of satisfaction every day. Even when I miss something, or have to rework an entire set of numbers because I've done it wrong, I can't help but feel accomplished. I feel almost immeasurable joy at the fact that I actually have a purpose.

It gets slightly better between my master and me as well. Things seem to shift, just a little. Like the way he nods at me when he passes me in the hallway, or the way he actually deigns to ask me what else I might be helpful with. I feel like a goddamn idiot, because I stutter and mumble when I do manage to speak, but eventually the words make their way out, and I realize that he really is interested in something about me, even if it's only what I can do to help make his life better.

I'm a slave. I should make my master's life better. And this is more than just cooking food that he could have afforded to order anyway, or cleaning instead of having a cleaning person take care of it. I'm providing him with something of actual value. I am needed, if only for this specific task. We work side-by-side, as much as we can from separate rooms. He still doesn't seem particularly fond of me, but he appreciates my help. I know that we're not going to cuddle up and share a soda while we work or anything, but he does come over and sit next to me sometimes while he explains the most recent project, and he doesn't seem completely opposed to having me in the same room with him anymore.

I don't forget that I'm a slave. It's clear, from the way that he gives me orders, to the fact that I'm the one doing the majority of the work around the house. Remembering it is necessary for my survival.

Remembering that I'm a slave makes me start to dread Bobby's visits.

Now that I'm helping my master with work things, he's suddenly got a lot more free time on his hands, and while he still goes out more often than not, he's having Bobby over more as well. I don't know why he doesn't have any other friends over, hell, maybe he doesn't *have* any other friends, but I am getting quite sick of Bobby's teasing and touching and suggestions of what he'd like to do with me.

I get it. I'm a sex slave. I'm cute. I'm like a fresh steak in front of a hungry dog, except my master doesn't treat me that way and I've gotten rather used to it. It makes my skin crawl when I feel an unwanted hand on my shoulder, or eyes undressing me. He never goes further than that, my master never allows it, and sometimes I feel ridiculous for being so bothered by it. After all, if my master wanted, he could just lend me out to him, and I would have no right to protest.

But he doesn't, just like he said he wouldn't, and on more than one occasion, I start to suspect that he's actually keeping me out of sight.

"Sascha, don't you have work to do?" He asks sharply one night, after I've finished serving them dinner and brought out a bottle of wine that he's ordered me to leave on the table.

I freeze, the tone of his voice startling me. "Uh, yes? Yes, Master." Great. I sound like an idiot again, but I didn't realize he wanted it done so soon. More importantly, I thought that my presence attending him and Bobby took priority.

"Well, then, I suggest you get to it." He looks at me, and the way he raises his eyebrows contradicts his harsh tone. It's like he's challenging me to figure out what he's really saying.

"Come on, Cash, let the boy relax a little," Bobby protests, although I suspect his protests are more about his own interests than my playtime. "I like having him around. He's nice to look at, and I'm sure we could —"

"Sascha. Now!" My master orders again, cutting his friend off. "Quit standing around wasting time. If you don't finish up by the deadline I gave you, there will be serious consequences. Go."

"Yes, master," I reply instantly, almost running out of the room. My heart is pounding, and I entertain the terror for minute, wondering how I am going to get everything done in time, wondering what "serious consequences" will entail...

And then it hits me. There was never a deadline.

Chapter 15
Enough

I drop a small box on Sascha's desk, full of papers and different kinds of data. Instead of the usual financial reports that I have given him from Dean & Chanu, these are performance ratings and compliance ratings from re-education centers around the world. While there are some financial statements included, the majority of the data has nothing to do with the usual aspects that my company deals with. No, these things are from my private research, the reboot of the project that almost landed me in prison last time around.

"I need you to be discreet with these," I say, quiet. "Not that I could imagine anyone asking you about them, but if you hear anything mentioned about the people or the companies or the other information mentioned in here, I need to know that you'll keep your mouth shut about them. Can you do that?"

I'm risking everything by having Sascha help me with this, but I need a second set of eyes, and from what I've had him do for me with my legitimate business, I can tell that he will do as well, if not better with this data. I can't handle it all myself; between my day job and the meetings I've been setting up with key players, I just haven't had the time or energy to devote to this project. I try to pretend that I'm just giving him an order, just providing him with work to fill his time, but it's far more than that. I need to know that he's capable of keeping my secrets. He could destroy me with this information, although it wouldn't be in his best interest to do so. I need to know that I can trust him.

"Of course, master," he replies. I can see how desperate he is to please me, not to mention find out about the secret project I'm working on, but he just waits, staring up at me hopefully.

"Good," I reply, nodding. I try not to let the relief show, but it is there. Having someone else involved in the project is a relief; having Sascha involved is a treat.

I thoroughly explain what he's supposed to do, telling him more than enough for his task. I don't explain anything about what the names and numbers actually mean, and I explain even less about why I am so attached and personally committed to it. It's better this way; if he's in the dark about it, he's safer than if he knows what I actually do.

"Can I ask what this is for, master?" he asks tentatively. "This doesn't seem like your usual work."

I glare at him for a moment, and he cringes away a little, like he's waiting for me to slap or berate him. But I would have asked the exact same question. I force my face back to a blank mask.

"I don't wish to discuss it," I answer, drawing a surprised look from Sascha. "It's a side project of mine and you don't need to know much about it to complete the tasks I've given you. Please don't ask about it again."

"Yes, master." His reply is instant, automatic in response to my tone.

"You show initiative. I like that," I admit. "But some things are not for you to know. Thank you for respecting that."

I walk out of the room in a hurry, embarrassed to have been so brusque when he's being so helpful, and unsure of how to continue after delivering the compliment. It's not that Sascha lacks things to compliment him on; I just don't usually mention them out loud. It doesn't happen quite as infrequently as it used to, but it's not a commonplace event, either. It's not the way I was raised, or the way I've been taught to treat slaves. It's better to keep strict boundaries.

I leave Sascha to his work, amazed by how diligently he addresses it. He tries so hard to please me, going over the details of the projects I give him again and again, making sure they are perfect. He seems to think I don't know, but I peek in on him occasionally, when he's too engrossed in what he's doing to notice. When he's working, he's extremely focused, and the terrified look on his face gives way to curiosity. He's attractive; I find myself growing more and more attracted to him, but I wouldn't sacrifice our comfortable relationship for base needs. I know enough about what he's endured to be horrified at the thought of forcing something like that on him, and he gives no indication of feeling anything but fear and perhaps grudging respect for me.

I try to smile at him when I can, remember to thank him for his hard work and excellent cooking. The way his eyes light up is enough of a reward for me, and fact that he is starting to seem more comfortable assures me that I am doing the right thing. I know how to train a slave to be obedient; I have never considered how difficult it would be to train a slave to be comfortable in my home. I never realized it would matter.

My home is my sanctuary, the place where I can escape from the demands of work and other people. Bringing Sascha home made it tense, and I resented him for that, even as much as I knew I had to have a slave, had to keep a slave around in order to present the correct social image. I snap at my coworkers far more than I do at Sascha, but at least they fight back. I don't like people around me when I work, but when they must be around, it inspires me to have some lively debate. I'd have it with Sascha, but it just seems too inappropriate.

Instead, I arrange for a night out with Bobby. I've started to spend fewer nights at home with him, because he insists on cuddling and groping and leering at Sascha. I pretend to be possessive, but I don't do those things with my slave. It's demeaning to watch, and Sascha deserves better.

Bobby arrives, and I leave him for a moment while I get changed to go out. As I do, I see him wander into the small office that Sascha has claimed as his own.

"Well, if it isn't the little assistant!" Bobby teases. I consider asking him to wait in the living room, or even out in the car, because I've been putting up my best effort to keep him away from Sascha. Bobby is far too free with my property, and I don't want to increase the friction between them. Still, I'll only be a moment, and I trust that Sascha can manage a few minutes alone with him without any sort of drama. If anything, he can outsmart Bobby.

I make quick work of finding an outfit, changing into it quickly and running a comb through my hair. I'm not sure why I bother; it's

Subjection

not like I'm looking to pick anybody up, it just seems like the thing to do. I used to enjoy the nights out with Bobby, but these days it just seems like a waste of my time. I wonder if we are outgrowing each other. I stand at the end of the hallway, using the decorative mirror that my interior designer placed there to fix my tie and taking advantage of the fact that I can hear more of the exchange between Bobby and Sascha.

"Everyone needs a little rest," I overhear Bobby saying, using the flirty voice that always works well for him at bars, but not so well with my slave. "If you were mine, I would never keep you so busy all the time! No time to play."

"I'm *not* yours, sir," Sascha reminds him, sounding rather annoyed.

I can't hear Bobby's response, but I do hear Sascha's next statement.

"It's up to my master, sir!"

I sigh, picking up the pace as I finish getting ready. Bobby is wearing on Sascha, and I want to intervene before anything else transpires between them.

"Aw, too much work making you grouchy?" Bobby teases. I can't hear what he does, but I can only imagine the foolishness he's subjecting Sascha to. "There, now you only have one thing to occupy your pretty little head."

Sascha's response is immediate and loud. "Unlike yours, *my* pretty little head is perfectly functional! I'm sorry if you're too thick to get it, but the only thing I'd like right now is for you to leave me alone so I can get some goddamn work done!"

I shake my head when I hear the appalling stream of curse words and insults spew from my slave's mouth. I pick up the pace, making my way down the hall in record time and storming into the office.

I catch Sascha's eyes, and as angry as I am at him, I can't be surprised. Bobby antagonizes him, and Sascha has difficulty holding his tongue. I shake my head as I try to decide how to deal with him. I would rather deal with Bobby, but he's been through so much with me. I can't bear to tell him off for being playful with my slave; it's just how he is. He never means any harm.

"Little bastard," Bobby mutters, flushing with embarrassment. "I

118

should slap you."

I go to Bobby and put a hand on his shoulder. I don't want him hitting Sascha. "I'll deal with him. His discipline is my concern."

I glare at Sascha until he remembers his place. He jumps up from his chair to move in front of us, dropping to his knees.

"I apologize, sir," he says, looking terrified. "I behaved disrespect-fully and was very rude. Please, don't allow my insolence to affect your view of my master. I know better, sir."

"I guess you were right when you said he wasn't trained all that well," Bobby mutters. "I've been nothing but nice to the beast."

I'm not sure who's irritating me more right now, Bobby, or Sas-cha. "Bobby, really, I apologize as well. He's usually not like this."

"You shouldn't let him work like a free man," Bobby suggests, frowning at me. "They start getting uppity that way."

From the corner of my eye, I see Sascha turning red, looking like he's about to cry. I know that he values his work as much as I do, and I wouldn't dream of taking it away from him. If Sascha is uppity, he's always been this way, and the fact that Bobby dares to criticize my lifestyle irks me almost as much as Sascha's defiance.

"Go wait for me in the hov-car," I tell Bobby quietly. "Drinks are on me tonight."

"You don't have to—"

"Just go and let me deal with my slave!" I snap at Bobby, and he finally gets the point, turning and leaving quickly. Sascha is looking sick and scared, and I want this all over with.

Once I hear the door close, I walk over to Sascha and grab him by the hair. I resent the rift he's caused between Bobby and me.

"Sascha, what the fuck were you thinking?" I snap, tempted to just punch him. But I can't allow myself to lose control like that. In-stead of waiting for an answer that will anger me further, I let him go and step back. "I want you undressed and leaning over this desk by the time I come back!"

I mean to take a moment to calm down, but I realize I'm getting more angry instead of less. I decide on the punishment quickly and retrieve the belt I used on him the other day. I return to find Sascha struggling to undress himself, kicking his pants aside and looking ter-rified. I have no idea what the boy takes so much time doing, but a glare has him leaning over the desk and clutching the opposite side of it.

I strike him instantly, harder than I did last time. It wasn't that long ago that he should have forgotten the lesson. He responds by squirming and yelping and crying more quickly. Just as before, he truly does seem to be in pain, but he's still with me this time. The squirming escalates until I wrap the belt around his skinny ass and catch his stomach, drawing an anguished cry.

I try not to feel guilty, but I know I am responsible for letting him get hurt unintentionally. My job is not only to discipline him, but to make sure he's still and safe throughout the punishment. Proper training would dictate that I restrain him, but I don't want to. Somehow, that seems crueler than the beating itself.

"Hold still," I order instead, continuing to beat him.

I can see that he tries, clutching harder at the desk. I stop when I reach twenty, as I did before, and I see Sascha go limp across the desk, sobbing.

"Thank you, master."

The words make me uncomfortable. Why is he thanking me for beating him?

I consider his actions. "I'm not finished," I tell him, forcing my voice to stay calm. I don't want to hurt him more, but I decide that I haven't quite made my point. "You obviously didn't learn from it last time if you did it again."

The change is dramatic, almost so dramatic that I reconsider beating him further. He slides down off the desk and onto the floor, turning to me in terror and clinging to me as if I'll protect him.

"Don't, please?" he whimpers, looking up at me desperately. "That's enough."

I pull back, horrified to evoke such a response. What does he think I'm going to do to him? I don't know if I could handle him following me, but he doesn't. He curls into a ball and sobs. I'm afraid of pushing him too far.

I keep my orders simple and calm. "Get up. Face me. Lean back against the edge of the desk."

I wait silently as Sascha processes the commands, pleased when he does as he's ordered. He looks at me and cowers, turning his face away, then covering his stomach with his hands, then lifting his legs to cover his genitals. I realize that he's trying to figure out where I'm going to hit him, as though I would ever strike such vulnerable places with an object. I lay the belt lightly against his thighs, glancing up at him until he nods his understanding. He calms slightly until I hit him.

I don't hit him as hard as I did before, but he's too scared to know the difference. He pulls away, pressing against the edge of the desk. It must hurt, given the bruises I just left on him. It wasn't my intention, but it should serve as a good reminder. I watch his face, and I see him start looking sick. I doubt it's from the pain, but fear can be just as painful. I stop at ten, well in advance of him dissociating. Even once I finish, he stays waiting, whimpering and trembling, his eyes fixated on my hand.

I can't bring myself to speak to him, so I walk out and retrieve the ball gag I purchased after his last outburst. He opens his mouth to receive it, a look of surprise on his face.

I glance at the work on his desk. "Don't work on any of this to-night. This is important, and I don't want you distracted. Just clean up and go to bed. You may remove the gag if you go to bed before I get home, I don't want you to choke. You'll wear this tomorrow, too."

I fasten the gag around his head, trying to reconcile the absurdity of treating him like an animal while letting him work as a human. Strangely, it's not the human part that seems out of place. I want to tell him that I'm pleased with his work, that I wish Bobby hadn't antago-nized him, that I know he can do better. But that isn't how I've been taught to communicate with slaves. I just shake my head and leave.

In the morning, Sascha comes to me with the gag in his hand, looking miserable. He doesn't ask, but I realize that he's giving me the choice of putting it on him. Submitting to my will, just like he was probably taught at some point. It's a good self-preservation tech-nique.

"Go have something to eat, first," I mutter, not looking at him. It's unnerving to see him so subdued.

He comes back in a few minutes, tears in his eyes. I hadn't meant for him to return, but I won't shame him more by telling him, and I won't give him the chance to do something stupid like fasten the strap too tightly. I take the gag from him and put it on, fighting back the urge to call the whole thing off, especially when he starts crying again.

I take a step away, planning to ignore him for the rest of the day, but I stop and look back at him instead. "I'll keep doing it, Sascha. I let you have a lot of liberties, and I don't mind, but I have a reputation to uphold and there are things in my life that you know nothing about. If I have to beat you until every inch of you is bruised, I swear to god I will. You're smart enough to know better, and you can hold your tongue when you want to. Do *not* try me."

He nods through his tears, and I wonder whether I've made my point or just terrified him. I've broken almost every protocol I've ever learned for training a slave, but strangely, I feel most comfortable when I'm breaking protocol instead of following it like I am now. I have a strange desire to comfort him.

"Get the house clean today," I order. "You can get back to what you were working on tomorrow, and I expect it to be done as well as it usually is."

He nods, and I'm not sure if he picked up on the subtle compliment. I push myself further in to my work, trying not to feel guilty about the lenient punishment I gave him.

Chapter 16

Spring Cleaning

I storm out and slam my tablet down on the secretary's desk.

"Why in the hell wasn't I notified that Kristine Miller was scheduled into my calendar?" I demand, pushing the boundaries of our thin professional relationship. Bethany isn't part of our Demoted staff, she's a free woman and one who I usually like quite a lot. But when I saw my mother's name on my work calendar this morning, I wanted to be sick, or at least to destroy whoever scheduled a meeting with her.

She has no idea that Kristine Miller has any personal relationship with me.

"Ms. Miller called after you left last night and requested that I set up a meeting with you," Bethany explains, not backing down in the slightest. "She had a few questions about the Torenze acquisition you're considering, as well as a few others. She's been in close contact with some of our top investors for years, and now that you're working on those projects, I assumed you would want to speak with her."

The acquisition that Bethany mentions isn't one that I'm working on, at least not yet. Not publicly, anyway. But I know my mother, and I know how many steps ahead of me she always is. Bethany keeps staring at me like I've lost my mind.

"Come on," she jokes. "You can't be that angry about an unexpected meeting with the creator of the Miller System. She's like a celebrity, at least for our investors. She's so friendly, too; whenever she comes in for meetings she brings the most beautiful flowers for the office."

I force a smile onto my face. Of course, everyone who doesn't know my mother thinks she is a delight, and she's been tugging at the heartstrings and purse strings of Dean & Chanu since she banished me here.

"Sorry," I mumble, trying to rectify myself. "I just... could you give me a little more time to prepare, next time? I really do want to make a good impression."

Bethany smiles, clueless. "She said it wasn't anything formal," she informs me. "Just a little meet and greet. She's so personable!"

I smile, get myself a coffee, and wait for my mother to arrive. She doesn't have herself announced, nor does she knock, she just walks into my office like she owns it, just like she used to walk into my bedroom when I was a child.

"Hello, mother," I say, trying to speak before her for once.

She ignores my greeting, taking a seat on the edge of the desk instead of in a chair. Does she really think I don't remember the way she always insisted on being placed physically above her slaves?

"Cash, I hear you're getting involved with a lot of the re-education center accounts," my mother says, glaring at me.

I look up at her, fighting for calm. "I've recently been promoted," I inform her. "Or did your best friend Bethany not tell you that?"

My mother shakes her head. "There are other departments you could have been promoted to," she reminds me.

"I'm just doing my job. Contributing to the betterment of society through investment in the Demoted population."

My mother's face is stiff from emotional deadening and anti-wrinkle treatments, but I still see the flicker of anger in her eyes.

"You know better than to push this issue, Cashiel," she warns. "I've put too much work into keeping you safe for you to ruin it all by running around with your old associates."

"You put me in prison," I remind her. No matter how many years have passed, I still can't let that go.

My mother leans in, coming close enough that I can smell the expensive perfume she has worn since before I could remember. The smell is enough to make me leave department stores; having it this close to my face makes the hair stand up on the back of my neck.

"I protected you, Cash," she hisses. "You were going down a dangerous path. I didn't want to see my only son imprisoned forever, accused of treason for real. I didn't know what your research was going to do, but it looked dangerous. I put you in prison to keep you safe while I worked everything else out. I got you out of prison, I got you this job—I did what I had to do."

My mother exposed me because I proved her theory wrong. "You betrayed me," I reply. "You destroyed the thing that was most important to me. You took away my name—you took away my life!"

"You need to prune things sometimes, Cashiel," she says. "Remember that year when my garden was infested with mites? It hurt me so much to dig up those plants, but I had to. For the betterment of the whole garden. I never wanted to hurt you, but it was the best for you."

My mother had cried for days about her garden. The flowers were and are her prize possessions; she never let any of our slaves go anywhere near them. It was fine for slaves to raise her son, but not her plants. When they became infested with mites, she researched for days, cried for longer, and dug up over half of her giant garden.

"The neighbors sprayed pesticide and theirs lived," I mutter.

"The neighbors were filthy degenerates who didn't understand the value of purity," my mother replies, her face narrowing into a scowl. "That's why their gardening license was revoked."

From what I remember, their gardening license was revoked because my mother paid the city commissioner more than a year's salary to declare that they were the source of the mites that were typically spread by birds. The city's gardening commission came in with backhoes, excised the entire plot, and replaced it with standard-issue grass that required no human involvement to grow. Kristine Miller is dangerous.

"Why are you here?" I ask, growing tired of the debate.

"To remind you to be grateful," my mother says. "And to remind you to stay where you belong. Your little hobby of playing in my re-education business was ended years ago. It needs to stay ended."

"I'm just doing my job," I reply, trying to make my tone as cold as hers. "I don't know what sort of problem you would have with it. After all, it's not like I'm the son of the creator of the Miller System. I'm just a financial analyst. An up-and-comer. A nobody. Remember the life you made for me?"

"I made a much better life for you, Cashiel," she says, shaking her head. "You just didn't deserve it. I hope you'll live up to my expectations this time around."

"I'm just analyzing the finances," I repeat.

"I do certainly hope that's true," my mother says, and for once, I believe her. It would be in her best interest if it was, and she always looks out for her own best interests.

She shifts, finally, taking a seat in the spare chair I have in my office. I notice the change, the deliberate attempt to be more casual and less intimidating. It doesn't work; she reminds me too much of a venomous snake, recoiling only to strike a moment later.

"How's the slave working out for you?" she asks, smiling like she really cares.

"Fine."

She smiles, waiting for more. When I don't offer it, she speaks. "You know, I wondered if you really had started something with one of the slaves, way back then. You never showed any interest in owning one, and you seemed so opposed to the researched methods of the Miller System. It's good to see you accepting your place in society. Strong slave ownership can benefit free people, too."

I just nod. I've investigated the research done on the Miller System. It's flawed, biased, and utterly incorrect. But I won't tell her that and bruise her ego.

"I would have thought you would have gone with a higher quality specimen, perhaps one from a good retailer, but you do like to be difficult," she says, shaking her head. "Ever since you were a boy, always doing things your way. To think, if I hadn't chosen prime locations for your house, you probably would have ended up in some hovel, just to spite me!"

I try to keep the irritation off of my face. She had given me a set of locations to choose from for my home, but I would have picked a nice one, anyway. I enjoy some domestic comforts, and I'm not that spiteful.

"I appreciate what you've given me," I say carefully.

"I do hope so," my mother replies, smiling. "I never have seen the house, though. I feel like I just don't see my family often enough, or my investments."

When she leaves, I com my security company and make sure that nobody is anywhere near my house, or the secure facility where I keep some of my information. I don't trust her, and in the past few weeks, I've been busy with my promotion at Dean & Chanu. Sascha has been doing most of the legitimate work for me, freeing up my time to network with some of the individuals and organizations who might be willing to partner with me on my research. I've met with a few of them, at home, and even in my work office, pretending that everything has only to do with my corporate finance job. Sascha's help has been invaluable; he's quiet, obedient, and he's better at the financial part of my job than I am. I try not to praise him too much, but I bring him dinner sometimes when I know we'll both be busy, or ignore when he forgets to clean up in favor of working on the projects I've given him. If he wasn't a slave, I could see us being friends. We both have a similar work ethic.

Part of that similarity lies in the ability to overlook details and cleaning, but the conversation with my mother has me worried. She was far too interested in my slave, and she mentioned visiting me, something she rarely ever does. For years, she insisted that she didn't want her reputation soiled by associating with me, something I was happy to support. The more I think of it, the more uncomfortable I am with the chance that something incriminating is in my house.

I come home to find Sascha working diligently on some of the outside work I've given him. "I want you to put that away for a while," I inform him. "And I'll need you to help go through some files."

"Yes, sir," he says, looking at me blankly, waiting for more orders. There's a hint of fear, as there always is, like I'm going to take it all away from him.

"I need to focus on some other projects," I tell him, which is partly true. "My promotion has come with more work, and we are about to make a big breakthrough. All this business with the re-education centers... that isn't a priority right now."

Sascha looks at me for a moment, unfiltered doubt on his face. If he's this transparent with me, my mother will be able to read him too easily.

"Something you want to say?" I snap, challenging him.

He cowers, looking down and shaking his head. "No, master. I'm sorry."

"Don't lie to me."

He's silent for a moment. "I just thought you said the other day that this was the top priority, sir."

I sigh. I'm not angry at him, I'm angry at my mother. I try to be a little more calm. "Regardless of what I said the other day, today your top priority is clearing away any evidence that any of this was ever here."

Sascha nods, even daring to look up at me. "Yes, sir. I'm sorry."

I shake my head, dismissing his concerns. "You're thorough and attentive. Those are great assets. But I set the priorities around here."

"Yes, sir," he replies immediately. "Can I ask what it is? The project? Why you're shelving it? It has nothing to do with your job."

The little shit is too smart for his own good. "You may not," I reply, keeping my tone mild. "I don't want you speaking about it or asking about it unless I bring it up. You've done good work so far, but I asked you when we started to be discreet. I trust you can still manage that?"

"Of course, sir," he replies.

He's disappointed, but it's for the best, at least for now. I tell him what things I need him to collect, from his files and mine, and I give him a box to place the hard copies in. I have him back up the data on his tablet and send it to me, and I run a program to clear any evidence of it from his tablet. The process takes a few days, but I feel more comfortable the less there is to connect me with the research.

In the meantime, we focus on my day job, and I find out soon that I am to host a "celebration event" at my house. I've never been less thrilled to celebrate anything, or more relieved that I've already started to clear any incriminating evidence from my house.

"Sascha, you'll need to ready the house for a celebration event," I inform him, trying not to turn my nose up at the thought. I'm not that social, and more than anything, I'm afraid. So many people in my house means a lot of opportunities for important information to be uncovered. "Rearrange the furniture to make space; there should be enough food and drinks and supplies for about forty people. Oh, and select some music to play in the background. Nothing too trendy or loud, this will be for work."

He nods obediently, immediately attending to his tasks. I need his help with the logistics, but I also need him out of the way.

I begin with the hard copies of the data. A quick call to one of my less legitimate associates finds me someone who will take it off my hands; a few more calls make it disappear entirely. So much work, scattered through the city, but these people make it their living to hide things. Usually it's things like drugs and murder weapons, but for enough money, anything can disappear.

The digital data is far more difficult to hide. I know I would be safer destroying it all together, but I can't bring myself to part with it. It's the heart of my work, the vital information I need to start my project over again. Unfortunately, it is the information that could do the most damage. I can't risk it being discovered, but I want access to it, immediate access. I have spent too long working on it to let it go.

"Sascha, bring me your tablet," I call out from my office. I try to keep my tone level, pretending like it's nothing out of the ordinary.

"What do you need it for, sir?" he asks, handing it over and giving me a curious look.

"Is it your place to question me?" I ask, giving him a dirty look. The last thing I need is my slave poking around where he shouldn't. It will put us both at risk.

"No, sir," he mumbles, backing away. "Sorry. I just thought I could help."

I'd rather scare him than let him know how worried I am. "You can help by doing as you're told and not asking questions," I tell him firmly.

"Yes, sir," he says quietly, turning to leave.

"Sascha," I call after him, stopping him in his tracks. "Bobby will be coming by to help set up with the party. I know he can be... distracting, I suppose you could call it. I'll be having him take care of errands outside of the house, picking up food from local vendors who don't deliver, arranging for parking, handling contracts, that sort of thing. Get any lists and addresses to me so I can give them to him without having to interrupt you."

I want to keep the two of them apart as much as possible, for my sanity as well as Sascha's. Bobby has gotten on my nerves lately by harassing my slave, and I worry that he might push Sascha too far.

"Thank you, sir," Sascha says, smiling like he knows exactly what I'm doing with Bobby.

I nod, and he leaves me with his tablet. I move the data from my own tablet to Sascha's, disguising it under layers of security. The slave's tablet is far less suspicious than mine is, and I doubt that anyone interested in investigating me would look too closely into a slave's tablet.

Besides, if anyone does look into Sascha's tablet, my plan is to place the blame on him. I can just say he stole it. Perhaps he found the old research somewhere and tried to recreate it. There's very little to place the data in context; and what I've found out about his past sets him up as a likely suspect. Unearthing juvenile browsing history can be difficult, but it is possible, and I've looked into Sascha very carefully. He was precocious, not particularly fond of rules, and he has made a game of sneaking into digital places where he shouldn't be since he was a child. Based on what I've found on his past, it wouldn't be hard to convince a jury that he discovered this old project and investigated it again just to see if he could. If anyone catches us, I'll work to protect him, but neither of us is safe if I am exposed. A criminal master can be excused or even redeemed more easily than a criminal slave.

I consider telling him, briefly, but we are both at increased risk if he is cognizant of the plans. The fewer people who know about this, the better. I give him his tablet back and feel relieved when he doesn't seem to notice anything different. As embarrassing as it is to depend on a slave, I trust that his discerning eye will catch anything that I might have missed. I review my security devices, the ones that alert me if anyone enters my home without the activation code, the ones that alert me if any police officers are dispatched to my home, the ones that alert me if anyone attempts to access my network from inside or outside of the house. Everything is tight, flawless, safe. I have only my own paranoia to deal with.

I invite Bobby to help, more to calm myself than anything else. Despite the friction between him and Sascha, he was there for me when my life collapsed years ago. To keep him safe, I haven't told him anything about my new research, but he knows about everything else in my life, and he has always stood by me. I start to relax, at least somewhat, and try to believe that my home and my research are safe. I focus on the party, pleased to see that Sascha has handled the majority of the preparations. I want nothing more than for the party to be over and for things to return to normal.

Chapter 17
White Knights

On the day of the party, I've been dressed up in suit, not as formal as my master's, but certainly nowhere near the extravagant show-piece I was made out to be for the Peace Day Celebration. Similarly, I am much more than a simple decoration on my master's arm; I run around getting drinks for people and taking coats and fulfilling a hundred different roles at once. I don't even think to talk back or be anything but the picture perfect slave. My master has given me exactly one warning, right before the party started, and it was simple: "Fuck up tonight and I'm selling you." He knows how to hurt me, and he's clearly willing to do it.

I don't dwell on it, though, because I suppose it would be an appropriate consequence. I want to stay with him, badly, so I perform perfectly.

Even when I'm trying to be good, I'm still underhanded. I purposely overhear his conversation with a coworker.

"Mr. Michaud, I didn't realize you owned a slave!" the older man exclaims after I hand them drinks and nod deferentially to my master.

"It appears that way." My master is all grave and displeased about it as usual.

He must be grave and displeased as a general rule, because his colleague doesn't seem bothered in the slightest.

"That's the same boy you had at the Peace Day Celebration, isn't it?" he realizes, and I resist rolling my eyes. "I almost didn't recognize him all formal and such."

"Yes, well, different atmospheres," my master replies, eager, as usual, to stop talking about me.

"I wouldn't have expected you to keep him," the man comments. "I've heard... well, I probably shouldn't listen to rumors, but I've heard that you weren't exactly in support of slavery?"

The man is clearly prying, and my master seems as displeased by his coworker prying as he does when I do it.

"Rumors can be misleading." His eyes are darker than usual, and if I wasn't so interested in the conversation, I'd be running away to hide.

Instead, I linger, pretending to adjust some drinks on a tray, pick up some dirty glasses. I know my master said he didn't want a slave—would I finally find out why?

"Of course, of course," the coworker amends. "It was just surprising; most young men are so eager to surround themselves with pretty slaves; especially those without a partner or family around to keep them company. When I found out you didn't even have one to keep up around the house, I couldn't help but wonder."

"Ideals of youth," my master dismisses the idea. "I thought things were easier on my own. I've found that having a slave around can be quite useful. I'm responsible for quite a lot more than I was years ago, and it only makes sense."

"Well, I can see that he's up to the exacting standards of the most stringent re-education centers," the colleague says, and I can feel eyes on my back. "Hasn't been idle a moment tonight."

"No, he hasn't." Shit, my master does not sound pleased. He'll know damn well that I'm loitering on purpose. "Sascha, I think you have quite enough dirty dishes for one trip. Don't look for more than you can handle."

I get his message to clear the fuck out, and I try not to rush too obviously to do so. "Yes, master," I reply, an innocent smile on my face as I duck out. I can tell he doesn't buy it, but the colleague does, smiling at me like I'm just a pleasant slave boy.

I hide in the kitchen, ignoring the dishes and pondering what I heard. The doctor that my master took me to had mentioned my master's mother, said he had known the family for years. How, then, did my master's colleague seem to think he was estranged from them? I wonder if there is any truth to accusation that my master doesn't support slavery. But then, why did he buy me in the first place? It is rather strange that in all this time he has never mentioned or even commed his family, at least not that I've noticed. If I weren't a slave, I would certainly still be in touch with mine. I think about them every day.

My thoughts are interrupted by the sound of footsteps, and I look over to see Bobby standing in the doorway, hands on either side of the doorframe.

"Hello, sir," I mumble, keeping my eyes cast down. I hope he thinks I look proper; really, I just don't want him to look at me.

"Hello, Sascha," he mocks, smiling.

He's drunk. I've brought him six drinks already, and god knows whether he's helped himself to any others. This is supposed to be a work event, but my master allowed him to stay because of all his "help" setting up the party. And the fact that he can't seem to say no to his best friend.

"Having fun?" he asks me.

"I'm performing my duties as my master requests, sir." As if to prove it, I grab up a tray of snacks and take a few steps toward him.

He doesn't budge.

"I need to take these out to the guests, sir," I try to sound assertive without being pushy. I think I just come off as scared, which I am.

"You need to relax," he says, smiling. "Put the tray down."

I pause for a moment, silent. "Please, sir —"

"Put the tray down, Sascha!"

I jump at the tone, and years of training have me reacting before I can even think to do otherwise. The tray is safely sitting on the counter, and I am growing more terrified with every second.

"That's a good boy," he says with a smile. "It seems like I never get to spend any time alone with you."

I blink back tears. "It is as my master wishes it, sir."

"Of course, of course," he says softly.

I dare to look up at his face, wishing I could trust that tone. Wishing I could give in like I used to, back at the brothel, when everything was clear and I could count on being raped and miserable every day. I curse myself for feeling safe.

"Your master wishes for me to have a good time, Sascha," he says, his voice low and sultry.

I shudder. "Yes, sir."

I stand, frozen, as he strides across the room to stand in front of me. His hand reaches out and I flinch, thinking he's going to strike me, but he doesn't. His hand tangles in my hair at the back of my head and he pulls me close and kisses me. His lips are rough and wet and too big, and his tongue is cold and tastes like alcohol as it forces into my mouth.

I don't resist at first, and I'm ashamed to be such a whore.

I realize what's happening and I try to pull away, managing only by ducking down and feeling him rip some hair out. He catches me again with his other hand and uses my own momentum to force me to my knees. I wince as I hit the floor.

"Cash is a good friend of mine, and he told me he wants me to have a good time, boy," he says again. "Now, why don't you be a good boy and show me a good time?"

I know what he wants. It's pretty fucking obvious, what with his dick in front of my face, hard and ready inside of his pants. But he would have told me! My master would have told me if he wanted me to do this.

Wouldn't he?

"Please, sir, he never said anything about this, I'm supposed to attend the party!" My attempt is pathetic, but it's the best I can do.

"Are you denying me, boy?"

The question is a threat. There is no right answer. "Please, sir, just let me check with my master." Please let him save me.

Bobby grabs my face and forces me to look up at him. "Now listen here, whore. I was with your master when he bought you, and I know what you've been trained for. If I tell my friend that you were being rude and uppity and defiant with me again, who do you think he'll believe? You either show me those skills right fucking now, or I'll help Cash to sell you back to a place that will make that one look like a god-damned beach resort!"

I know he's lying, and I know my master wouldn't want this, but this bastard has just laid out my worst fear, and I'll do anything to avoid making it happen. I let the tears fall as I nod, whispering "yes, sir," as my hands begin to unfasten his pants as quickly as I can.

It's just a blowjob. It's just. A fucking. Blowjob.

I may be out of practice, but it's a skill you don't lose easily, like riding a bike, and even the fact that he's gripping me by my hair and thrusting down my throat doesn't throw me off balance. Hell, this is what my training was like; if anything, it puts me back in the right mindset. Just another hole to be used. It doesn't matter that I have a comfortable lifestyle now, and it certainly doesn't matter that my master has never, ever required anything like this of me. It's just a blowjob, and I'll finish, and I'll wash my mouth out with mouthwash or soap or bleach and try never to think of it again.

Except he doesn't finish.

He's almost there when he pulls my head back by my hair. I close my eyes, figuring he's going for the facial, which will be a bitch to clean up, but I'd almost rather that than have to taste any more of him.

"Get up," he orders.

I'm confused for a second, so I do, and he starts grabbing at my pants.

It dawns on me that he's going to rape me, and I start to struggle.

Let's be clear. I've had sex that I wanted, I've had sex that I didn't want, and I've been raped, and there's a difference between all three, and I know that he's about to do the third thing to me.

"No!" I snap, twisting out of his grip. "Let go of me!"

"You're telling me no?" he asks, in disbelief. "Wait till your master hears this. He'll whip you until the fucking sun comes up and *then* he'll sell you!"

I know it's not true, if only because my master would never sell damaged goods. I doubt that he's authorized this exchange, either. But I can't help thinking about my master's words to me before the party tonight, his orders not to fuck up, and I can't help thinking that that's exactly what I'm doing right now. "Please, sir, just go back to the party?" I try, hoping he'll give up.

No such luck. He comes forward again and I back away until my back is pressed against the stove. I realize I'm trapped. He reaches out and grabs at my pants again, and I squirm, trying to move sideways, down, anything. I want to push him off of me, but no matter how terrified I may be, I'm not stupid enough to lay hands on a free man.

"Stop it!" I yell, half-angry, half-pleading.

He backhands me hard enough to spin me and I taste blood where my teeth graze my lip. I'm dazed for a moment, and he uses it to his advantage, turning me away from him and pinning me to the counter with his body.

"Been wanting to do this since the first time I laid eyes on you, fucking whore," he mutters, pressing my stomach painfully into the counter while he rips through the button on my pants and tears apart the zipper. "And don't you go crying to Cashiel about this, either, or I'll tell him what a rotten little shit you've been. What should I say, should I tell him that I saw you stealing? Touching yourself? Lying? What really makes him upset, huh?"

I struggle, but it's hard, and I want to give up. It's easier to just give up and let him have his way, at least then I won't end up hurt, too. "There's olive oil," I mumble, squeezing out the words through my sobs. "You can reach it... for lube."

He laughs as he jerks my pants down. "You'd like that, wouldn't you, whore?" He cuffs me on the back of the head. "Beg me for it, then. Beg me to fuck you, and *maybe* you can earn some lube."

I can do it. I know I can. I've begged for worse, and I can feel my lips starting to form the words. "Please help!" I scream instead. "Help me—"

His hand clamps around my mouth so tightly I can barely breathe, and I redouble my efforts to struggle and escape. I've gone this far now, all I want is to finish it, to escape his grip, to avoid the inevitable.

"You son of a bitch!" he growls in my ear, and I can feel the hand that's not around my mouth reaching down between us. I know he's grabbing for his cock, and I know what he's about to do with it, and I start to try to grab anything; the kitchen sink, the cabinets, anything that I might use as a weapon or a distraction. The animal instinct that I thought had been beaten out of me suddenly kicks back to life, and I feel his cock missing its goal, ramming just barely too high. I thrust back against him again, purposely aiming to press my tailbone into his cock, hoping I can hurt it or break it. It doesn't matter now; I've been about as defiant and uncooperative as I can be, if my master wants to punish me for it later, let him.

Bobby twists my head to the side, and for a second I think he'll snap my neck. For a second I want to let him, but he doesn't. Instead, he takes his hand and forces two fingers inside of me, roughly, and I try to scream but I fail.

He's not preparing me. He's holding me in place like that and it burns. My arms still flailing in front of me, I grab a dirty glass in the sink and I do the only thing that I have left to do.

I throw it, hard, against the wall. It shatters, and I hear the noise from the party dim the tiniest bit. Breaking glass. People always want to hear.

"Fucking little bitch!" Bobby mutters. He rams his cock into me, replacing his fingers, and as the pain intensifies I throw another glass, trying for a third before he captures my hands and clenches them tightly, slamming them down against the corner of the countertop with enough violence that I hear something crack.

I let myself go limp, sagging despite the pain so he has to work to hold me up, much less fuck me. I wish that one of the blows to the head would have knocked me out.

And then, I hear the most wonderful and terrifying voice I have ever heard.

"Sascha, what in god's name—"

It's my master, and he's furious, and he's apparently speechless. Bobby releases his grip on my head, and I turn to look at the man who owns me, and I can't say anything.

"Cash, it's not what it looks like!" Bobby says quickly, pulling out of me and releasing the death grip he had on my hands.

I crumple to the floor, whimpering and crying.

"He seduced me! The fucking whore seduced me, begged me to fuck him!" Bobby protests. I can hear his pants zipping up. "He was being aggressive and rude, and he wanted to tease me, and then when I started going, he, he asked me to be rough, and—"

"Get out of my house."

The words barely make sense, because all I can hear is the fury in my master's voice. I can hear him saying that if I fucked up he would sell me, and I can hear how angry he is, and I know it's because of me and I know it's my fault.

"Cash, come on, he's just—"

"I will *not* repeat myself!"

I curl into a ball and start sobbing. This can't end well. I can't see any way that this will end where I don't end up taking the blame. I've interrupted the party, and I've come between my master and his best friend, and I let myself be raped. I should have just taken it, should have just spread my legs and complied, because what good am I at anything else? I've ruined my chance to stay here and it hurts more than all the physical pain combined.

I don't hear Bobby leave, but he must, because the next thing I know, my master is crouching down in front of me.

"Are you hurt?"

These words don't make any sense at all. I'm expecting to hear threats, beratements, anger. And I do hear anger, but not like I think, and the words don't mean anything to me. Bobby will come back, he'll finish what he started, and then my master will have him help arrange for me to be sold. It always works out like this, the slave is always the one to pay at the end, even when all I was trying to do was to be good and to behave and to do everything right.

"Get up."

He's pulling me to my feet and I force myself to comply, to put weight on my ankles, and my legs, and he actually has his hands on my shoulders, steadying me. I struggle to pull my pants up, but they keep falling down because the closure is broken. He shakes his head at me, a look of disgust on his face.

There's no words, I just keep sobbing. I wish I had been killed instead. I wish I had never come to a place where I had a taste of decency, only to have it ripped away.

He reaches his hand out toward my face and I flinch, ashamed that I'm so cowardly and weak. He is barely deterred, and a second later, he has me by the chin, and is carefully looking at my lip.

"I'm sorry, master," I whimper. He probably won't sell me like this, not until I heal up. He'll be stuck with me for days.

He says nothing. He notices that I'm cradling my left hand in my right, and he pulls that toward him as well, frowning as he looks at it.

"Son of a bitch," he mumbles, taking a step away from me.

I drop back to the floor, curling into a ball and waiting for the beating to start. He already has to wait for me to heal up, he'd be right to add a few more bruises first. I can't look at him. I feel my pants sliding down again as I try to make myself invisible, and I try not to whimper when I hear the unmistakable sound of his belt being pulled from his pants. Just check out, disappear, stop being here. I've done it so many times before, how have I forgotten?

"You can't walk through the house like this," he mutters. "Come on, on your feet."

I drag myself up, not bothering to look at him as I lean over the counter. It doesn't matter that my ass is half exposed; he's just going to hurt me more anyway. I feel him come up behind me and I can't help but whimper when I feel his hands on the waistband of my pants.

He pulls them up and holds them there, fiddling with something I don't understand.

"Turn around," he orders, and when I do, he finishes putting his belt through my belt loops and fastening it. "I don't need you tripping over yourself."

He goes to put an arm around me and I jerk away, shaking. He shakes his head and curses, but grips me by the upper arm and leads me instead. He takes me out the back door and starts leading me around the house. I am terrified. Would he really just drag me out back and shoot me or something?

We arrive rather anti-climactically at the patio that connects to his bedroom. Pulling keys from his pocket, he unlocks the door and opens it, half-shoving me through.

"Stay in here," he says quietly. "I don't need my guests to see you. As far as they know, my friend was intoxicated and you helped him to get home. You can shower if you'd like, or just rest."

"Yes, master," I mumble, still confused. What does he want from me? "Please, master, I'm sorry. I'm sorry I fucked up."

"Sascha..." he turns away, and I think he's going to leave. "This was never supposed to happen. I'm sorry I didn't stop him sooner."

He leaves me no less confused than I had been just moments before. Maybe he regrets having to sell me? I have become pretty helpful to him, at least to his business.

He's gone, and he's even locked the door behind him, making sure nobody can get in. I want nothing more than to wash the tears and the sweat and feeling of Bobby's hands off my skin, but I curl up on my master's bed instead, breathing in the faint smell of him that's left on his pillow. I shake and sob in confusion, and eventually I drift off to sleep.

Chapter 18

Lavender

"Get up."

The words catch me off-guard, which is surprising, because it means I was sleeping deeply enough to be off-guard. I can't even remember the last time that happened, but then, I can't really recall why I'm not in my bed, or why my hand hurts so much, or the party last night...

I blink, and my master's face comes into view and I remember. I start to feel sick.

"Go change," he orders, not looking at me as he throws clothes at me.

He's selling me today. He's selling me today and I didn't even get a chance to wash the feeling of Bobby's hands off of me. The lingering smell of his cologne seems embedded into my nose, and the feeling of his fingers and his mouth and his cock... I fight back the urge to be sick again, sidestepping my master's order to change in favor of using the bathroom first.

I frantically begin strip last night's clothes off, not caring if they rip. I don't want to see them ever again. I pause when I see my master's belt around my waist, realizing now why he had taken it off in the first place. He hadn't hurt me any more, not like I thought he was going to. It's a bitter comfort in the face of being sold.

I wash my hands, rinse out my mouth, and grab a towel and scrub violently at my skin. It isn't enough. I can still feel him touching me. A towel and hand soap will never be enough to erase the memories and the mistakes that were made last night. Throwing caution to the wind, I step into the shower, my master's shower, the one he said long ago that he didn't want to share with me. Fuck it. He's selling me anyway.

His shower is slightly nicer than mine, with one of the massager things on the handle and a variety of shampoos and soaps to choose from. Which ones will smell like him? Can I at least hold on to that?

I find the right one, some sort of manly scent, stone or something ridiculous. I think it actually smells more like lavender, but of course lavender wouldn't sell well. I'm rubbing it across my skin when it hits me that I might not be in a warm shower again, or using scented soap, or attending parties or eating or helping with work or being with my master ever again.

I drop to the floor and sob, heedless of the consequences. I'll look weak, maybe even defiant again, but it doesn't matter anymore. I've failed enough, what's one more thing? He's going to sell me anyway.

I don't know how long I'm there, because the water has gone cold when I hear a knock at the door. I don't answer. I will myself to die, to pass out. Anything would be better.

"Sascha?" he demands, pounding on the door more forcefully this time.

I still don't answer, curling in a ball and hoping illogically to freeze to death.

I hear the door opening, and I regret not locking it. I curl up tighter and put my hands above my head, whimpering when the left bangs against the edge of the bathtub. It aches.

I hear the shower curtain open.

"Jesus Christ!"

I'm dragged up roughly by my shoulders and I go limp, expecting the inevitable slap that should follow such a move. Maybe he'll slap me hard enough to snap my neck.

He shakes me instead, not hard enough to snap my neck, but hard enough to make my eyes open against my will like a toy doll. He looks more relieved than angry when they do.

"For fuck's sake, Sascha, I thought you were dead!" he snaps, finally refraining from shaking me. I don't understand why he looks so scared at the thought. I won't bring him that much money when he sells me; why else would it matter if I die?

"I'd rather be dead than sold, master," I mumble, sitting up only because he's forcing me to. It's easier to go along than it is to fight him.

Holding me up with one arm, he reaches to shut the water off with the other, slamming the handle down with significantly more force than necessary. "Goddammit, get up now!"

I do. I'm trained that well, at least, and when I do it he pulls me out of the shower and proceeds to dry me off with excessive vigor, although he's not quite as violent as he was with the shower.

"I'm not selling you, I'm taking you to the goddamned doctor!" he snaps. "So if you're going to martyr yourself or whatever the fuck you're doing, you can knock it off right now!"

The words sink in as he finishes drying me off and shoves the clothes into my hands.

"Put these on!" he orders, stepping out as if I have some dignity. I'm half-surprised that he doesn't dress me himself.

I move robotically. I think of the robo-clerks at fast-food chains and clothing stores, and I laugh unexpectedly at the image of myself as one. I can't stop laughing any more than I can stop crying. This is it, then, I've lost my mind. I can't tell how long it takes me to regain my composure, but I do eventually stop laughing. The crying... I just hope it's okay.

Reality moves like a dream as I step out of the bathroom and follow my master down the hall and out to his hov-car. He doesn't say anything to me, doesn't even look at me. He focuses on the road more intently than I've ever seen before, and he grips the steering wheel until his knuckles are white, despite the fact that the indicator light says that the auto-drive is in use and he doesn't have to steer.

"Master, you said... if I fucked up..." I hear the words leave my mouth and I regret them.

"You did nothing wrong. I'm not selling you." My master grinds the words out between his teeth. His face grows red and I cower away when he slams his fist against the steering wheel. "I meant if you were mouthy or rude or something. *Not* if my supposed best friend assaulted you in my kitchen. Bobby and I are the only ones who fucked up last night, not you."

I sit there quietly, trying to process it. He's not selling me. He's not even angry at *me*, I don't think, although it's hard to tell with how angry he is. I guess he's angry at Bobby? That makes sense, it was Bobby who damaged me and interrupted his night, but the strange thing is, it seems like my master is angry at himself. He's acting guilty, like he had just allowed someone he cared about to get hurt, but I'm just a slave. Can he really be that possessive over his property? I don't understand him, but that's nothing new. All I can do is wait and respond to whatever he decides to do with me.

I'm silent as we drive to the doctor's office, and I sit stupidly in the car until he comes around and takes me by the arm, half-dragging me out of the car. He's not trying to hurt me, but I guess if I don't want to be hurt I should walk instead of sitting here, frozen.

We don't even sit in the waiting room, he just takes me straight back to the office. Of course, he must have called first. Everything is always so smooth for him. I wonder if we've kept everyone waiting while I cried in the shower, and I wonder how my master is able to make everything work so perfectly. I can't help but think of how difficult I make his life, and it starts a fresh round of tears down my face.

The doctor looks at me and frowns.

"It wasn't me." My master's voice is trying to be an angry growl, but he almost sounds sad.

"You explained that," the doctor says quietly, guiding me to sit on an exam table, my master standing nearby. "And I believe you. Are you pressing charges?"

My master shrugs. "It's petty destruction of property. Nothing more than a fine. I have other means."

I don't understand what my master's talking about, and I don't care. I wouldn't expect him to press charges against his friend for using me like the whore that I am. It's enough that he stopped him.

The doctor nods. He looks at me, and I turn my head away.

"Let him see your lip, Sascha," my master orders.

I'm surprised enough that he uses my name that I do it, and a second later the doctor is poking and prodding at it. He frowns at it, but he's not really hurting me, so I stay still.

"Well, if he had been in last night I might have recommended stitches, but it's stopped bleeding. I'll clean it up and bandage it. What else do we have?"

My master doesn't even bother to answer, he just grabs my left arm, lifting it up. I try not to wince, but my hand hurts, more so than it did in the shower, and it's an ugly shade of purple and blue and green that I don't really want to look at. I whimper instead, resisting the urge to pull it back against my chest and hold it there where it's safe.

The doctor takes it and touches it and makes it hurt, and mutters something about x-rays. I don't want x-rays; I just want to be left alone. Haven't I had enough done to me? I just want to hide and cry for days until I feel better. At least when I was hurt badly enough at the brothel, I was allowed that.

"He's also..." my master hesitates, fidgeting uncomfortably. "I should probably let you check that part out alone. The, uh..."

"Sexual penetration," the doctor fills in with a nod, clinical and calm. "You said it was rather violent?"

My master shrugs; I can see that he's clearly unwilling to talk about this. "I guess, I mean, I didn't see it, but from the state he was in... just check it out."

The doctor nods again, walking over and opening the door to the exam room we're standing in. "Certainly, just step out—"

"Please, master!" I yelp, clutching his hand in terror even though I know how horribly inappropriate it is. "Please, no!" I shouldn't touch him, and I shouldn't beg him to do anything, but I can't help it.

He looks shocked, but he doesn't pull his hand away from me, and he doesn't move. "I didn't think you'd want me in here."

I don't, not really, but I don't want him to leave me alone with someone else, either. "Please, don't go, master." I can feel my face burning with shame at the request.

"I'll stay," he says quietly, glancing at the doctor. I hallucinate him squeezing my hand, because, surely, that can't be real. "Do you have a chair I can sit in?"

I zone out a little bit during the next part. I'm aware, vaguely, that my master is given a chair, and he sits next to my head, looking uncomfortable as the doctor does what he needs to do. I comply when I am asked to take off my pants, and I feel the doctor's hands on me, cold and clinical like they are when he passes the x-ray scanner over my hand, and when he disinfects my lip and places a tight bandage over it to pull the freshly lacerated skin back together. That part probably hurts the worst, but even then I just cry silently and wish it was over. I wish it was all over, and even though I've been hurt so much worse, I've never had someone take care of it afterward, never had to see my master looking uncomfortable and angry because I needed taking care of.

My master never wanted a slave, because slaves are a problem, and I'm nothing *but* a problem. I challenge him, I waste his time, I eat up his money and food and time and I make him look bad and I ruined his relationship with his friend. I'm sinking into despair when I hear the doctor state that a variety of bones in my hand are broken, and I'll need a cast, and I realize exactly how much of a useless problem I'm going to be. I curl into a ball on the exam table and sob, heedless of the free men who are staring at me in shock. A hand touches my back lightly and I jerk away, whimpering and sobbing even harder.

"Give me a minute alone with him," I hear my master saying.

"I don't know if that's really the best idea." The doctor sounds apologetic, but I'd be apologetic, too, if I was arguing with my master. "You know how I feel—"

"Just do it." My master cuts him off in the same demanding tone that he uses with me. "I'm not going to hurt him."

"Your family's training methods would dictate otherwise, Cash."

"I'm not going to hurt him."

There's silence for a moment, and I let the words wash over me. I don't understand them. I don't understand the comment about my master's family and their training methods, and I don't understand my master's insistence that he's not going to hurt me. Why else does he want me alone? A few seconds later, I hear someone walking out, and a hand lands firmly on my shoulder.

My master pulls me up to sit and face him. I can't help but look at his eyes.

"I'm sorry this happened," he says, all curt and businesslike. "And I'm sorry that you're in pain. You did nothing to deserve it, and I'm working on making it go away, but I can't have you sit here and lose your goddamn mind because someone says they're going to put a cast on your broken hand. Is that understood?"

"Yes, master," I reply automatically, but I'm still terrified. "I won't, I won't be able to—"

My master gives me a shake, firm, but not nearly as hard as he did when he found me in the shower. His grip is tight on my shoulders and I don't want him to let go. "Do you think I don't realize that you won't be able to do a goddamn thing? It's not the end of the world, Sascha. You'll heal in a few weeks and then you can catch up on everything you've gotten behind on. I'm not going to make you do what you used to when your goddamn hand is busted up — what kind of person do you think I am? Do you think I'd blame *you* for this?"

I can't answer, because I don't know. He's decent to me, but he's not exactly kind, he demands some sort of fucking perfection, but he's not overly harsh, even when he punishes me. I'm terrified of him, but still I cling to him. I let my head drop against his hand and I think I'm hallucinating again when I feel him go from clutching my shoulder to holding my head. I wish he wouldn't ever let go.

"You'll be fine, Sascha," he says firmly, gripping my shoulders one last time before stepping away. He walks to the door and leans out, beckoning the doctor back. "Give him a painkiller and something for the anxiety. I don't care what it costs, just do it."

I flinch when the needle slips into my skin, but within a few minutes, I feel the cessation of pain throughout my body, and the worries that I had about upsetting my master seem far away. I'm at a doctor's office, and I'm comfortable, and everything seems great. Even the slight pain in my hand as the bones are set and placed in some sort of cast material doesn't bother me, and I smile at my master. He's a nice man, I decide, and so is the doctor. Another small machine is brought over, and my hand gets warm, and maybe it should hurt, but it feels good, and I start to fall asleep. I think there should be a nurse to catch me, but there's no nurse here, and the doctor is doing something with the cast, so it must be my master who catches me and holds me up gently and leads me to the car a while later. He does smell like lavender.

Walking in on Sascha and Bobby made me aware of two things I was trying desperately to avoid: I care far more about Sascha than a master should about a slave, and my best friend is not the kind of person I want to associate with any longer. Slaves are property; they can be used, hurt, sold, destroyed — it doesn't matter. I should have been simply irritated to see Bobby on top of my slave, as I would have been if he had borrowed a sweater from my closet without asking me, but I felt so much more than that. If I had been armed, I would have shot my best friend without blinking.

I can't stand the thought of him being around Sascha again, ever. It's not enough that I deny myself the pleasures of his body; I want to make sure that nobody else takes advantage of him. I've always been a little uncomfortable using slaves for sex. Everyone does it. I've even sampled a few, but it seems wrong, and I rather prefer the challenge of finding a willing, eager partner. But it's more than principle with Sascha. I see the way he flourishes when he's safe, and I want to make sure he can stay that way. I have my rules and demands, but at the end of the day, I have my idle fantasies, too, that one day, he'll stop grouping me with the other people who have hurt him. People like Bobby.

Once Sascha is taken care of, I can deal with the other problem that has arisen from this ordeal. I place a few calls, make a few arrangements, and set up a dinner date with Bobby to remove him from my town and my life.

Bobby is the only person who has been with me through the first run of my research, through the scandal I caused, through all the changes. He was the only one who never judged me, not by my birth name, nor by my new one. He's been my best friend since we were twelve and we've shared everything. But I arrange dinner with him, and all I can see is him brutalizing my slave.

We barely speak, focusing awkwardly on our food.

"I found a great job for you," I mention, pushing the food around on my plate. "It pays well, it has good benefits, and they're looking to fill the position soon." Most importantly, it's far away from me and Sascha.

Bobby gives me a curious look. "I didn't know I was looking for a job."

"I know," I mumble, trying to downplay it. "One of my colleagues mentioned this great position, though, and asked me if I knew anyone who might be interested. I thought of you — you'd fit perfectly. I can give you a recommendation and everything. You're pretty much guaranteed the job, and it will nearly double what you're making, unless you've gotten a raise recently. I think you'd be really happy there."

"Where is it?" he asks.

Good. He's considering it. The offer should be good enough that he can't turn it down. When my mother did this to me, so many years ago, I tried to fight it at first. Now I am just amazed by how easy it is to follow in her footsteps. I only hope that Bobby accepts it as passively as I did back then.

"It's out of state," I tell him. I give him a little more information, launching into the story of the city he'll move to and the company he'll work for like a paid salesman. He looks surprised, at first, and then I can see him starting to put it all together.

"Cash, are you trying to get rid of me?" he asks, looking shocked. "Look, I'm sorry about the slave. Christ, if I realized you were going to get this upset, I would have asked permission—"

"You knew exactly what you were doing," I reply coldly. I had heard the rumors before, but I never believed them. Slaves, interns, pretty girls at bars... Bobby was "fun," and everyone knew that, but a few had stepped up to suggest that his fun had gone too far.

"You can't make me move," he mutters, looking hurt.

I'm hurt, too. I'm losing my best friend. But Sascha was hurt worse. And making people do things they don't want to do is simply a matter of finding adequate motivations and punishments for disobeying. The thought of what he did to Sascha turns my stomach, makes the pleasant aroma of cooking food seem vile and nauseating.

"I don't want you anywhere near me," I let him know. "Don't com, don't visit. Just go."

"I've got family here," he complains.

"I'll pay for them to visit you. They can visit you there, or in jail."

"You don't go to jail for fucking a slave," Bobby snaps.

"No, but for enough money, you can go to jail for raping a free person," I reply casually. For enough money, almost anyone can be bought and sold, Demoted or not. I glance at our server. "How much do you think it would take for him to sell you out? Or the one over there? She looks fitting. Or maybe I'll find someone you really did it to."

Bobby goes quiet, and suddenly, it's over between us. Twenty-some years of friendship destroyed by a single action.

"This is blackmail," he mutters. "You can't do this. I know secrets about you."

He doesn't know the important secrets. The only one who really knows anything about my work is Sascha, and he doesn't know half of it. "The secrets you know are public record," I remind them. "Any journalist worth their paycheck could find them. Yours aren't. You can take my offer and live in comfort, or you can try to ruin my reputation. You won't win."

He nods, knowing I'm right, and knowing that I'm perfectly aware of how this works. After all, it was done to me. We work out the details, have our food boxed up to go, and he's gone.

Chapter 19
Simplicity

I'm surprised when I find a bunch of information on re-education centers hidden away on my tablet.

Since my master brought me home from seeing the doctor, it's become clear that he isn't getting rid of me. He puts me to work, at least a little, carrying stacks of paperwork over to my office and flashing over file after file onto my tablet. It's all legitimate work stuff, not his secret project, and he never rushes me as I work one-handed. I know he would have rushed me before, demanded that I perform to the best of my ability.

I become depressed, and I wonder how long he'll tolerate it, how long he'll tolerate me. I can't even bring myself to say anything to my master when he goes out of his way to do nice things like replace my wardrobe with pullovers and drawstring pants and slip-on shoes, or order takeout food for me. My master notices. He makes no secret about monitoring what I eat, and how much, and during the first few weeks, he gives me a little blue pill along with my painkillers. They make me feel nice, floaty, and content. Bobby doesn't come around anymore. I don't know what happened to him, and I don't care to.

Instead of thinking, I waste time, playing with new mods and enhancements and all sorts of things that I probably shouldn't. When I come across a file I didn't install, I investigate, making sure it's nothing that could harm the system or get me in trouble.

I don't look too closely; I know it's not for me to see, and I remember my master's insistence a few weeks ago that I not pry into his project. I look just closely enough to see what it is, and to put it together that it's not anything to do with his legitimate business. Then I consider what to do with it. He obviously tried to hide it; it's disguised under layers of protection and security. Of course, that's what tips me off in the first place. It's too obvious, too perfect, too well-hidden. He's done the equivalent of putting a giant safe in the middle of a banquet hall—it's drawing attention, and once it draws attention, it's only a matter of time before it will be broken into. I consider his secrecy, the giant house cleaning we completed right before the party. Maybe he's in trouble; maybe someone wants something from him. I'm alarmed at first that he used my tablet to hide the data, but I realize it makes sense. I'm supposed to be a stupid slave; nobody would ever suspect me of hiding anything more than a stolen cookie. His logic was sound, but his final method of hiding it wasn't.

I don't have to think long before I decide to fix it for him. I break into the first few layers of encryption easily, pulling out any of the data that looks suspicious. I encrypt the data with much simpler security methods, making sure that it is protected without drawing attention to itself. Finally, I compress it and hide it in a system file that controls the brightness of the screen. It's simple to find if someone knows where to look, but if not, it is so easily overlooked as to be invisible.

I hide some porn in the other location, as a detour, and I encrypt it again. Once again, it is glaringly obvious that something is hidden.

With this finished, I decide to research my family. It's been so long since the Assessment, since I've seen my family. I wonder if they still remember me. I finally find Abriel's college registration, and read the same graduation notices that I assume he's reading. I think about our parents going to watch him, how proud they must be. He was always the more loyal son anyway, the responsible one who helped dad out and remembered to tell mom that she looked nice. I spend some time looking up our parents, but there's so little information on them. I'm just relieved when I don't find an obituary or anything terrible like that.

It's only after I've exhausted searches on my family and friends that I have the idea to run a search on my master. I don't really know why I do it—I suppose I've been living with the man for seven months now, and I know so little about him. I assume he grew up wealthy— was it normal wealthy, or over the top? Does he have siblings? Is he even from around here? He's so closed-off all the time, and I doubt he'd answer if I asked.

He doesn't seem to exist, which is frustrating. Could he really have no electronic presence? Everyone does. Everyone has records and schools and businesses and embarrassing photos from when they were twelve. I certainly have my share—the question is, where are his?

I'm completely engrossed in my hunt for my master's history when I feel a rush of air near my head. The tablet goes flying and I recoil in an instant, covering my face reflexively.

My master towers over me.

"You just don't fucking know when to stop, do you?" he snarls, glaring at me like I'm lower than an insect.

I don't say anything. Agreeing with him seems like a terrible idea, even though it is true, and contradicting him might even be worse. I cower and say nothing.

"I let you do damn near anything," he says quietly. It's true. He does, and I just keep pushing.

"It stops now."

He strides over to the tablet, grabs it, and carries it out of the room. I stop to breathe a sigh of relief. He's just going to take the tablet. He's angry that I'm wasting time on it and stealing things again and investigating my family, and so he's going to take the tablet to punish me. That's okay. I can deal with that.

He comes in a few minutes later with a piece of paper and a pen. He drops them in front of me.

"Write."

Once I do, he rifles off a list of tasks, everything from mopping the kitchen floor to oiling the hinges on the doors to cleaning the grout in the bathroom. Mindless tasks, but the list fills almost an entire page. When he finally stops, I look at him, questioning.

"Since you have enough time to go behind my back and look up my family and myself, you obviously have *all* the time in the world to get through this list," he says, scowling at me. "I don't want you to eat, sleep, or so much as use the toilet until you finish. And if you *ever* pry into my life again, I'll make this look like a reward."

The words terrify me, because I know it's impossible. If I had two good arms, it would be impossible, and I don't, and I'm out of shape because I've spent the last few weeks doing next to nothing. I feel my heart start to race, and I become aware of a sudden pressure in my bladder.

"I wouldn't just sit there if I were you."

"Yes, master," I mumble, jumping up and mindlessly tackling the first task.

I don't really need to use the bathroom, it turns out, I'm just nervous, because it passes as soon as I get into the work I'm doing. Three hours later is a different story, however, because I'm squirming and miserable. I can't even imagine the punishment for pissing myself. I want to give up, lie down and sob until I can't any more, but I can't. I have to keep going.

My master is checking on me often, making sure I'm still working, glaring at me every time. I can tell he wants to hurt me more, but he doesn't. For once, I'm glad he's so reserved.

"Use the bathroom," he says suddenly, brusquely. "I shouldn't have said that. Use the bathroom if you need to."

I immediately drop what I'm working on and head in that direction. "Thank you master, thank you so much!"

"I just don't want you pissing all over my floor," he mutters, but I can tell he's covering for something else. Shame, perhaps.

He pushes me for hours, although I know we both should be sleeping, and I feel the fingers on my hand start to grow sore from scrubbing and raw from chemicals. I'm starving, and the fact that I'm not allowed to eat makes me hungrier. I slip while attempting to clean the floor in the kitchen, and with only one good hand to catch myself, I land on my ass with a thump. A shock of pain radiates up from my tailbone. I fight the tears and the pain and try to stand up, but it's too much, and I sit there in a pile of mop water and resent the tears that are rolling down my face almost as much as I resent my master.

I don't feel better when I hear the door open, knowing my master has come to yell at me or punish me for slacking. But maybe if he hits me it will be over.

He stares at me for a few minutes, silent and angry. "Go have something to eat and go to bed," he orders, shocking me.

He wakes me up early the next morning with a shake, and it's all I can do not to start crying again. The glove he gives me protects my hand from chemicals, but it does little to ease the rest of the pain in my body from the unexpected physical labor.

The next few days are similar. He doesn't hit me, doesn't even yell at me, he just works me endlessly, forcing the most pointless tasks on me and making them redo them over and over again until they are done to his satisfaction. I don't know what he'd do if I just refused to do them, and I'm not willing to find out. He wakes me early, orders me to eat breakfast, and then forces me to work. I don't cook. He orders food for himself and orders me to make dull, quick meals that keep me alive but not happy. Lunch and dinner are the same, as are bathroom breaks. He's even gone so far as to work from home for a few days so he can supervise me more closely. He never seems to want to stop until I break, until I give in and cry and can't stop myself from lying on the floor in misery.

He takes me to get the cast removed from my arm, but continues to torment me. It's the kind of tasks they had us do at the re-education center, the same kind of food, too. Short of the beatings and the sex, I'd feel like I was back there, but I'd rather not recreate that experience. He doesn't speak to me, doesn't look at me, except to bark orders or to glare. All this, because I was looking up information on my tablet?

I start to feel sick as he wakes me up earlier and earlier each day. I don't even bother looking at a clock any more. The strange thing is that he doesn't seem any less angry, in fact, he seems more angry with every passing day, and I start flinching away when he comes near me. It doesn't make sense, and I know it infuriates him every time I do it, but he's so out of control and explosive that I can't override my own self-preservation instincts.

He never says anything about it though, he just snaps at me to keep working.

By the eighth day, I'm crying within an hour of waking up. I'm down on my knees again, on the tile floor of the guest bathroom, scrubbing the already white grout with a small toothbrush and cleaning paste. My knees are bruised and my back hurts and I sit there in tears until he comes in to check on me. He orders me to continue, and I just can't. I don't move from the spot, and when he comes back in to check on me, I'm in a ball on the floor, whimpering and covering my face. "Just beat me, master," I mumble, wishing I wasn't saying it. I've never willingly asked to be beaten before, but it would be better.

"What?" he demands, standing over me. I curl away, expecting a kick.

"Please, just beat me, master," I repeat. "Just get it over with. I can't take this."

He grabs me by the shoulder and jerks me up, and it's all I can do not to go limp under his grasp. "Whatever gave you the idea that I was going to beat you?" he demands.

The endless torture, maybe? "Please, master, I know that what I did was wrong. I get it. I can't keep doing this, sir, I can't keep working like this, it's killing me, and it's not helping you. I just... I'd rather you beat me than drag it out like this. I won't do it again. I won't look anyone up and I won't try to find my family and I won't do anything wrong, I promise!" I've turned into a sobbing mess, and I'm shaking, half from the exhaustion and half from the terror I feel.

"I thought you wanted to learn more about me and my family," my master says, his voice low and dangerous. "I thought I'd show you first-hand what I'm about."

"This isn't you, master!" I protest without even thinking about it. He's silent too long and I dare to glance up, surprised when he looks back at me in shock. "You're not like this. This is just... pointless suffering, and cruelty. None of these things even need to be done, and you're not getting any work done in the meantime because you're trying to prove some stupid point! It's inefficient and wasteful and — "

He backhands me, which I know damn well I deserve, and his iron grip on my arm is all that keeps me from flying into the wall. I taste blood where I my teeth catch on the inside of my cheek.

"Don't *ever* speak to me like that again, Sascha," he hisses. It's the first time he's used my name in days. "You don't know the first thing about who I am."

"I know you're smarter than to waste perfectly good help on scrubbing grout!"

He draws back his hand to hit me again and I don't flinch or back down. I stare into his eyes, bracing myself for the hit, knowing I deserve it as much as the last one, but refusing to give him the satisfaction of seeing my fear.

"Get out of my fucking sight," he growls. "Take one step out of your bedroom before you're told otherwise and I *will* beat you. Try me and I won't even bother selling you — I'll give you away."

I nod, not trusting myself to speak. He's still clutching my arm, and I glare pointedly at it. He shoves me away, making me stumble as he does it. Before I can get myself into further trouble, I rush down the hall and into my bedroom. I manage to hold in the tears and shaking until the door is shut and my head is hidden under my pillow. I don't know whether I won or lost the fight.

Chapter 20
Threats

I watch Sascha leave, barely able to contain the rage I feel toward him. I was supposed to be training him, putting him in his place, making him feel stupid and afraid and inadequate, just like the best training methods dictated. I wanted to feel vindicated when he worshipped the slightest hint of kindness, to see him so broken that he could never forget who owned him again.

I wanted to force both of us to remember our respective places before we got too comfortable.

Instead, I feel ashamed. He's still not the perfect slave that the treatment was supposed to produce. He's worse; he's smart, and he saw through my game as clearly as I saw through my mother's. I've always been taught that fear accomplishes something; when it fails to accomplish, it is clear that I am just being cruel. It sickens me. The threat to sell him wasn't much better, but I had to get him away from me. I still own him, and the disrespect he subjected me to was enough that I wanted to lose all control, beat him until he screamed and bled and begged me to stop.

I want to wash all of my mother's influence from my mind.

I try to decide what to do. A part of me wants to give him the beating he asked for, another wants to just leave him to stew in his own anxiety for a few days. I thought I was prepared to deal with a slave; slave training is in my family, in my blood. I know all the right things to do. I just never expected to get a slave like Sascha.

A knock on the door draws me away from my thoughts, and I answer without a thought.

I'm shocked to see Kristine Miller standing there with a smile on her face.

"Why are you here?" I ask, too stunned to worry about being polite.

"Can't a mother visit her son?" she asks, her voice false and sweet-sounding. "I've never seen your place. I gave you the money for it, but I've never seen more than a picture."

"You said you didn't want anybody to associate your good name with mine."

"Well, then, I had better come inside."

Without waiting for an invitation, my mother steps into the door, glancing expectantly at me until I close it behind her.

"Most people have their slaves do that sort of labor," she comments. She's barely inside of my house, and already she's criticizing me. "Where is your little pet, anyway?"

"In his room," I reply, curt.

"In the room you let him use," my mother corrects. "Never forget who owns who."

She's not talking about the slave anymore, she's talking about me and her. "He doesn't know," I inform her. "What happened, the research. He doesn't know."

"So, I take it you want to keep your secrets safe, Mr. Michaud?"

I can see her mocking me, but I don't care. I'm furious at Sascha, but I don't want him to be a pawn in this exchange. I subjected him to her style of training; the least I can do is protect him from experiencing it firsthand.

"Why are you in my house?" I ask again.

"To visit," she repeats. "You don't mind, do you? If I have a look around, see what you've done with the place."

"I'm sure there are neighborhoods having home tours right now."

"But none are as interesting as yours," she reminds me, her eyes cold.

"You have no right to be in my house," I mutter, uncertain of how to remove her. "You don't have a warrant, or an official investigation, or—"

"Cash, I wouldn't have anything to do with those, anyway," she reminds me, a smile playing on the edge of her lips. "I'm not a law officer. I'm not even a quality inspector. There are people that review my human products, but I would never debase myself by doing that work on my own. I research. I think. I design. Surely, you understand that after all these years?"

I nod. I do understand, but just because she doesn't have the official titles doesn't mean she can't make my life hell again.

"Of course, I could probably pull a few strings and get one of my friends in the judicial department to find a way in here," she says, as if she's just musing out loud. "I mean, it does demonstrate a commitment to quality. And if my very own son refused to let me into his house... well, I'd say that seems suspicious, don't you? Suspicious enough for a formal investigation. It would be terrible to see all those armed officers swarming the house; they always track mud in on their boots.

"Welcome to my home," I say, not meaning it in the slightest. I just can't fight her. It's not worth it.

"I'll let you know if I see anything that's non-compliant," she says, winking conspiratorially at me.

I stand back and watch her take over my home. She rifles through everything she can, looking for something to incriminate me. If I protest, she'll have her evidence, but if she finds something, she'll find even more. She questions me as she does it, talking about my job, my friends, my social life, my slave. She spends a lot of time talking about Sascha, and I get increasingly worried as she does. I don't know that I can trust the slave, not after what just happened. I hurt him, I tormented him, and the last thing I did before leaving him in panic was threaten to give him away like an unwanted puppy.

Like a predatory animal, my mother senses my fear.

"Does your slave spend all day in his room?" she asks.

"No," I shake my head. "He annoyed me and I told him to get away from me."

My mother purses her lips. "Avoidance isn't a good strategy, Cash," she chides.

I wish I could avoid her.

"Take me to him," she demands, and I comply. I don't know what else to do.

As we walk down the hall, I can feel her frown getting larger. Sascha's door is closed, as it always is, and it's in violation of the Miller

System training that demands that slaves not have any privacy. I can feel her judging me and my slave.

"I didn't want to see his face," I mutter, feeling ridiculous for making an excuse.

"Our associates make punishment hoods for a reason," she comments, throwing open the door like it belongs to her.

Sascha is lying on the bed, quiet, curled into a ball. He jumps when he hears the door open, but he doesn't move.

"Sascha," I intone, praying he won't fight it. "Up and on your feet."

He responds immediately, tears forming in his eyes, quickly replaced by confusion as he sees that I am not alone. I want to pause everything, to tell him what's going on, to let him in on everything I can. I don't want him to know, but I need him on my side. I realize just how badly I might have ruined this for myself.

"Sascha, this is my mother," I say, carefully keeping my tone level. "You will answer any questions she has and treat her with utmost respect."

Sascha nods. "Yes, master," he replies. He studies my face for a moment, then turns and bows his head deferentially in my mother's direction. "It is a pleasure to meet and serve you, ma'am."

I breathe a sigh of relief. He's putting on the good slave act, at least for now. He studies her for a moment, a confused look on his face, but then he lets it pass, standing there silently and waiting.

"How long has Cashiel had you, boy?" she asks, starting a series of demographic questions. Sascha stands at attention in front of us, answering perfectly. I am amazed by how well he performs; he still looks like he's had the life beaten out of him, and there is a bruise on his face from where I hit him earlier. It bothers me to think that my mother would be proud of that fact, if not the specific placement of the bruise. She asks Sascha what he thinks I do, what I use him for, if there have ever been any problems that a "mother" would want to know.

She's investigating me without really investigating me. I would almost rather suffer through a formal investigation, except I know she would stage that in her favor. This is a hunting expedition, but it's also an intimidation tactic. She will have me submit, or she will force it. At least this way, I have some illusion of control.

She orders Sascha to follow us around the house, continuing to interview him. She asks about the kinds of food we eat, the correction tools I use on him, the freedoms and restrictions he has. Again, he surprises me, providing appropriate stock answers at every turn.

"Cash, would you mind me meeting with the boy alone?" she asks, smiling coldly. "A mother is always so concerned about her boy."

I seethe. Just when I think I am getting ahead of her, she outwits me again. I can't say no, but I don't want to say yes. "Of course not," I reply. I turn to Sascha, trying to disguise the apologetic look on my face. "Go with her. Obey."

My mother looks like an animal about to devour her prey.

"If I find him to be unsatisfactory, do I have your permission to implement some corrections?" she asks, like she's trying to be polite.

I see Sascha going pale, and I want protect him. I think about it, instead.

"I'll handle it," I answer, finally. "After all, he is my responsibility. I know how much you hated when I neglected my responsibilities."

She shoots me a glare, the one that tells me she's furious at me for making her lose. She's underestimated me.

"Come, boy," she snaps, grabbing Sascha by the arm. "We'll see how well you remember your training."

I try not to think of how bizarre it is that my master's mom is basically kidnapping me. She digs her fingernails into my arm and drags me into his office. It seems weird that he's not here, just like it seems weird to see the same dark eyes on his mother as I see on my master every day. They look so much alike that I start to wonder what his dad looks like, if he and his wife are as alike as my master and his mother. She looks familiar, but I can't quite place her. I attribute it to her familiarity to my master.

"Do you know who I am, boy?" she asks, the moment she has me alone.

"Yes, ma'am," I reply. "You're my master's mother."

The look on her face suggests that she wants to slap me, but I can't figure out why. She interrogates me, asking about my brother, my master, my life before and after my master bought me. I answer honestly for the most part, omitting the incriminating things and keeping the answers simple. I'm just a stupid Demoted slave: I cook, clean, and serve my master. She seems to grow increasingly angry as she talks, desperate for me to slip up. I wonder if this is why my master is estranged from his family, but I can't figure out why he allowed her in the house. She asks me about re-education centers, which one I was at, which ones I've heard of, whether I've ever seen or heard my master doing anything with them. I tell her about the one I was at, but mention nothing else. The sheer fact that she wants to know makes me want to hide it.

"Nothing else to tell me, boy?" she asks, glaring at me.

"No, ma'am," I reply, innocent. "I just follow my master's orders. I wish I could help you find what you're looking for."

"Maybe you need a little inspiration," she suggests, a vicious smile on her face.

I have no idea what she's referring to, but she pulls out her com device. "Yes, come on in. We're in his office. If he gives you a problem, just tell him I requested your company. Tell him you have valuable information for me."

I stare at her, confused, and then I hear a knock at the door, followed by my master's voice.

"I told you not to visit!"

"I'm not visiting you. I'm visiting your mother."

The visitor's voice evokes a physical reaction, one that only worsens as the door to the office flies open to reveal Bobby's overly casual style and fake smile. "Bet you didn't think you'd be seeing me again.

Chapter 21
Intimidation

I've had so many people hurt me, I never thought that any one in particular would stick out above the others, but the memory of what he did to me is still too fresh, and I have stupidly allowed myself to believe that I would be safe.

My master storms in just seconds later, glaring at his mother. "What is he here for?" he demands.

"Your little friend says that you have an unhealthy relationship with your slave," my master's mother replies, giving him a dirty look. "He tells me that you threatened to spread lies about him, that you threatened to have him destroyed, just for using him like the little whore was meant to be used."

"I can use my property however I want," my master reminds her. "I don't fancy sharing with someone who touches my belongings without my permission."

"Bobby tells me that Sascha knows some secrets that he shouldn't," my master's mother says. "He called me up just a few days ago, told me that you and your little secrets were what really drove you to try to silence him. What a pity, Cash, that's no way to treat your friend!"

"He's lying," my master responds.

"Well, then, you won't mind if Bobby and I both speak with Sascha, will you?"

I freeze, fighting back the terror that threatens to take hold of me. He won't do it. He won't let them hurt me, do what they want to me. He'll save me, even if I was looking into his secrets. I look at my master desperately, wanting nothing more than to run to him and hide.

"Go ahead," he says, and I feel my heart sink. "But don't you dare lay a hand on him. I don't want so much as a hair out of place."

"Of course not, Cash," his mother replies. "After all, I have a reputation to uphold as well."

My master turns and slams the door, leaving me alone with them.

Bobby smiles at me. "How's your hand, Sascha?"

Hearing my name come from his mouth makes me want to vomit. I clench my hands into fists at my side and force myself to reply. "Almost healed, sir."

"And the rest of you?" he continues. "How's that sweet ass of yours?"

"Fine, sir."

"Maybe you should show us," he suggests, a smile spreading across his face.

I stare at him, confused.

"Take off your clothes," he clarifies.

Trembling, I obey. I have nothing to hide; just like every day since I was Demoted, my body is not my own. In a few seconds, I stand naked before my master's mother and his former best friend.

"Ask him about it," my master's mother orders, glaring at Bobby.

"Tell us about the secret your master has," Bobby orders, a smile on his face.

"I don't know what you're talking about, sir," I reply. My master has a secret research project, but as far as I know, Bobby knows nothing about it.

"You're lying!" Bobby snaps. "Touch yourself."

"What?" I'm confused. The order is out of nowhere, and it makes as little sense as this conversation.

"Touch your little cock, or I'll do it for you," Bobby threatens, taking a step toward me.

I grab myself, because I don't want his hands on me. My master told them not to touch me, but why did he leave me with them in the first place? I take my dick in my hand like it's a foreign object, wondering what sort of test this is that I'm trying to pass.

"Well, go on, enjoy yourself," Bobby taunts, stepping close enough that I can feel the warmth of his breath on my face. "Play with yourself like the little whore you are, unless you'd rather tell me about your master and his secrets."

I don't reply, I just start sliding my hand up and down. It feels so wrong, like I'm being controlled by someone else's whims. I bite down on my lower lip as I feel the tears start to fall down my face. When Bobby moves behind me, I feel the revulsion, and I wonder when I should scream, call for my master. He saved me once, will he do it again?

I feel warm breath on my ass and I yelp in terror. This is too real, too close to the last time, only now we have an audience.

"Tell us the secrets," Bobby demands, each word puffing against my skin, more painful than any whip. "Tell us, unless you want more of this."

"Please, sir, I don't know what you're talking about!"

"Ask him more directly," my master's mother suggests, watching and looking almost bored. "Stupid animals can never figure things out on their own."

"You know, Sascha," Bobby demands. "The secrets. Tell me. Tell us both."

I realize that he doesn't even know what he's talking about. If he did, he would have been more direct, but he's just fishing, and he's doing a terrible job of it. I gag as I feel his tongue slip down the crack of my ass, and I try to pull away, only to find myself securely restrained by an arm around my waist. Before I make up my mind to scream, Bobby rises, clamping a hand around my mouth as well.

"Tell us what you're hiding or I'll make you," he whispers in my ear.

I close my eyes and brace myself for what's to come.

"Ask him directly!" my master's mother snaps, angrily enough that I peek to see her glaring furiously at Bobby. "You said you knew what the secrets were. Ask him!"

Bobby's arm moves from around my waist. I pause, repulsed that I'm still touching myself, and I hope this can all be over. My master's mother isn't stupid enough to think Bobby really knows anything, is she?

"Don't stop, little whore," Bobby snaps, grabbing my arm and moving it up and down. Somehow it's even worse than doing it my-self, more intimate.

I don't speak, not even when I feel his fingers brushing over my back. He's not hurting me, not yet; if this were another situation with another person, it might even feel good. But it's Bobby, and he's doing this in front of my master's mother. I'd rather have bees swarming over my skin. I squirm, but I don't pull away. I can't give either of them a reason to think I'm so uncomfortable.

Bobby's hand snakes forward, covering my own, working it up and down over my cock.

"Cash told me about how beat up you were," he comments. "I never really got a chance to look at it for myself. Looks like someone carved you up like a little piece of meat."

I feel myself flushing, but I stay silent. It stings to think of my master talking about me with Bobby, providing him with more fuel to hurt me. I know that was never my master's intention, but it doesn't change anything. I yelp as the soft caresses turn rough, fingernails digging into my skin.

The pain catches the attention of my cock, and I'm mortified to feel it growing hard.

"You like that, don't you?" Bobby taunts, forcing my hand up and down over my cock while he claws at my back. I don't want it to feel good, but my body disagrees.

I look at the door, wondering what my master is doing on the other side of it. Why isn't he in here? He was so angry at Bobby after what happened at the party; why isn't he stopping him now?

My master's mother seems to be growing impatient as well. She takes a few steps closer to us, her face and body language clearly communicating her displeasure. "You don't know anything, do you? My son did nothing but chase you out of his life!"

"He's hiding something!" Bobby protests, jerking his hand and mine up and down over my cock while digging harder into my back with his fingernails. "Just give me some more time with Sascha, I can get him to talk."

I clench my teeth, resolute in my desire to stay silent. My body betrays me; I grow hard and excited from the rough treatment and humiliation. I close my eyes, pretend I'm not standing in front of these two people. I want my master, but he won't come for me. Still, I keep his secret.

I hear my master's mother moving toward us, and I keep my eyes closed.

"You're a filthy creature!" I hear her say, and when I hear a whoosh of air, I brace myself for the slap.

I'm surprised to hear Bobby yelp, retreating away from me a moment later. I glance up, shocked to see a bright red handprint on his face.

My master's mother is glaring at him. "You stupid, disgusting man. You wasted my time so you could have another chance to molest a slave? You humiliated me and lied to me? You know nothing. You never knew anything!"

"But I did!" Bobby protests, cowering away from my master's mother. "Cash was always secretive, and he wouldn't share Sascha! That's not normal, Ms. —"

Another slap. "Shut your dirty mouth," she orders Bobby.

I have never seen so much hatred directed at another person who wasn't me. I'd feel bad, but Bobby deserves everything he has coming to him.

"You will take the job that Cashiel arranged for you, and you will never return to this town," she threatens. "Not to see your family, not for a vacation, nothing. If I so much as *think* that you're anywhere around me or my son again, I'll report you, and not for assaulting a slave, but for assaulting a free woman. My little boy might have money and connections, but it's a child's game compared to what I can do to you. I asked for your help in keeping my son out of trouble, and you come up with this? If we were anywhere else but here, I'd have you arrested right now!"

Bobby just stares at her in shock, as do I. The information about my master getting Bobby out of town is news to me, and the way his mother is acting makes me realize exactly where my master got his evil streak.

"Get out and visit a whorehouse or something," she says, shoving Bobby toward the door to the office before turning to me. "And you. Get dressed."

I do as she orders, numb and still terrified. I hear the door slam as Bobby leaves. He was my biggest threat; the woman who made him cower is that much more powerful by comparison.

When I'm finished dressing myself, my master's mother walks

over to me, and I brace myself as she grabs me by the face. Her fingers dig into my jaw, and I wonder for a moment if she's going to just strangle me to death and end it all right here.

"I'm onto you, you little shit," she hisses. "You and Cashiel think you're so smart, but I brought him into this world. He's mine, and so is everything he owns. I should have had him Demoted when he was a child."

I stare at her, silent. I have no idea what I've done to anger her, or what my master has done to anger her, but I'm afraid of her. My master spent the past week bringing me to tears every day, and I would much rather return to that than spend another minute with this woman.

We finally return to meet my master, who is looking nervous.

"What did you do to him?" my master asks. He's pale, panicked, and clearly relieved to see me coming out in good physical condition. I'm surprised that he's so concerned about it; it's like he's forgotten about his secret research.

"I stopped your repulsive friend from molesting him," she says. "Bobby misled me, but he won't be bothering either of us again. We just asked your slave some questions. He was evasive. I think he's hiding something."

My master takes a breath, and I wait for him to tell her to leave. He doesn't. "If he's hiding something, I know nothing about it," he says, his voice carefully controlled. "How would you like to proceed?"

His mother laughs. "So formal, Cash," she teases. "I don't want to hurt your little pet. But where do you keep your tablet?"

I watch in amazement as he retrieves his tablet, handing it over to her without a word. What power does this woman have over him?

She pulls out a small device and plugs it into the tablet. It makes a low whirring sound, and lights flash across the screen. A few minutes later, she frowns. "What about yours?" she asks, glaring at me.

I'm caught. She makes it sound like she knows I have one, so I can't deny it. "My master took it away from me, ma'am," I reply, hoping that he'll think of something if he doesn't want her getting at it.

"Bring it," she orders. I watch in amazement as my master obeys.

A few moments later, the device is whirring in my tablet, and in just a few moments, it flashes bright green.

"What do we have here?" my master's mother asks, a gleeful smile on her face. "Cash, I didn't think you had any secrets from your mommy. Why on earth would you need this level of security? I thought you were being a good boy, these days."

My master stands there, jaw set. I'm worried about him, and even more worried as he opens his mouth, looking crushed.

"Mother, please—"

"It's mine," I say, immediately. I see my master's eyes fly open.

"You did this?" his mother asks, giving me a doubtful look. "What does a slave need with security?"

"Sascha," my master warns, looking at me with alarm on his face. "She doesn't even know what's in there."

"But I do," I say. "It's not hard to open, ma'am." I explain the process, watching as my master gets increasingly pale.

Smiling, my master's mother breaks through the security, looking more and more gleeful as she gets in further. Suddenly, her face drops, and I realize she's reached the final point.

"What is this?" she demands, scowling.

"I'm sorry, ma'am," I mumble. "I wasn't supposed to be looking at it. I just liked it, and even though I wasn't supposed to be pleasuring myself—"

"Shut your mouth!" she snaps, glaring at my master, who is utterly confused. "Porn, Cash? You let the boy watch porn?"

My master looks confused for another moment and I try to catch his eye. Suddenly, it dawns on him. "Well, I certainly don't allow him to," he replies coolly. "That's probably why he tried to hide it. The little delinquent that he is. It's why he no longer has access to a tablet without supervision."

The scowl on the woman's face is frightening. "I have other matters to attend to," she snaps, turning to glare at my master. "See that he's punished," she cautions. "If you let them get out of hand, it will come back to bite you later."

My master just nods. His face is slack, like he's waiting for the next blow to fall, but the rest of his body is tense. He doesn't speak, doesn't even say goodbye. He watches silently as his mother turns and opens the door in a rush. Without turning back, she storms out, slamming it behind herself. A few seconds pass, and I wait, terrified that she'll return. My master is just as nervous, and I don't think he breathes until the slight sound of her hov-car tearing away from the house has faded into silence again.

We're left alone.

"You know she wasn't looking for porn," he says quietly.

I nod.

"You found the other data?" he confirms.

I nod again.

"Is it still on the tablet?" he asks, his voice wavering. It's so unlike his usual confident, arrogant demeanor. He looks at me with wide eyes, almost more afraid than he was when his mother was prying into his life.

"Yes, sir. I hid it."

"Why didn't she find it, then?"

"I hid it better than you did." I realize how offensive the words are the moment they leave my mouth, but they're true. He owes me this recognition.

My master goes quiet for a few moments, and I start to worry. Am I some sort of risk to him? Was I wrong? Or is he just angry that I outperformed?

"You protected me," he says, looking down at the tablet. "Why?"

I don't answer. I can't. It doesn't make sense, but nothing with my master makes sense.

"Sascha, I treated you like a dumb animal and threatened to give you away," he reminds me. "Why would you protect me?"

I don't know how to explain it. I could tell him that he's better than the brothel, he's better than Bobby, he's better than the unknown, but those would all be lies, and he's told me so many times not to lie to him. I don't know how to tell him that I want to be his partner. I can't deny my feelings for him, no matter how illogical they are.

"Why do you think?" I challenge. Isn't it obvious that I'm infatuated with him?

He shakes his head. "Just go back to your room, Sascha," he mutters.

I don't argue. I go back and lie in my bed, wondering if I will ever be enough for him.

Chapter 22
Raising Stakes

I need to be alone to think, to revel in my good fortune. The good fortune that my little good luck charm brought me. I had worried so much about that data, and here he had hidden it with some sort of magic, or so it seemed. I try to focus on the tablet, trying to figure out how he did it. It crosses my mind only briefly that he might have just deleted it from the tablet; he said he didn't, and I trust him. I shouldn't trust the deceptive little slave, but I do. It's a strange feeling, one that is made stranger by the fact that I can't get his face out of my mind, even though he stays in his room for days, obeying my last order. I bring him plates of food without speaking to him, wondering why it's so important to me that he eats. I can't sell him; even if I could bring myself to be so cruel, I couldn't afford to have the limited secrets he knows out in the public. Besides, I want him around.

If our roles had been reversed, I would have let me sink and drown under my own lies and cruelty. I would have enjoyed the spite and the power, and I would have enjoyed the suffering. It frightens me how much I am really like my mother, no matter how much I try to avoid being so.

After a few days, I summon the courage and make my way to his room. I open the door and stand there, stunned when he jumps up, smiling like he's excited to see me.

I pull away, startled by his unexpected happiness. I've grown used to his pouting; the desperate reverence throws me off.

"We need to talk, Sascha."

I lose my nerve, turning away and walking down the hall to my office. After a few steps, I realize he's not following, and I wonder if he thinks I'm testing him or something. He's smart, but sometimes he has no common sense. I would never waste that much time, except that I did last time I punished him. Sometimes, I have no common sense.

"Don't take all goddamn day," I call over my shoulder, pleased when I hear footsteps behind me.

I go to my office and sit at my desk, leaving Sascha to stand awkwardly in front of me. I feel safe here, in control, and it helps to clear my mind. I think of the first time I brought him in here, how I ordered him to kneel and proceeded to grill him about his life. He was just as terrified of me then as he is now, but for different reasons. He doesn't need to be, now. He moves to go to his knees.

"Don't you get *enough* rest now?" I snap, irritated that he's acting like this. It's easier to snap than to tell him how I feel.

He stands again, thrown off, and puts his hands behind his back, like it hides his fidgeting.

I can't say anything for a few minutes. I'm still furious at him for snooping, but I'm grateful for his help. More than anything, I'm curious about him. I can't figure him out, and it bothers me.

"Just what were you hoping to find out about me?" I demand.

"I don't know, master." He cringes as he says it, and I can see him growing more afraid the angrier I get

"You don't know." I repeat his words back, unbelieving. "And you didn't know why you helped me, either? Or are you just not telling me?"

"I don't know, master," he says again, looking miserable.

We're silent for a moment he looks like he's waiting for me to hit him, or at least yell at him.

"Did you find what you were looking for?" I ask.

He stands there, looking trapped. "The search results didn't tell me anything, master."

"From what I can see on the history of your tablet, that is perfectly correct. Do you remember why I said I never wanted a slave, Sascha?"

"Yes, master," He says, looking away. "I believe you said they were pesky and underfoot."

Sascha has proven to be exactly that, but he is so much more. If he didn't look so terrified, it would be comical. "You're that, but you're helpful, too," I concede. "I really appreciate what you did for me the other day, with my mother. You know, I've never outsmarted her, before. I thought I was hiding so well, but she caught it. You fixed it before I even knew it was a problem."

"Yes, master," he responds.

I stare at him for a moment, trying to figure him out.

"Did you want me to show you where the data is hidden on my tablet?" he offers, as if he's reading my mind. I want to tell him no, to tell him that I've already figured it out and don't need a slave to help me do it, but I've spent days, and I've gotten nowhere but the decoy information.

"Yes, please."

With a satisfied smile on his face, Sascha comes over and shows me his amazingly elegant disguise. In just seconds, the entire dataset is available. I haven't lost anything. He's saved more than my reputation.

"Did you read it?" I ask, curious as to how much he knows. The second the question leaves my lips, I realize he won't answer. My mother's training system used tricks like that all the time, setting a slave up for perceived success, then tricking them into admitting that they had lied, or cheated, or stolen. They were shown over and over again that there was no way to win, and I don't want Sascha to fail again. "Never mind. That sounds like a setup for punishment. Forget I asked."

"I didn't, sir," Sascha replies, glancing up at me. I study his eyes, for once seeing nothing but honesty there. "I knew you didn't want me looking, you had told me not to pry into it before. You're good to me. I don't want to mess that up."

His words are so bold, so painfully true and stark that I have to believe him. He is so much more trustworthy than I am. I was going to sell him out and place the blame on him. He has to know that's why I put the data on his tablet. As much as I tried to justify it to myself that we would both be safer, it was a lie. I was hiding behind him, cowardly, and still he stepped up to take my place without question. As much as I've tried to avoid feeling anything but annoyance toward Sascha, I can't help it now. I am not only grateful, I am in awe of my slave, and ashamed of my own behavior.

I've never seen my master look as scared as he did when his mother was here, and I've never seen him at such a loss for words as he is now.

"Is everything all right, master?"

"It's fine."

I can tell that he's lying. Something happened when his mother came here, something far more important than a visit from an estranged mother. "This isn't just a family conflict, sir, it's obvious. There's something else going on, something with the research you're doing."

"Good, you figured it out," my master replies, looking away from me. "Now you can stop asking questions and sticking your nose where it doesn't belong."

His tone tells me to shut the hell up, and common sense does too, but I ignore both those things. "What did I hide for you, master?"

"Leave it, Sascha!" He warns, glaring at me. "You know nothing about it!"

Nothing about it? I've worked on this project with him for months. I lacked the details, but it didn't stop me from putting hours of labor into it, and it didn't stop me from outsmarting his mother. When she was here, I watched him act more strangely than I've ever seen him act before, and as a slave, my well-being is directly linked to his. "Nothing, master? Is that because you never tell me anything, or because I'm just a stupid slave?"

If he wasn't sitting at his desk, I'd be wincing, because I deserve to be slapped for a comment like that. He doesn't move, though.

"You are most certainly not stupid," he says, rolling his eyes. The dismissal hurts more than the slap would have. "And I don't think I treat you that badly for a defiant slave who has no respect for limits. Do I?"

I think back to the first few weeks that I was here, the harsh orders, the threats, the way they continued. And I think about the free rein I have around the house, the tablet that I used to have before I pried into my master's life, the meaningful work he's given me, and the care he's taken to make sure I'm healthy and at least somewhat content. And then I think again about his orders, or the way he ignores me, or the punishments he's subjected me to, no matter how deserved they were.

"You beat me, master," I mumble, unable to put any other thoughts into words.

"Yes, because you can't keep a civil tongue in your mouth," he replies, calm. "What was I supposed to do? Give you the day off without pay? I hate to repeat myself, but you know nothing about what's going on here. I've done my best to give you what I can, but there are boundaries, especially when other people are involved."

I think about all the times I've been sullen and defiant, all the times that I'm sure any other master would have hurt me or sold me. The only times he's done anything of the sort has been when I've taken my childish actions public. His image is the only thing he spends more time protecting than he does me.

He stands up, grabbing my tablet off of his desk as he does. He walks over and shoves it at me as I stand there gaping at him.

"What is this?" I ask, old training making me wonder if he really wants me to read it.

"The data that you hid from my mother," my master replies. "It's my current research project."

I go silent, reading through the information that I had only scanned when I found it, afraid of punishment, afraid of finding out more than I should have known. It's only the raw data, though, that, and a collection of names and addresses. I know there's more to it; for all this tells me, my master could be completing a research project for the State Department of Demoted People. What's more; I know from hiding the file that there is far more information than what I'm looking at right now.

"Happy?" he asks, still not looking at me. I realize it's how he handles lying to me, or hiding things. I can't tell if he's embarrassed or if he just doesn't want to give anything away.

As a good slave, I should say yes, kiss his feet for the tidbit of information, smile like a fool and pretend to be happy. I should be grateful and not let him know that I know there's far more to the project than what he just revealed to me.

"Where's the rest of it?" I ask, instead.

"That's it," he lies. "You're looking at it."

I go quiet for a minute. He should have punished me for questioning him, but he gave me an out. He'll let this go if I do, but I don't want to let it go. I set the tablet back down on the desk and push it back at him.

"We both know that there's far more than this, sir," I say quietly, wishing he wasn't standing close enough to hurt me. I've been hurt before, but it's been a long time since I've been this interested in something.

He finally looks at me, shooting a glare at me like he's trying to burn me with his eyes. I don't back down.

"I've told you enough," he replies, his voice restrained. I can see the way his shoulders tighten.

"You don't tell me anything, master!" I contradict him like an idiot. "You don't tell me anything about this big secret, you don't tell me about half the work you do, you didn't tell me where Bobby went or what your mother has to do with anything or why your image is so important! Your mother showed up out of nowhere and was really weird, and scary, and I saved your ass and I don't even know what I saved it from! How am I supposed to work with you if you don't tell me anything?"

He grabs me by the shoulders and pins me against the wall, his face hard and angry. "You don't work *with* me. You work *for* me. You're a slave, and don't you dare forget that."

"Then use me like a slave."

He shakes me, once, and draws back his hand to hit me. At least, I think that's what he's going to do.

I close my eyes. Instead of feeling flesh striking flesh, I feel a hand cup behind my head and as I'm slammed against the wall again, my head is cushioned and I feel lips pressing against my own.

Chapter 23

Used

I've never understood the way that books and movies describe sudden kisses. They say that kisses happen "unexpectedly" or "out of nowhere," but this one does really catch me by surprise. Maybe it shouldn't have, because what else should I expect; I'm a sex slave, and I demanded that my master use me.

I'm in shock for all of a quarter of a second, wondering if my master really hit me hard enough to knock me out, and then I realize that's not the case, and he's actually kissing me, and *holy fuck*.

I waste no time before I start kissing him back, ignoring logical things like fear and common sense and focusing instead on the rough grip of his hand on the back of my head and the forceful, demanding pressure of his tongue as it invades my mouth. He's hard and unrelenting, pressing his body up against mine, and I feel my cock starting to rise. It's as hot as I ever imagined. And I've imagined it a *lot* of times.

Of course, it ends more quickly than my fantasies do, and he shoves himself away, staring at me with a mix of lust and horror. He doesn't say anything, but the look says enough. I've see it enough times. The pity. The disgust. It's the look that you give a washed-up whore who's stupid enough to still have emotions left. It's the look that you give a stupid boy who doesn't have the common sense to know that his master would never dream of lowering himself by fucking such a washed-up whore, even if the washed-up whore is supposed to be a sex slave.

I feel rage and tears rising up where my hard-on used to be.

"You liked that," he says, finally. He doesn't sound happy about it.

"What did you think, master?" I snap, wishing it didn't hurt that he's looking at me like that. I wish he would have slapped me instead. "You know what you bought. A whore."

"I didn't think..." he stops, looking confused. "I was trying to scare you. Threaten you. You didn't like it. Before, I mean. Bobby. Mr. Dean. You didn't like what either of them did to you. I doubt you were enjoying yourself at that brothel, either. You don't like people to touch you — you don't even like when other people *look* at you for fuck's sake."

"I like it when *you* look at me, master," I mumble, figuring I may as well come clean. He's seen and felt enough of my "excitement" that I may as well. Shame be damned.

My master stands in front of me, glaring, for a few more minutes.

I wait for him to hit me, or yell at me, or walk away, or do something. He just stares into my eyes like I'm some kind of goddamned alien. At that moment, I don't care that he's my master and I'm being disrespectful, all I want is to get away from him. I turn to flee and he grabs me again, pinning me back against the wall and slamming his lips against mine again, longer this time, giving me enough time to fight back first before I give in and start kissing him back. I drop the tablet he shoved at me earlier, letting it hit the floor without a second thought, and my hands come up to clutch at his chest. I want to feel more of him, to prove that this is really happening.

He pulls away again, still pinning me to the wall like he's afraid I'll run away. His eyes are wide, but not disgusted this time. He seems pleased.

"You really liked it," he says again, softly this time.

"Yes, master," I whisper, afraid to move. I feel like speaking too loudly or moving might break the spell, and we'll go back to not-touching.

"You have some sort of crush on me."

I can't tell if it's a statement or a question. "You would have realized that if you had ever paid attention to me, master."

"All I ever noticed was you being terrified of me," he replies, not taking my bait. "That's all the more I thought I needed to know."

"I'm that, too, master." I shrug. The two things aren't mutually exclusive in my mind. I'm terrified of him *and* I have a crush on him.

So what?

"You should be," he says, less terrifying than any number of other things he's said. He leans in and kisses me again, slower this time, until I feel myself starting to melt into him. I feel one of his hands move from my shoulder, where he has me pinned against the wall, and down my body. He doesn't caress my skin so much as demand that it yield to him, laying claim to every inch as he moves down. He presses his hand between my legs, cupping against my cock and pressing in just the right places to make me whimper and want to beg for more. I settle on kissing him back.

He doesn't pull away this time, he just migrates from my lips to my neck, biting hard enough that I know there will be a mark tomorrow. The thought appeals to me. My legs threaten to sag as he grinds against me, and I finally give in and clutch at his arms, steadying myself. I stare at the wall across from us, my vision blurring as the world shrinks to nothing but the dark shade of green paint on the wall and the way my master's body feels pressed up against mine. Nothing else matters right now.

"I want to fuck you," he growls in my ear.

It's not sappy or romantic, but I'd never expect that from my master. I'd expect... this. I think I moan, I'm not really sure at this point.

He bites at my ear, the sharp pain focusing me for a minute and making me realize that I should probably say something.

"Please," I reply, realizing that my eyes are closed and forcing them to open.

He pulls back a little, frowning at me. "Please what?"

"Please, master!" I correct myself instantly, horrified that I got so caught up as to forget. It's sobering, but didn't he just remind me a few minutes ago that I shouldn't forget that I'm a slave? He scowls at me and shakes his head, worrying me even more.

"Sascha, I don't care about *that*—please do what *to you*?" he clarifies. "Are you begging me to fuck you like I want to or to leave you alone? I can never fucking tell with you."

"Oh," I say, startled by his consideration. He has always been direct, though. "I, um, please fuck me, master?" In all my fantasies, I'm wantonly begging when I say this; right now, I kind of whimper it. Not exactly the mood I want to convey.

The hand on my cock presses harder, and I suddenly find myself gasping for breath.

"Is that a question?" he asks, half-rhetorically. There's a dangerous glint in his eyes.

I shake my head, unable to speak. I want him so bad, but suddenly there's not enough air to use to make words.

"Sascha, don't try to be subtle. Neither one of us is any good at it," he orders, looking me in the eyes. "Do you want to fuck or not?"

I fight the dryness in my mouth until words form. "Yes, master. I want you to fuck me. I do. I've wanted it for a long time."

He holds me there for a few more seconds before releasing his grip.

"Go into my bedroom and wait for me."

I nod, unable to tear my eyes away from him until I start walking. I go into his bedroom, standing next to the bed awkwardly. Do I dare to sit on it? No. I'm so shaken up that I don't even have any idea if that would be okay, and I'm not quite sure what he wants from me, anyway. Actually, I have no idea why he ordered me to come in here while he stays out in the hallway or wherever he is. A part of me wonders if he just wants to make me more anxious, but I'm about to start hyperventilating, so his plan is probably going to backfire.

My questions are answered soon, as he comes in with two bottles of water.

"Strip," he orders, casual and confident.

I move slowly, my hands and limbs not cooperating like I want them to. I'm scared, fuck it, I'm goddamned terrified, but I do want this. I think. I do want to do this, but I also want to run and hide, because everything is moving so fast, and what if I screw up, and what if I don't please him? I have so many questions in my head, now that it's actually happening, that I wish everything could just be as easy as it is in my fantasies. I can barely work the buttons on my shirt, although I've managed to get them all undone. Now to figure out how to take it off my body.

He comes up to me and rolls his eyes as he grabs the waistband of my pants and jerks me close.

"You always do take forever," he growls in my ear, making me whimper.

The thing is, I can't tell if it's a good whimper or a bad whimper.

I don't think about the sounds I'm making for much longer, though, because he's unfastening my jeans with ease and jerking them down along with my boxers before I know what's happening. The only other time he's done this it was for punishment, and this feels so different that it seems like some sort of sacrilege to even compare them. The cool air and the fact that I'm nearly naked gets me turned on again, and I feel some of the anxiety starting to recede in the face of the excitement.

Once he's shoved my pants down, he pushes me back onto the bed and I sit immediately, awed when he takes the pants from around my ankles and tosses them aside. He finishes by grabbing my shirt and yanking it off in one fluid movement. I'm speechless and hard. Could he really be as eager to get this started as I am? I didn't know it was possible.

I yelp as I feel his hand encircle my cock, and my eyes fly up to meet his. He's grinning, a predatory look that should be scary but is also so fucking sexy that I have to catch my breath. I want to say something, but I can't speak. I settle for breathing, because if I don't, I might pass out.

"Lie back," he orders, stroking my cock.

I do, staring up at the ceiling and wondering if this is all some sort of strange dream. His hand feels so good, and his other hand is resting lightly on my leg, and all of a sudden I feel him shift positions and then my cock is in his mouth and I yelp again. It feels wonderful, being sucked like this, but it's so wrong, so different than I ever expected. I start to sit up, horrified that he's the one sucking my cock instead of the other way around. It feels amazing, but I'm supposed to be the slave, and he's supposed to be the master, and everything is just too good to believe, so I guess I feel like I have at least try to fuck it up.

"Sir, you don't have to—"

"I told you to lie back, and I will be deciding what I do with you." His words are blunt and harsh, as usual, but the usual coldness is replaced by a sort of teasing tone. He's still the one in control, here.

I lie back.

His lips wrap immediately around my cock again, and I try to push away the uncomfortable feeling. If anything, his insistence makes it better, because I know that this is what he wants, and I guess I shouldn't protest. I do protest, a few moments later, when I feel him pull off of my cock. I whine and crane my neck to look at him, eager for him to continue.

"You are enjoying this, I assume?" he asks, that teasing tone still there.

"Mm hmm," I manage, moaning and twisting my hips up in hopes of more. My wish is quickly granted.

He treats me to the most wonderful blowjob. I don't know what I did to deserve this, because he always acts like I annoy him, but if that's the case, I should start annoying him more. He does things with his mouth that I didn't even learn during two years of slave training. When he lent me out, his boss went down on me, but it wasn't like this. My master seems to do some sort of acrobatics with his tongue, and he's putting pressure in just the right places, and sucking just enough, and he's using his hands to stroke and touch around my cock and balls and ass and the more I think about it, the more I want him inside me.

He toys with me for a while, making me moan and squirm, and finally I feel myself starting to get close, wishing I could let go.

"Please, master," I whimper, appalled by how pathetic and desperate I sound. Still, I wouldn't trade it for the world.

He pulls away, and it's all I can do not to grab him by the hair and tug him back down. It's really nice to not be hurt, though.

"I'm enjoying you," he informs me, his voice all low and sultry and content.

If he was still going down on me, those words would have sent me over the edge, training or not.

"I can see that you're enjoying me, too," he continues. He presses his fingers against my ass. "Do you still want to fuck?"

"Yes, master," I reply instantly, spreading my legs so he has better access. I want to fuck more than pretty much anything, at the moment.

The very tip of his finger breaches me and I take a deep, gasping breath, my hands clutching the sheets tightly. He knows exactly what he's doing, and it's not long before he's twisting ever so slightly inside of me, biting at the inside of my legs as he does it.

"You're sure?" he teases, pausing for a moment. "Because if you really want, I can get you off right now and we can call it a night."

I force my eyes to open so I can see his face, familiar, but still so unusual. He's smirking at me. He doesn't smirk!

"Oh god, yes, master, please, I want you inside of me." Christ, I'm desperate. "Fuck me!"

"Don't move," he orders, moving away.

It's all I can do not to cry when I feel his hands and mouth leaving my body.

It's not for long, of course, he returns with what I assume is lube. My suspicions are confirmed a few seconds later when his hands return, slippery now, and he forces two fingers inside of me while gripping my hip tightly. I arch and moan and almost try to move away before I realize it feels good.

I hear him make a low sound of pleasure and it sends sparks through my body. I rock with his movements, wanting more of him.

He plays with my cock while he fucks me with his fingers, alternating between licking and sucking and biting and jerking it with the hand that he's not using on my ass. Between the attention my cock is getting and the attention my ass is getting, I want to come, I need to come so bad I can almost taste it, but I know better, and I want to wait for him to be inside of me anyway.

"Please, master, don't make me wait any longer," I beg, giving up all hopes of shame. "Fuck me before I come!"

My master laughs, pulling his fingers out of me and making me squeal with frustration. "Don't you fucking dare," he warns, clamping his hand around my cock. "Move back."

He uses my cock like a joystick, guiding me back further on the bed. I'd be offended, except it feels so goddamned good, and despite his actions he's surprisingly gentle. When I have the presence of mind to look at him, he's smiling.

"Much better," he decides, climbing onto the bed with me. "I hate being uncomfortable."

He's half-sitting, half-kneeling between my legs, and I watch as he takes a moment to apply a generous amount of lube to his cock. I'm surprised, because I'm sure I'd be ready as it is, but I appreciate it anyway. All I want is him inside of me.

After what seems like forever, he leans forward, guiding his cock toward me. He pauses, just barely pressing against my body.

"What—"

"Shh," he says, holding a finger to my lips.

I stay silent, staring up at him as he waits for some unheard signal before slipping himself into me in one long, smooth motion. I try to keep focused on his face, but it's too much, the pleasure and the denial and the absurdity of the situation, so I close my eyes and give in to the sensation.

He's slow for that first stroke, but after that he speeds up, thrusting in and out so fast I lose track and simply hold onto the sheets as if they'll protect me. He has one hand on my cock, pumping in time with his own thrusts, and the other is on my hip, pressing me down as if I'm about to go somewhere.

The feeling is amazing. He's fucking me hard enough that it hurts, just a little, enough that I can get off from it. The hand on my hip is probably going to leave bruises, too, and I love that just as much. I struggle to contain myself, knowing I won't last long. I want to wait, hoping he'll order me to come for him, but he doesn't, he just keeps driving into me and stroking my cock, and I'm afraid I'll ruin it by coming too soon.

"I need to come, master," I finally give in. "Please? Let me?"

He doesn't say anything, he just smiles and increases the pace, fucking me and stroking me harder.

I panic a little. It feels too good. He's going too fast, this has been too much of a fantasy. I won't be able to stop myself and I know it and somehow the anxiety gets me more turned on.

My eyes are pressed shut as my orgasm rips out of my body, accompanied by screams and shaking and trembling. I almost don't care if I've done something wrong, because it felt so good and it still feels good. I could be killed right now and it would be worth it.

I hear my master make a little sound of pleasure, and when I finally look up at him, I see him smiling. He can't be angry at me, I realize, and it occurs to me that his goal the whole time was to make me break, to force me to lose control like this. I don't mind, because it seems like he is perfectly aware of how turned on the whole situation made me, and I'm still elated from the orgasm he just gave me.

He keeps fucking me; it seems like he could last forever. In reality, it's probably only a few minutes more, and when he comes, he grabs my hips in both of his hands and jerks me to him, making me cry out at the deep thrust. I feel him come inside of me and shudder a few times before pulling out, his hands still holding me down.

He takes a few deep breaths and I follow suit, not eager to disrupt the moment. Finally, he slips off the bed, looking at me pointedly and ordering me to stay before disappearing into his bathroom.

My head reels. Did this just happen? Reality comes back quickly once I'm alone, and all the anxieties and fear and uncertainty that had been chased away by the wonder of sex start flooding back in, and I wonder if I just made a mistake. I start to tremble, slightly at first, and then all over, everywhere, my skin breaking out in goosebumps. I close my eyes and try to figure out what the hell just happened.

"You okay?"

My master's voice cuts through the panic.

I open my eyes to look up at him, surprised that they *can* still open, surprised that my heart can still beat. Didn't that just throw the world off balance or something?

He sits next to me and I try not to flinch when he raises his hand with an object in it.

"Relax, Sascha," he orders, his voice calmer than usual. He doesn't say anything else, but he takes the towel he brought with him and carefully wipes my body clean with it.

I don't say anything as he takes care of me, because I don't know what to say. Anything I think of seems inadequate; besides, I think words might break the spell that seems to have come over him. I'm still nervous, but I don't want this moment to end.

He finishes washing me up and opens a bottle of water, passing it to me with an expectant look on his face. Right. Drinking. Hydration is good.

While I'm trying to remember how to swallow, he goes to the other side of the bed and makes his way under the covers, leaving me lying there confused. Do I stay with him? Go back to my room, slinking away like a whore? I shouldn't even consider thinking that this changes things; I am still his unwanted slave, he is still my cold and distant master. This had to have been just sex. I set the bottle of water down next to the bed, suddenly aware that I'm naked and exposed. The fact that he's naked as well makes no difference; something tells me that he could show up at work naked and claim that it was the latest fashion trend and nobody would question him.

"The light's on your side," my master says calmly, as if this is nothing unusual. As if he didn't just subtly invite me to sleep in his bed. "Just above your head."

I reach up and hit the switch wordlessly, plunging us into darkness. It's not cold, but it's awkward to lie on top of the blankets, so I scrunch my legs up under me until I can get under them, stretching out hesitantly and lying on the pillows. I remind myself again that this had to have been just sex, but even the harsh reminder doesn't make me feel any less happy to be here right now. I try to tell myself it's just because his pillows are *very* comfortable.

Chapter 24
Coming Clean

I wake the next day to see Sascha fast asleep next to me, curled up in my blankets like he's meant to be there. I watch him, just for a few moments, while I think about what we did last night. The sex was undeniably amazing; there's no doubting that there is chemistry between us. I just never thought it would be acted upon. I'm not sure what provoked me to kiss him like that. I wanted to scare him, but he ended up liking it. I did too, far more than I expected. The fantasies I have tried not to have about him are nothing compared to the real thing.

I'm not sure what to do with it, so I creep out of bed as quietly as possible. I return to my office, make sure my tablet is still working after we dropped it last night, and keep working, trying not to let myself get distracted with memories of last night. It's a while longer before I hear Sascha up and about, showering in my bathroom again. He's bold, spending quite a while in there. I wonder if he'll find the towel I left out for him.

After a while, I hear him walking down the hallway. "Sascha, start coffee?" I request. "And get back in here when you're done, I have some projects for you to pick up on."

I have the work ready for him, but he takes even longer than usual, returning with a toasted bagel like we're on vacation. He hasn't been allowed out of his room for days, and he's already putting aside my orders. I frown, wondering how much I'm spoiling him.

"When I tell you to get back in here, I mean immediately," I point out. "Now, look at this."

He looks wary. I push it aside, just like I push aside the newfound realization of just how attractive he is. I've ignored it successfully

189

for months, but today, it's like a spotlight follows him around, high-lighting his best features as I try to ignore them and think platonic thoughts. I have no interest in abandoning my work because I have a pretty boy to fuck; I've gotten behind enough with the power struggle I engaged Sascha with.

"I need you to research some figures for me," I explain, giving him a list of the companies I'm interested in. If he resents the past two weeks, he doesn't show it; he seems excited to be working again, if not a little distracted.

"Is this public information, or will I have to hunt a bit?" he asks.

I realize he's asking whether he'll need to break through anyone's security to get what I need. "It's not public," I admit, still uncomfortable with him helping me commit these sorts of crimes.

"I'll need my tablet," he says, eyeing me warily. "And some of the blocks that you put on it..."

He won't just ask me to remove them; that would be too easy. "Restore it to the last point you had it at," I concede. "Stick to work."

"Yes, master," he agrees, keeping his eyes down and focusing on his breakfast.

He doesn't question me further, and we go about our day as we used to, no indication that last night ever happened, nor the punishment I subjected him to. I don't know how to bring last night up, especially not the questions we left unanswered in exchange for a night of passion. More than anything, I don't know how to tell him why I was so angry without revealing everything. I wonder if I should; after all, he's as deep into this as I am. I've been burned before, though, and I don't want him pulled into this if it will put him in danger.

Of course, being involved with me and opposing my mother has already put him in danger. I need to put that lie aside and give him the information he needs to keep us both safe.

"I found a way to distract you from asking about my research last night," I start, a little hesitant. He glances up, a shy smile that encourages me more than anything else he could possibly do. "But you deserve to know about it."

He stands there quietly, waiting for me to make the next move.

"Bring a chair over here, and give me your tablet for a moment," I order, moving my own aside so he can sit next to me at my desk.

When he does, I open the files I have hidden, not only the benign data that I showed him last night, but incriminating data. I hand it over to him. "That's all of it."

The files outline my current project. It is one of the secrets I've hidden from Sascha for months, the information I once smacked him for looking at accidentally. It's the project that he puts at risk every time he speaks out of turn.

Ten years ago, I started to research the Demoted. In particular, I was interested in the re-education centers, the industry my mother had shaped into the cold system of torture and brainwashing that it is now. My research started as a spiteful vendetta against my mother, but what I found had far-reaching implications. Simply put, the re-education centers made slaves less useful. I wanted to find a better system, but that meant defying my mother and challenging the current system; the system that the governments of many nations had adopted. I was young, careless. My mother found out. She reported me to the state officials and had me arrested on treason charges. She insisted that she was protecting me, but she was just protecting herself. The Miller System had always been more important than her son.

Fortunately, she didn't find all my data. I was able to recreate most of my original research proposal.

Everything I've hidden so carefully I'm offering to Sascha. It's uncomfortable; I've never shared this much of my work with anyone, not to mention this much of myself. My plans for funding are all laid out, potential associates, risks, benefits. The research proposal itself is simple, just a reboot of what I did before. It's the sharing that is a challenge.

He could destroy me with this, if he wanted to. While I should be able to silence him, I doubt I could go through with it. That's not the biggest thing that concerns me, though. He could be in danger from knowing everything, especially about the past project, the failure, my family's connections. My mother is a threat, but I can't see how knowing about that threat will make Sascha any safer.

The decision not to tell him everything is easy enough to justify. It will keep him safe and it will simplify things. A part of me wants to start new with him. The way he looks up at me, waiting, trusting, only makes it that much easier. I want to be the person he sees when he looks at me like this.

"I ran a pilot test a few years back," I tell him, disguising the truth. I can tell him about a pilot test without telling him about my mother, or my imprisonment, or just how dangerous this really is. "I had researched the Demoted in college, and I knew that the whole Demoted system was flawed, starting with the re-education centers. We waste valuable intellectual resources by Demoting people who might otherwise be key in innovation and invention."

Sascha raises an eyebrow at me, looking impressed.

"So I bought a *lot* of slaves, all sorts, but especially the ones who seemed bright. Those who did things like you did, when I found you at the brothel. The ones who were bold, defiant, willing to take risks. I hired some university students as well, and I subjected both groups to the same testing procedures, and do you know what I found?"

"They weren't all that different," Sascha hypothesizes.

I smile, pleased that he's thinking along the same lines that I did. "Not only were they not that different, but in more cases than one, the Demoted people came out *higher* on practical tests. Following instructions. Attention to detail. Creative thinking. Despite many having lower Assessment scores and often lower IQ scores than their free counterparts, there was a certain subset who outperformed them on every task."

Sascha sits there, looking utterly unsurprised. My involvement seems to surprise him, but not the research himself. Then again, he's part of the group who I'm sure would have excelled on any of the measures I used to test my subjects. He looks a little angry, probably that I haven't told him this before, but more than anything, he seems curious. I know he's thinking about everything he's seen, integrating it flawlessly with the way I've acted and what he knows. He puts things together so quickly that I don't worry about dumping this much information on him. Even when he drops the tablet and looks away, I'm pretty sure it's more a case of emotional overload.

"Come on, Sascha, you've had eight thousand questions for me since I bought you," I point out, apologetic. I should have answered all of this so much sooner.

"I've done a bit of research on the Demoted myself," Sascha mentions, casual. "I never noticed anything legitimate about the differences, just a lot of fringe stuff. Questionable methods; most of it is easily discredited."

No, he wouldn't have found my research. It was silenced, thanks to Kristine Miller. But I don't tell him that.

I shrug. "It didn't amount to much. Research like that surfaces every few years, abolitionist movements try to bring it to light and nobody cares. But that wasn't the most important thing I found. I noticed that slaves from different re-education centers performed vastly differently from one another, enough that it stood out in the data without even having to run statistical analyses on it. That suggested a problem, and a far more interesting research question. The re-education centers run on a standardized curriculum of sorts, government mandated, but the implementation of the rules varies from place to place. And it's in this variation that I noticed that some slaves were performing better, others worse, others... well, let's just say that some were unable to perform at all."

Sascha waits, staring at me intently, eager for more. I continue.

"The re-education centers with the most violations — that is, record of the most humane treatment — produced the brightest slaves. The ones who had been cited repeatedly for inadequate punishments, overfeeding, coddling — those were the ones who produced the brightest and most capable slaves." I stop, bitter at the thought of all the research I wasted. But I have a chance to try again now, and I have someone to help. "I made it my mission to figure out how we can stop wasting potential, how we can fix the Demoted system. It's been my obsession since I was a teenager."

"Why aren't you working for the State Department?" Sascha asks.

It's a reasonable question; State Department jobs are lucrative and provide quite a bit of security for their employees. Unfortunately, my mother ensured that I would never have that opportunity. Without telling Sascha what transpired in the past, I can't answer that honestly.

"The system is too broken to fix from the inside," I say. "Besides, the money is to be made from privatization. The re-education centers are privately owned, just government contracted."

Sascha nods. "The Miller System," he recalls. "I bet the woman who invented that has more money than she knows what to do with."

I nod. My mother never worried about money. It was her security and her weapon. It still is. Sascha hasn't made the connection yet, and I'm pleased to see that I can still keep some secrets to myself.

"So, why did you stop?" he asks.

The court order played a big part in it, as had the fear of going to prison. But if I tell Sascha, he might back out, turn against me. I've given him enough reason to, and even if he wants to stay, the knowledge could still be used against him. "It wasn't the right time," I say instead.

Sascha gives me a doubtful look. It's the same look I give him when he's doing a poor job of lying to me.

"I needed to have a stronger case," I try again. It's partially true. "I didn't want to get dismissed like the rest of the research. I wanted to succeed; when I finally finished my research, I wanted it to be flawless. Besides, I'm not completely removed from that world. Even my position at Dean & Chanu is helping me gain legitimacy in the field. I started working there as a financial analyst, but I became their expert on the slave industry. Clearinghouses, matching organizations, research, re-education centers. Medical research, that's how I found out that a good portion of the Demoted are used as medical test subjects. For every brilliant pathologist who is discovering the cure to new diseases, thousands of Demoted are killed testing the cure. I orchestrated my position carefully, and now I have relationships with all the major players. I know which ones will provide data, which ones won't, which ones are in a poor enough financial position that their silence can be bought while I test their slaves."

Sasha's look is somewhere between hopeful and cautious. I can see him battling with himself and the new information. "What does that do for you?"

"It gives me connections," I answer honestly. "I can start my research again... for real, this time, not just my test project." It can protect me from my mother, but if I do it right, Sascha won't need to know about this threat.

"And when your research is finished?" he asks.

"I can destroy the Demoted system as we know it."

Chapter 25
Trust

I'm stunned. My master? An abolitionist? "So, then, your results could actually destroy the Demoted system? No more slaves?"

"What?" My master looks surprised. "No, I'm not against the Demoted system at all—I think it's rather logical, especially the sterilization part; it's been humanity's only successful response to overpopulation. Unemployment is virtually non-existent, crime is down, parents work harder to prepare their kids, who are getting smarter with each generation—the benefits far outweigh the costs. I think that slavery is practical for now; it just needs to be reworked. And I think that the research I am doing has the potential to leave a mark on the world forever—imagine, *my* name on the list of top researchers, my brand on the re-education centers. I want to revolutionize the system, give brighter slaves the chance to prosper and take the whole Demoted system to a new level."

"Oh." I guess every slave kind of hopes his master is a closet abolitionist.

"Don't look so crushed; I am not a fan of the current system. I strongly disagree that anybody needs to be treated worse than animals, which is how it usually works now. And still, plenty of people who are Demoted do well enough in life. I believe that they wouldn't have done well elsewhere, although they certainly aren't allowed to reach their full potential," my master explains. "The brighter ones are usually Demoted in the first place because of some stupid *choice* that they made, not because of any real lack of intellect. I mean, what if the person who could have cured a terminal illness never had the opportunity to do it just because he or she decided to party too much before the Assessment?"

I feel myself crashing back down to the real world a little bit. I suppose it's for the best, but for just a moment, I had allowed myself to hope that my master might be opposed to the system that hurt me so much. Instead, he wants a piece of the pie. "So, you don't think slavery is wrong, or anything?"

"Not inherently," my master dismisses the thought. "People are always subjugated in one form or another. At least this way, it's regulated. It's the treatment that appalls me, and more importantly, the destruction of potential and possibility. We live in a time when intellect is valued over all else, and yet we squander it so quickly?"

Right. Intellect *is* valued over human life, dignity, shame... "So it's like... an intellectual pursuit?" I manage. "Like finding the next prime number?"

My master shrugs. "It's that. It's a desire to change the way things work. It's prestige as well. I want my name to live on for recreating the Demoted system, particularly the re-education centers. I want a research institute in my name. If it's successful, it will be extremely lucrative as well. The money that can be made from something like this is astonishing."

I kind of think he makes enough damn money, but I don't say that. I don't say anything, and I certainly don't ask him if he ever feels some sort of moral compunction. I doubt he does, from what he's saying.

"I envision something more along the lines of job placement; apprenticeship, maybe," my master explains, no doubt seeing my disheartened look. "Involuntary job placement, with a side of sterilization, but still. The current system attempts to work like that in a way, but too much emphasis is placed on attitude and personality destruction. Sascha, I know you're smart, and I know where you ended up. You didn't end up being a brothel whore because you were unintelligent, you ended up there because you have a shitty attitude and you act like a spoiled brat when you're bored."

"Pretty much," I admit. It's true, even though it stings to hear it spelled out so clearly.

"Don't you think you would have been better off being treated with some respect, given work that interested you?" he suggests. "It would have been easier on you, and I think it honestly would have been easier on the trainers as well. If you need to transport something across a river, you don't stop the river from flowing; you use a ship *in* the river. I know you're not the only one who suffered needlessly, inside the re-education centers or outside of them. It's waste, all over, waste of time, waste of resources, waste of people."

I nod, allowing myself to consider the possibility. "If I had been placed with you immediately, I would have been a lot happier," I admit. "I would never have fought against the chance to work with you; I would have seen it as a perfect opportunity to learn more and have a secure life.

"Of course you would have," he nods. "Don't think you'd be the only one who would have been happier—I would have loved to take you on before anyone got a chance to torture you in the name of 're-education,' much less what happened at the brothel. Part of what's always frustrated me about you is that I *know* you're smarter than you act, I can see it just yearning to get out. You wouldn't have had to hide that, and I wouldn't have tried to treat you like a dumb beast."

I fume, thinking back to the early days, the days when he treated me like some sort of non-entity. I think of all the time he wasted, all the fear he caused. "You didn't talk to me or explain anything or do anything but order me around! You say you knew I was smart, why didn't you treat me like I was? You treated me like shit."

"I know," my master says. "And I shouldn't have. I wasted a lot of time ignoring you, but it was the only thing I knew to do. I didn't think you would have believed me if I had told you about the project earlier, and I wasn't sure I wanted you involved, anyway. I'm still not sure about that, but I can't continue to keep you in the dark. I didn't ever want a slave, Sascha. That much was true, and I certainly didn't want one like you."

I keep glaring at him.

"I felt like I had to have a slave so I could keep up appearances," he explains. "I resented that. I resented having to change my lifestyle to fit the image of the good slaveholder, to avoid the wrong kind of attention, and I resented that I had gotten caught up in some bull-headed slave from some cheap brothel that wouldn't be exactly what I wanted, because you weren't and you aren't. You don't look the part, except when a premiere makeup artist coats you in latex paint. And for a while, I thought you actually might be as stupid as you pretended to be, because you didn't make any moves to prove otherwise, and I thought... well, like I said, I never wanted slaves."

"You never gave me a chance to prove otherwise," I mutter. "Not for a long time."

"I know," my master says, nodding. "I should have. I should have done a lot of things differently with you."

I'm silent for a moment, letting the words wash over me. "You bought me for show," I realize, trying not to sound hurt. I fail. It's not like I think he fell in love with me at first sight, or that I was so clearly brilliant that he couldn't imagine life without me, but the cold fact that he needed a slave for his method acting hurts.

My master shrugs. "In part."

I try not to *look* upset, either, but I'm pretty sure I fail at that as well.

"I knew I needed a slave," my master explains. "I wasn't expecting to buy one when I did, and I certainly wasn't expecting to buy one from a place like that," my master explains. "But I'm glad I did."

"So, what, you just needed someone for the Peace Day Celebration? You really just picked up the first pretty whore that wasn't already claimed?" It hurts to know he thought that little of me.

"That was part of it. Although, you weren't so pretty back then. You looked sickly, beaten. I didn't know if you'd ever stop cowering away. But if you really want to know, it was that little stunt you pulled with the cards. I could have found a far more suitable slave practically anywhere else, but Bobby insisted on dragging me there. When you did that, I couldn't *not* be interested."

So my plan had worked back then.

"It wasn't just that it was a useful trick to bring out at the party, it was the fact that you could do it, and you thought to do it, and you risked yourself to make that offer to me, someone you didn't even know. You knew you would be severely beaten by that woman, but you calculated the risk and you did it anyway. It reminded me of the brighter subset of the Demoted that I tested years ago. The thought of leaving someone like you in a filthy brothel in the slums horrified me."

"Thank you," I mumble, trying not to blush now. I had always known I was taking a risk, but I never realized that the risk itself would be what drew him to me. Then again, I never planned for him to exploit me like this.

Slaves are made to be exploited, but somehow my master made me feel like I'd be exempt from that treatment. Maybe it's because he refused to lend me out, maybe it's because he ate with me sometimes or bought me nice clothes or let me help with important projects, but I stopped thinking he would use me like that months ago. The realization that he will use me if he needs to hurts, but it reminds me of my place. It also reminds me of how far we've come. He can only hurt me because I trust him; I haven't trusted anyone else to do anything but hurt me since being Demoted.

He lets it go quiet for a moment.

"Am I right in assuming there are other things you're not telling me?" I ask. He's given me so much already, but I have to know.

He nods. "Details. They could put you at risk, or me, or my project. But mostly, they could put you at risk. I hope you understand... Sascha, I've come to care about you a great deal. The harder I try not to, the more I do. But there are secrets that are better off left alone. I look forward to working with you, now that you know more, but I am still your master. It is my responsibility to make sure you're safe."

I accept his explanation. I don't like it, but I believe him when he says it will keep me safe, and I respect that he isn't lying to me outright. Out of courtesy, I will avoid digging deeper.

"What about your mother?" I ask, giving him a curious look. I can't figure out why she was here the other day, or why she was so interested in exposing my master.

"She's overbearing, and she feels like she's keeping me safe by hindering my progress," my master explains.

I wonder if he sees the parallel.

"Did she know about the test study you did?" I ask. For a moment, I think my master is going to shut me down again, tell me it's none of my business. Then he nods.

"She found out about it," he admits, looking away like he's uncomfortable to even talk about it. "She was part of the reason I decided to hold off, to build a stronger case. I'm her only child; she made it very clear that she thought I was in danger. Challenging the status quo... it can come with risks. And there are a lot of powerful people involved in the Miller System. My mother has done everything in her power to keep me out of that world, even when it hurts me. She says it's for my own good. I'm sorry you got caught in the middle of it."

I nod. My master is paranoid, so careful. I assume it's a family trait. The Demoted system makes parents very invested in their children's well-being, and if my master was endangering himself, it would only make sense that his mother would interfere. It feels like there is something more to it, but I can't put a finger on it. I've been given so much already; I won't pry into family conflict.

Sitting here, I almost forget that I'm a slave. Not because we lie about it, but because it suddenly fails to matter. I have a purpose, I have a question to investigate, and I have a have a man who likes me for more than sex or cleaning. Judging from the hungry look on his face, though, he's thinking of the first thing.

"You should probably get back to work," he suggests. "I hope I've answered your questions adequately."

"You have," I assure him, knowing that the remaining questions won't get answered anyway. "Thank you, sir. This means so much to me."

"You've exceeded my expectations from the moment I set eyes on you," he admits. "Even with the problems we've had, I don't regret buying you. I know I've threatened to sell you in the past, to give you away, even... that will never happen. You have a place with me as long as you want it."

I blush, stunned by his heartfelt confession. It's all I've wanted, from the first moment I set eyes on him.

Neither of us speaks another word, and I return to my office, starting on the work we discussed. He leaves me to it, and our few interactions are business as usual. By the end of the day, I've started to wonder if last night was a slip of judgment, a poor decision, a fluke that will never, ever happen again. Maybe we've reset, so to speak, to before the sex, before the incident with the tablet and my master's mother. Maybe it's better this way. I'm walking down the hall toward my room when I hear him stand up from his desk and come up behind me.

"Sascha?"

I freeze, not even turning around. "Yes, master?"

"If you're going to sleep in my bed again tonight, you should bring some clothes in for the morning. I have some things I need to do and I'll need you up early."

Chapter 26
Cashiel

Sascha turns to face me, surprise evident on his face. It takes him a few moments to process, and I start to wonder if I've made a mistake. I thought there was something between us, but he tries so hard to please me. I don't want it to be fake. Maybe it is for the best that he and I go our separate ways.

Then his face lights up. "Yes, master," he says, but his face shows his excitement, as does the speed with which he dashes off.

He's still excited when he meets me in my bedroom, but nervous as well. I look at the sliding glass doors that make up the better part of my east-facing wall, undressing slowly. We went so fast last night, I want to take my time tonight. I turn my head to see Sascha standing there, uncertain.

"There's some space in the nightstand that you're standing next to," I tell him.

He sets his clothes in the space that I've indicated, as well as his toothbrush and toothpaste. I consider telling him to put them in the bathroom, but I decide he can put his things where he feels most comfortable. He waits for me to tell him what to do.

"Come here," I order, taking the pressure off of him.

He comes to my side quickly, still looking nervous and excited. I doubt it's the act itself; he's not a blushing virgin by any means. It's me, us, the change in how we're interacting. I look at him and nod. This is good.

"Stand over there and strip," I order, pointing toward the doors. "Slowly. I want to watch."

He does as I ask, and turns to face me as he starts to remove his shirt.

"No, turn around," I correct. "Look outside."

I see him tense as he turns his back to me, but I trust he'll relax with time. I want him to see the view. The glass doors themselves are of excellent quality, and subtle etchings decorate the edges, framing the cityscape. We're close enough that the buildings are clearly visible, not just dots or outlines, but the greater expanse of the city dissolves into sparkling lights that complement the stars in the sky. Everything is visible from this spot, my own take on being on top of the world.

"The view is the main reason I bought this place," I mention, watching as Sascha twists, almost turning, then stays where I've ordered him, slowly continuing to remove his clothes. I smile at his self-control.

"That, and it's just far enough outside of the city that I can do pretty much whatever I want." This was my biggest concern when I bought the place. Privacy, seclusion. I had had enough of people; I wanted space. For years, it belonged only to me, and I never thought I wanted anyone else in it until I bought Sascha.

"It's beautiful, master." Sascha is down to just his underwear, and he slips them off seductively, leaving him naked.

"You should see it at sunrise," I comment, wondering if that will ever happen. I sit on the bed, getting comfortable before I give him his next order. "Turn around."

He obeys, turning to reveal his body to me. He's hard, as I am, and he looks scared and exposed, but not unwilling.

"One day, I'll have you stand there at sunrise," I decide, smiling at the thought.

I'm quiet, giving him the chance to take the lead if he wants to. I glance over his body, admiring it, thinking of the way he felt underneath me last night. He's covered in scars and marks, but even that doesn't make him any less attractive. He looks down after a moment, going red and starting to squirm. I wonder what he's terrified himself thinking about this time.

"Do you like to give head?" I ask, hoping I can bring him back from the hole he's lost himself in.

He responds automatically. "If it pleases you, master."

I sigh, hating the words. I may as well be working in a re-education center. "Sascha, how is it that you can be so goddamned annoying and difficult and obstinate when I ask you to do the simplest things and then when I ask you an honest fucking question give me some stock slave answer?"

He doesn't answer, he just looks ashamed.

"Let's try this again," I say more firmly. "Do you like to give head?"

This time, he actually thinks about it. "To the right person, master."

I laugh. He goes so quickly from disgustingly trained to almost offensive. "I suppose that's a little better," I admit. "What kind of people do you *like* to give head to?"

He looks confused, but he answers.

"I guess, people who enjoy it a lot, master?"

"Have you really met people who don't enjoy it?" I ask, laughing. "Go on."

"People who are gentle. And don't hurt me when they do it, master. People I find attractive."

Such simple preferences. I want him to ask for so much more.

I beckon him closer with my finger, and he obeys immediately. He stops an arm's length away from me, and I respond by reaching out and grabbing his hips, pulling him between my legs. I'm demanding, but he seemed to enjoy that last night. He looks nervous. I reach around him, stroking his legs and ass and lower back, pretty much everywhere I can reach. He relaxes the tiniest bit, but he still looks wary.

"You're so tense," I comment. Ordering him to stop would be counterproductive, but I'm not much good at comforting, either. "I'm not going to hurt you; relax."

I don't ask him to speak, yet, because he always struggles with that when he's scared—whether it's for a valid reason or not. His body is enjoying what I'm doing, I can feel his cock pressing against my leg. I showed him a good time last night, and I know he's attracted to me. This must be a huge change for him.

"You have my express permission to stop whenever you want to, or to say no," I remind him, hoping it will calm him. "I thought I made that clear enough last night, but it bears repeating. I don't want you to do this unless you're genuinely interested, and I won't be upset with you if you want to stop. I hope I've been clear enough with my expectations in the past that you can believe that, because it's the truth. So, with that in mind, would you like to go down on me?"

He looks shocked, but after a few moments, he replies, looking a little more secure. "Y-yes, master."

"Good," I say, smiling at him. I wait, letting him set the pace. I'm in no hurry, and I'm not about to put more pressure on him. When he sinks to his knees and looks up at me, I glide my hands over his back and shoulders, waiting eagerly.

He leans in tentatively, taking only the tip in his mouth. I feel him hesitating, taking my cock only slightly deeper into his mouth, swirling his tongue around it carefully. I could sit here for hours and let him explore my body.

I watch him, see his hair falling to frame his face. I reach up to run my hand through it, feeling the silky softness for only a moment before he takes a deep breath and braces himself, his lips and tongue going pliant.

"I'm not going to pull your hair or force your head," I assure him, carding through his hair calmly. "I've been taught manners, you know."

I keep moving my hand through his hair, soothing him, letting him take his time to do what he wants. He focuses after a few moments, taking me deep and working the muscles of his throat around my cock. I feel myself growing harder, and I start to breathe faster. It's been so long, and he is skilled at what he does, I rock back and forth with his motions, holding back, making sure to be careful with him. I can feel him relaxing, and when I make a low sound of pleasure, I can feel him shivering and working my cock more excitedly. I want to come, but I keep my promise and stay gentle with him. It gets to be too much all of a sudden, and I grip his shoulders, pushing him away as lightly as I can before I come.

"Master?" he asks, looking up at me with confusion.

I smile down at him. "How sore are you? From last night?"

He blushes, only increasing my desire to have him. "Only a little, master."

I consider it for a moment. If he's sore, I don't want to press him for sex. I want this to be good. "We could just continue—"

"Please, I want you to fuck me!" He blurts out, cowering the second he does.

I hate to think that someone would hurt him for such a request. "Go grab the lube. Top shelf in the cabinet. And relax, for fuck's sake, or you'll be a hell of a lot more sore tomorrow."

He grins at me, darting off to retrieve it. I climb into bed and lean back against the pillows, watching him. He joins me hesitantly, searching my face for direction.

"Come here," I order, and he crawls up between my legs. He hesitates at my cock, but I have other plans for him.

I grab him by the hair carefully, trying to be playful, and once he starts moving with me, I stretch him out over the length of my body, face-to-face with me. I move my hand to grip the back of his neck and pull him down to kiss me. My cock throbs as he moans for me.

I pull the lube from his hand and reach behind Sascha's back, carefully pouring the lube onto my hands. I reach around and press my fingers inside of him, preparing him for what's about to come. I feel him shiver in anticipation and I work my fingers in deeper, enjoying the way he stays, held up by his elbows, kissing me as I take possession of him. He rolls his hips, working my fingers deeper inside of him. I can't wait to have him on my cock, but I still want him to take a more active role in this. I slide my fingers out, pleased when he writhes on top of me, and I caress his legs.

"Come down when you're ready," I whisper into his ear, keeping my voice low. "You can take it slow if you want."

The surprise comes first, and then the confusion.

"You said you were still sore," I explain, nibbling lightly at his ear. "I don't want to be the one responsible for hurting you."

He smiles, for real this time, and he gently works himself around the head of my cock. He takes his time, and I wait patiently, stroking his arms, brushing his hair back, letting him have his way with me. I see him wince a little as he slides all the way down, but I wait, letting him do what he needs to do. He finally finds his rhythm, sliding up and down my cock. His breath catches and I realize that he's finally enjoying it, breaking past the uncomfortable barrier of tension. I lock eyes with him and start to thrust in time with him. For months, he's been a mystery, but right now, it's like he's a part of my own body.

I bring my hand between us and grab his cock, stroking it in time with our motions until he gasps in pleasure. Suddenly, he moves faster, thrusting down harder, clenching his teeth. I smile a little, waiting for him to come, and I can feel myself getting closer as well.

He sits up a little, changing the angle, allowing me to drive deeper into him. It feels wonderful, and I feel myself approaching my own edge. I look up at him, wanting to see his face as I come, and I'm startled to see his hands on his legs, his fingers digging into the sensitive skin of his thighs. I see his fingers pressing in harder, and the slight look of pain on his face.

"Sascha, what are you doing?" I demand. I grab his hands and pull them away, revealing angry red crescent-shaped marks. One is bleeding.

"Um..." He squirms for a moment, looking guilty and desperate, like an addict in need of his next fix. "I just..."

"You need the pain," I say quietly, realizing what he had been used for in the past and how much it must have affected him. I brush my thumb over the marks he's put on himself, trapping his hands in mine. Last night was rougher, he was scared, that must have been good enough. Tonight is too gentle. "It's not enough to be fucked, you need the pain."

He looks horrified, flushing bright red. He twists, pulling his hands away from mine, and moving off of my cock.

"Where are you going?" I demand.

He squirms his way off of me, and starts to get out of the bed. "I'm sorry, I just—"

I catch him around the waist easily and flip him onto his back, pinning him to the bed. I smile down at him, knowing I'm scaring him a little. He got off on the fear last night, he liked it when I was controlling. I'm not going to kick him out of my bed for that.

"Put your arms above your head," I order, smiling when he obeys.

I pin them together with one hand, keeping them in place without putting too much pressure on his shoulders, or the hand that's still healing. He looks up at me, uncertain, but definitely not unwilling.

"Do not hurt yourself," I order, my free hand tracing down his chest and scratching ever so lightly against his skin. "If anyone is going to hurt you, it's going to be me, and I'm going to enjoy it."

Sascha whimpers, a sound filled with need and longing. I slide back into him, thrusting slow and deep, wanting to fill him with my cock. He tries to stay quiet, but that ends quickly, and he cries out as I make him feel good. It turns me on, bringing me back to the point I was at just a few minutes ago. I like the confirmation that he's enjoying the sex I give him.

I keep his hands pinned above his head as I lean down and start biting him, covering his neck and chest with little red marks. He squirms, and I laugh at how worked up I've gotten him. I move up to nibble at his earlobe some more, pleased when I feel him shudder.

"Is this good, or do you want more?" I ask.

He moans for a while before realizing he should answer. "Um, good. Master."

I move to the other side, stopping to bite at his collarbone on the way. I whisper in his other ear, "Then I want you to come."

I keep biting him, just hard enough to make him cry out, and I thrust deeper into him. I'm getting close, and so is he. I wrap my hand around his cock and stroke, hard, as I bite down on one of his nipples. I feel him come, struggling against my grip, and I come just seconds later. We move together for a few more seconds before I collapse on top of him, one hand still pinning his above his head. I enjoy being on top of him.

But I don't want to hurt him, and we should clean up. I get off of him carefully and retrieve a towel, tossing one to Sascha as well as he lies there shuddering and smiling.

I slide into bed next to him, feeling the warmth of his body, tracing my fingers along the faint impression of teeth I've left on his shoulder. He shudders even more, responding to the pain and the reminder even now that we're finished.

"Is it always like this?" I ask, curious.

He blinks up at me.

"The pain," I clarify. I've known some slaves who have been conditioned to respond to pain, but then, I've known some free people who just prefer it. I've always enjoyed giving it to a willing recipient. "Do you always need it?"

He looks embarrassed. "Um, since I was Demoted, master. They, uh..."

He lets his sentence trail off, looking ashamed again. I finish for him, sparing him the humiliation. "They trained you to respond to pain, right. Do you like it, or do you just need it?"

He looks startled, not to mention embarrassed. "Um... I guess a little bit of both, master," he mumbles.

"Nothing wrong with that," I tell him, shrugging. I wouldn't fault him for enjoying something he's been forced to enjoy, even if it wasn't something I shared. "Some people enjoy causing pain, some people enjoy receiving it."

"Yes, master."

I can see him thinking about it, and I give him a moment to do so. I want to bring him to a point where he doesn't just enjoy it, he enjoys it without guilt.

"Don't hurt yourself again when we're having sex," I order. "I can take care of that."

He stares up at me, shy and silent.

"And don't call me master when we're having sex," I add on after a few moments. It's too subservient, too real. "Call me nothing, or sir, or call me by my name. In fact, if you're going to scream anything out, scream out my name."

He hesitates for a moment, then nods.

He tries it out. "Cashiel."

I grin, enjoying the way the name rolls off of his tongue. "You make it sound good. Just don't let me hear you calling me anything inappropriate at other times."

"Okay," he agrees, gazing up at me like some sort of lovesick puppy.

All this, over a name? I don't want to think of what it means, so I grab his face and kiss him again, continuing until he's breathless and his cock hardens against my leg. It's amazing that something as insignificant as permission to use my name can make him so happy, but he's not the only one who enjoys it.

I look forward to hearing my name roll off his lips on a regular basis.

If you enjoyed this story, you can sign up for a free membership at
ForbiddenFiction and discuss it with other readers
and the author at the *Subjection* story page
at http://forbiddenfiction.com/library/story/AC2-1.000202.

We do our best to proof all our work, but if you spot a text error
we missed, please let us know via our website
Contact Form at http://forbiddenfiction.com/contact.

Author's Notes

"A simple story about a sexy, domineering master and a pretty, rescued slave boy." This was the first description I ever wrote about what would come to be *Subjection*, and the *Demoted* series.

The *Demoted* series has come a long way from my original idea. While I was in the middle of writing the *Inherent Gifts* slave stories, I wanted something light and fluffy to fill my time — proof that I have no idea of what I want, ever!

I made it only two or three chapters into *Subjection* before falling in love with Sascha and deciding that he deserved to be so much more. By the time Cash came around, the rest of the world had been built up to support them both, and the questions of how two very vibrant characters could coexist in a harsh world guided the rest of the story. Their world isn't nice, and neither are their friends or families. Such a world demands some calluses.

At the end of *Subjection*, the sexy, domineering master and his pretty, rescued slave boy seem happy, but there is so much more to their story! The next book, *Sedition*, follows the couple deeper into the political mess that they have barely touched upon so far — making their connection to one another that much more important.

About the Author

Alicia Cameron has been making up stories since before she can remember. After discovering erotica during a high school banned books project, she never really turned back. She lives in Denver, Colorado with two tiny dogs and a rabbit who conspire regularly to distract her from doing anything productive. By day she works in the mental health field and is passionate about youth rights and welfare. In her spare time, she enjoys traveling, glitter, and punk rock concerts.

ForbiddenFiction works by Alicia Cameron

Inherent Gifts Series
Inherent Gifts
Inherent Risk
Inherent Cost

Short Stories
Cuts so Deep
Dangerous Steps
In Other Hands
Jingle Boy
Twisted Gifts
Party Favors
Hot Rain
Lessons Learned

Demoted Series
Subjection
Sedition
Succession

DEMOTED

The superior lead. The inferior are DEMOTED.

Cashiel and Sascha aren't revolutionaries. Cashiel just wants to use his privilege to make the world a better place. Sacha just wants to save his brother from being Demoted. Unfortunately, they're both trapped within the system.

In the past, lesser people rose above their natural station, and greater persons found themselves stifled under the incompetent leadership of their inferiors. Today, the Miller System conditions the Demoted to serve; persons otherwise lost are given purpose, and placed under the ownership and guidance of responsible citizens.

Cashiel's mother invented the Miller System, and trying to prove that the Demoted should be treated humanely sets him against his mother and all her political power. Sascha succeeded in saving his brother from the system, but only by taking his place and being made into a brothel slave.

It isn't exactly love at first sight when Cashiel buys Sascha. If they can work together, though, they might be able to bring down a system of institutionalized abuse, and find some happiness for themselves.

About the Publisher

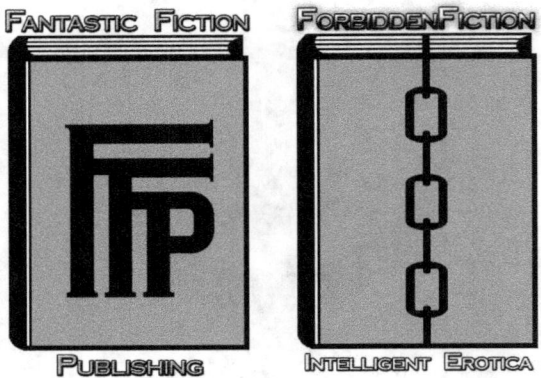

ForbiddenFiction.com is a publisher devoted to writing that breaks the boundaries of original erotic fiction. Our stories combine intense sexuality with quality writing. Stories at Forbidden Fiction.com not only arouse readers through sensations, but also engage them emotionally and mentally through storytelling as well-crafted as the sex is hot.

ForbiddenFiction.com is also designed to be a social reading environment. You'll have fun even if just reading the latest post each day, yet you will have the chance for so much more. Readers and authors can be part of ongoing discussions of specific works and individual authors as well as more general topics.

Sign up for a FREE Membership today at ForbiddenFiction.com